"You okay?"

Nora asked when we were finally alone.

I groaned. "Yeah, just Dad being Dad. He's all up in my face about Roman. Not like it's going anywhere anyway."

Nora gave me a conspiratorial grin and playfully punched my shoulder. "Yeah, but you two looked like you were hitting it off, so who knows?" She grabbed her coat from under the counter, put it on and buttoned it up, although I didn't know why she bothered. It wasn't like she had a long walk home. The four of us lived in the apartment over the store.

I shrugged. "I guess it wasn't meant to be. He gave me the old 'I'll call you' line."

"Don't write him off just yet," Nora said. She put up her hand to stop the inevitable *but*. "I'm off." She tossed her handbag over her shoulder. "If Ty asks, I went to bed because I have an early shift tomorrow."

"Do you?"

She winked at me. "What Ty doesn't know won't hurt him."

I snickered and started closing out the register.

"Oh, and by the way," Nora said, sticking her head back through the door. "About Roman. It took me a while but I finally figured out why he looked so familiar."

My heart started racing again at the mere mention of Roman. "Why?"

"He's Roman Montgomery, heir apparent to the Montgomery Designer Footwear fortune."

I stifled a gasp. "Are you kidding me?" But she looked as serious as a heart attack. I was pretty sure all the blood just drained out of my face.

Praise for Pamela Woods-Jackson

After reading a sample chapter of *SOLE MATES*: "Oh my! I want to continue reading! Are you planning any more installments? I can't wait to read the book!"
~*Janet Benedict Barnhart, high school English teacher*
~*~

"Pamela Jackson's characters come to life under her pen. I got so caught up in *CONFESSIONS OF A TEENAGE PSYCHIC* that it was hard to put it down."
~*Jane Hall Rodkin, Oklahoma City TV, radio, and theatre personality*

~*~

"I read your book *TEENAGE PSYCHIC ON CAMPUS*! It was very good and entertaining!"
~*Nancy Scott Fields, Healer, Psychic/Medium*

Sole Mates

by

Pamela Woods-Jackson

Sole Mates

Cover Art by *Debbie Taylor*

The Wild Rose Press, Inc.
PO Box 708
Adams Basin, NY 14410-0708
Visit us at www.thewildrosepress.com

Publishing History
First Fantasy Rose Edition, 2018
Print ISBN 978-1-5092-2080-9
Digital ISBN 978-1-5092-2081-6

Published in the United States of America

Dedication

To my ever-supportive family.

Chapter 1

Honolulu, Hawaii, 1946

How did I get here, standing over some poor girl's hospital bed? My hangover must be worse than I thought. Was she a friend from my campus dorm? She was part Japanese, young and pretty, with olive skin and long, dark, silky hair. She looked vaguely familiar, but I couldn't quite recall...

A nurse walked into the room, checked the pulse of the young woman lying motionless on the bed, gasped, and ran down the hall, shouting for a doctor.

I followed her into the hallway. The nurse took the arm of a handsome doctor, very handsome in fact, and with a few furtive glances in the direction of the girl's room, whispered something in his ear. The doctor strode purposefully toward the room, a grim set to his jaw. He brushed past me as if I were invisible and rushed to his patient's bedside. He took her pulse, shined a light into her vacant eyes, and listened to her heart with a stethoscope. With a huge sigh, the doctor shook his head and exchanged knowing glances with the nurse.

"I'm so sorry, Dr. Montag," the nurse said. "She's beyond pain now. Take comfort in that." The nurse's words offered solace, but her gleeful expression and the affectionate way she stroked his arm spoke to her true

1

intent.

I didn't like the looks of that woman. She was young, probably mid-twenties, overly thin and wearing too much makeup. In addition to her crisp white uniform that was a bit too tight, and a nurse's cap sitting atop overly-coiffed red hair, she had on fashionable navy blue pumps instead of more practical white oxfords. I didn't even know her, but every fiber of my being was screaming not to trust her.

Pity and sadness overtook me as I stepped to the patient's bedside. Was this girl a friend of mine? I wracked my brain but I couldn't seem to remember. And just as I was about to get a close look at her face, the nurse covered her with a sheet.

Dr. Raymond Montag, according to his nametag, said, "Rosemary, uh, Nurse Williams, is the family nearby?"

Nurse Williams curled her lip. "The Japanese folks?"

He gritted his teeth. "Yes, Nurse."

My crush on this cute doctor was growing, especially when he seemed put off by the nurse's intolerant attitude. I was sure I could do a better job of comforting him than Nurse Williams, and I hoped to get a chance.

The nurse rolled her eyes but leaned out the door, crooked her finger, and stepped aside to allow two people to enter the hospital room.

A man probably in his fifties, with blood-shot eyes and uncombed hair, came through the doorway, followed closely by a nun. I didn't get a chance to study his features because as soon as he caught sight of the girl on the bed, he buried his face in his hands. The nun's face was obscured by her dark blue habit and white headgear. Since no one attempted to shoo me away, I stayed right where I was, hoping to glean information as to who these people were and why I was intruding upon their grief.

"Thank you, Nurse," the doctor said. "That will be all."

She paused to smile at Dr. Montag and touch his arm seductively before making her way out. Good riddance.

"I'm very sorry for your loss, Mr. Chinen," Dr. Montag said.

Mr. Chinen? Why did that name sound familiar? The man removed his glasses and wiped them dry with a handkerchief, swiped at tears with the back of his hand, and replaced his eyeglasses. I scrutinized him and the nun by his side. And then it hit me as surely as if I had been struck by lightning. That was my father! And my sister Norma.

"Father! I'm right here."

He and Norma ignored me.

"But, doctor, you said there was a new drug…" my father stammered. He was wearing a colorful Hawaiian shirt and khaki pants, but his cheerful clothing belied his somber mood.

"Penicillin, yes," the doctor replied. "It's still experimental, but unfortunately Julie's bacterial meningitis was too far advanced for it to be effective."

"Doctor," Norma said, "this is…" She took a deep breath and paused a moment. My sister was always in control of her feelings, never letting anyone see chinks in her armor. Today was no different. She leveled a firm gaze at the doctor. "This is so unexpected."

Dr. Montag nodded. "I know it's a shock."

"It's more than shocking," Norma said. "It's a devastating blow. You see, my brother Henry was killed in the attack on Pearl Harbor, and then my mother died of a broken heart two years later. Julie was never the same after that, and our family…" Much to my surprise, my sister allowed a tear to trickle down her cheek before hastily wiping it away.

What was she saying? That couldn't be me in that bed. I had so much to live for. I looked from my sister to my father and then to the handsome doctor, trying to comprehend what was happening. To them. To me. "Norma," I shouted. "I'm right here. Look at me!"

"Norma…" Father said as if I hadn't spoken, squeezing her shoulder.

I stomped my foot. "Father, why are you so concerned about her? I'm the one who's sick."

"I understand," Dr. Montag said, speaking right over me. I turned to gaze up into his deep-set blue eyes and felt the urge to brush away the stray lock of blond hair that had fallen out of place. I'd be angry he interrupted me if he weren't so handsome. "And you have my deepest sympathy, Mr. Chinen." He turned to Norma. "Sister, do you have any idea about arrangements?"

"I will speak to Father Anthony immediately," she said.

My father shook his head and sobbed. "My little girl was only nineteen."

I put my hands on my hips. "Yes, I'm nineteen and I'm right here."

"Indeed," the doctor said, again ignoring me, "too young to die."

I looked around at the sterile hospital room, at my grieving family, at the sad doctor, and then at the inert body under the white sheet. What happened to me? I couldn't remember anything. And I certainly didn't feel dead. After all, I was standing right next to my family.

I waved my hands in front of their faces. Neither seemed to notice me. I reached out my hand and smacked Norma's shoulder, like I used to do when we were children. She shivered, clasped her arms tightly about herself, and took a step away.

"Doctor," she said, "if you don't mind, we would like to see Julie one more time before we make arrangements…"

The doctor nodded and led them back to the girl's—my—bedside. I peered over their shoulders and gasped as the doctor pulled back the sheet. I barely recognized myself, so unlike the reflection I usually saw in a mirror. I was half Japanese on my father's side, half Caucasian on my mother's, but this empty shell of a girl wasn't me. It couldn't be. My silky dark hair was spread across the pillow and my normally olive skin now appeared ashen.

My father's eyes were red and swollen as he hesitatingly stepped to my bedside. Suddenly I felt very sorry for myself, dying so young, and worse, having to spend eternity in an ugly hospital gown. But when I looked down at myself, instead of the shapeless white gown, I had on a colorful sundress and open-toed sandals. These were the clothes I remembered wearing before… Before whatever happened to me, I suppose.

Norma removed the rosary dangling from her belt, kissed it and began to pray. She and Father hugged each other as they sobbed, but I had to look away. It was all too sad. I stepped to the window and peered out onto a beautiful sunny day in paradise. All the people below wore summer clothing, and I could see the beach way off in the distance. I live—lived—on the island of Oahu, Hawaii, a U.S. Territory. The Japanese attacked Pearl Harbor in 1941, but despite our family being part Japanese, no one blamed us, and we were not rounded up for the internment camps like our Japanese friends on the mainland. Everyone on Oahu worked together to rebuild what had been destroyed, and five years later beauty and hope had been restored.

I turned back to my family and my heart ached for them. Norma was only twenty-nine, but at that moment she looked to have the weight of the world on her shoulders. I felt deep regret about the irresponsible teenager I'd become after the deaths of my brother and mother.

Father sobbed. "She had so much to live for."

My sister nodded. "It's in God's hands now."

I'd never felt so alive, yet there was my body to prove I wasn't. I focused, trying to recall what had landed me here, dead in a hospital with a gorgeous young doctor by my side. Slowly it came back to me.

Everywhere at home were reminders of the family that had been destroyed. Photos of the five of us on the beach. A cross and photo from my confirmation, drawings my brother had done in school, dresses my mother had made for me, Norma's Bible. It was all too much, so I avoided home more and more. I spent all my time at the beach and ignored my studies, yet somehow, I managed to graduate high school. By then, my reckless behavior was ingrained, and it carried over to college. I'd been skipping my classes and spending too much time at the naval base, socializing with the enlisted men. After the tragedy of war, I told myself, I was young and entitled to some fun. Yet in the back of my mind there was this nagging feeling that I was supposed to be doing something, something important. I never could quite put my finger on it, so I indulged in dancing, drinking, and smoking cigarettes. I assumed I had years to figure out my life. If I had only known.

I recalled returning to the dorm after a weekend of partying, to find that some of the girls in my college dorm had come down with the flu. At least we thought it was the flu. Soon many girls, including my roommate, were in the campus infirmary, desperately ill. I was all alone on my dorm floor, but then I got sick, too, and there was no one to take me to the infirmary. I took some aspirin and got into bed, but my fever spiked and frightening hallucinations set in. Yes, I'm sure that's what they were, because otherwise why would I see myself dressed in what looked like a Shakespearean costume? Was I in a play? No, I'd never been an actor, but in this dream I was speaking to a handsome man who looked like Dr. Montag.

The next thing I knew I woke up in this room. I'd opened my eyes and looked around. Everything was white: the bed sheets, the pillow, the blanket, the plastered walls, the nightstand, the closet, the water pitcher. Even the Bible on the nightstand was white with gold embossed lettering. I felt sick and afraid as I put a cold, clammy hand to my throbbing head. I called out, and in came Nurse Williams, all fake smiles and feigned concern, to fluff my pillow, offer me a sip of water, and take my pulse.

"What happened?" I squeaked out. "How did I get

here?"

"The dorm mother found you unconscious in your bed and called your father," the nurse replied as she wrote something on a chart at the end of my bed. "He brought you here last night."

I tried to sit up, but my vision blurred and my head throbbed, forcing me to collapse back onto the feather pillow. "What's wrong with me?"

"I'll let the doctor speak to you about that." She turned on her heel and left.

I dozed on and off until Dr. Montag, Raymond Montag, came to see me.

"Well, Miss Chinen, how are you feeling today?"

"Terrible," I groaned. But as sick as I felt, I still noticed how really cute he was, probably not more than twenty-six or twenty-seven. And something about him seemed familiar. Like we knew each other, even though we'd never met until this moment. I noticed he wasn't wearing a wedding ring. "What's wrong with me?"

The doctor took my pulse and listened to my heartbeat with his stethoscope. "Bacterial meningitis, I'm sorry to say. But there's a new medicine I'd like to try. I just need to consult with the resident doctor on call." He patted my hand and left.

I was in and out of consciousness for hours, but I remember doctors and nurses coming in and out, all of them wearing white masks over their faces. All I wanted was to get well so the cute doctor would ask me out once I was no longer his patient.

Even though Dr. Montag wasn't married, it seemed to me that Nurse Williams was more than a colleague, or wanted to be. When in his presence she pretended to care about my condition and recovery, but out of his sight she scowled at me every time I glanced the doctor's way. And then I overheard another doctor tell Dr. Montag that the new medicine wasn't working. I got progressively worse, and of course I died this afternoon. The timeline was now clear, but what I didn't understand was how I was still standing in the room, watching helplessly and unable to communicate.

My father's shoulders drooped and he appeared to have aged years in the last few minutes. My sister took his arm and together they left my bedside, holding tightly to each other for comfort. Dr. Montag pulled the sheet back over my head. He seemed deeply saddened, staring at my cold, lifeless form as tears came to his eyes. I wanted to reach out to him, but then Nurse Williams returned, took his arm, and led him sobbing from the room. I was all alone in a sterile room with my dead body, and I didn't know what to do.

"Lettie, are you ready to go?"

That name sounded familiar. I turned around to see a beautiful woman, glowing inside and out, smiling at me from the corner of the room, which was now bathed in a peaceful white light. How did she get in? The door was closed. She was about forty years old, dressed in a flowing white robe with a circle of brilliantly colored flowers around her hair. She beckoned to me, but still I hesitated. "I thought my name was Julie."

"Think about it, dear. You're Juliet, Lettie for short, and now it's time to go Home."

"I wasn't supposed to die, was I?" She shook her head, and then what I'd been struggling to remember about my life came back to me. "I was supposed to get sick, yes, but Romeo—Dr. Raymond Montag—was to help me recover, and then we were going to be together.

We belong together." A terrible sadness overtook me. "Celeste, what went wrong?"

Celeste put her arm around me and led me away from the sterile hospital room, away from my cold, lifeless body. "We try to plan for all eventualities, but sometimes the unforeseen occurs. Your grief from the loss of your brother and mother, coupled with this illness, your weakened body from overindulgence of alcohol…"

"I know." I nodded, as tears flooded my eyes. "It's my fault."

"We'll talk about it when we get Home." She gently walked me into the welcoming white light that surrounded us both.

Chapter 2

Celeste dropped my hand as we walked across an open bridge that led us Home. I took in the vivid green grass and foliage, inhaled the sweet fragrance of the flowers that were all around us, and thrilled to the bubbling of the peacefully flowing brook. In the distance stood the Great Hall of Records, with heavenly music emanating from inside. On Earth I enjoyed listening to a symphony, but there were no words to describe the beauty of the notes here.

An idea started churning in my mind. With growing excitement, I said, "Celeste, we have to go look at Romeo's chart, what's next for him in this current lifetime." A chart was the blueprint each soul wrote in preparation for a new incarnation. It was supposed to be a guide, but sometimes events took the soul off course, as I'd just experienced for myself.

I pointed Celeste in the direction of the Great Hall of Records, the immense building of Greek architectural design, which housed all the records of mankind. It was the largest building on This Side and it spanned hundreds of miles visually. Yet when inside, it didn't feel any bigger than a large library on Earth. Files were easily accessed, or if research wasn't the purpose of one's visit, a soul could hear a concert or lecture in one of the expansive meeting rooms.

Celeste lifted an eyebrow. "What difference can it

make now?"

"Maybe it's possible for me to go back right away and join him." Without waiting for her answer, I started walking toward the building.

I hurried up the marble steps and through the floor-to-ceiling oak doors that were always open. Since the temperature here was a constant and very pleasant seventy-two degrees, there was never a reason to close the doors, which would deter people from coming in whenever they chose. I looked up and down the massive hallways, unsure where to go next. I'd need Celeste to help me find the room with Rom's files.

"Lettie," Celeste said, close on my heels, "it's too late for you to go back. With your death, Romeo's life will take a different turn."

But I wasn't ready to give up, especially since I was the one who caused this shift. "I have to know if it's possible," I insisted. "Which way?"

She blew out a puff of air and tilted her head for me to follow. We wound our way through corridor after corridor, passing rooms where concerts were being played, not just classical music but the new jazz that was just being introduced down on Earth. How I would have loved to experience that. As we passed another room, an instructor was giving a lecture on another form of music that would be coming later, something he was calling Rock and Roll. Finally, we arrived in the biggest card catalog section anyone could imagine. Celeste easily found the right drawer, thumbed through the cards, and finally withdrew one.

"Romeo," she read as she showed it to me. "This way."

I followed her through narrow rows of copper

shelving, each one crammed with what looked like unpublished manuscripts or school research papers, but were really written records of lives lived, until she arrived at the correct shelf. She ran her finger up and down the bindings. "Here it is." Celeste pulled out Romeo's charted plan for this life. "Let's go to a private room so we can study it."

There were hundreds of private viewing rooms, each one with a table, comfortable leather chairs, and study lamps, reminiscent of luxurious university study rooms on Earth. Many were already filled with spirit guides in conference with their clients. We walked and walked until Celeste found an empty room.

I took a seat next to my spirit guide as she opened Rom's file, searching from the beginning of his life in 1919 in Arlington, Virginia, page by page until she reached the year 1946. She pointed to the spot. "You may read it for yourself, if you'd like."

I took a deep breath and began to read the new addition that was appearing in fresh ink as I watched. Romeo, Dr. Raymond Montag, would now marry Nurse Rosemary Williams in 1947. He would then accept a position at Johns Hopkins Hospital in Baltimore, Maryland, closer to his family. I thought for a moment. "He'll be successful there, I'm sure, but he isn't going to be happy with her."

Celeste glanced at me sympathetically. "True, it will be an unhappy union. But like many other Americans, Rom's parents have deep-seated prejudices against the Japanese. A match between you two was destined to be difficult. Unfortunately, Raymond isn't aware that you and he had a future, so he will never quite understand why his marriage to Rosemary isn't working."

"Will there be children?" I asked.

Celeste flipped through a few more pages. "No, apparently not."

"Good!" I stood up and shoved the chair aside. "Then I can go back right now. I can meet him again by 1965. I'll be about nineteen or so and he will be mid-forties. We can have a May-December romance."

Celeste didn't look convinced. "Come along, Miss Homewrecker," she said, taking me by the arm. "You're not going back without first conferring with Counselor Everman."

She marched me out of the Great Hall of Records, out into the soft light of day, and through the gardens toward the Hall of Wisdom, where the Council members met with those needing advice. The magnificent smell of the flowers again struck me, more fragrant than anything on Earth, and their colors were so vibrant they shimmered. The water in the fountain was playing its own tune, a Brahms lullaby if I was correct. We walked through the gardens, past people who were reading, playing tennis, or simply chatting happily. Suddenly I stopped and gasped.

"Henry!" It was my brother from this most recent life, the one who died during the attack on Pearl Harbor. He sat under a tree on an ornate cement bench, completely engrossed in charts, graphs, and what appeared to be mathematical equations.

Henry looked up, startled. "Julie! What…?" But he saw Celeste behind me so of course he knew the answer to his unasked question. He stood up and we embraced, and then he held me at arm's length to look me over.

I sighed. "Another life wasted. I didn't take care of

myself, and I completely forgot my purpose."

He nodded. "I'm so sorry, Lettie. I suppose Rom's..."

"Still alive, yes."

Henry looked wonderful. So handsome, with those soft brown eyes and slender but muscular build. He was young when he died—only twenty-three—but he seemed happy now.

I cocked my head to the side. "How are you?"

He shrugged and grinned. "I'm in Heaven. How do you think?" He bounced up and down on his toes as he pointed to the charts. "And I've been assigned to work on technology that will benefit mankind in the coming century."

"That's wonderful!" I smiled. "Have you seen Mom?"

The smile drained from his face. "No. She's in isolation. They're trying to counsel her, but she was a mess when she got here."

"Oh, right." My mother's spirit had never fully recovered from the shock of my suicide in my first incarnation. And after losing Henry this time, and then seeing me turn wild, Mom just couldn't handle life anymore. The doctors said it was heart failure, which was a good description of the despair she felt after losing her son and watching me drift away from the family.

"Well," Henry said to lighten the mood, "what about you? Off for your life review?"

I shook my head. "I'm going to ask Counselor Everman if there's any way to salvage our plans."

"Oh, Lettie, I don't know..." Henry said.

I stamped my foot, just as stubborn here as I was

on Earth. "I ruined this chance for Romeo and me, but I'm hoping it's not too late to fix it." I took Celeste by the arm and pulled her along.

"Good luck!" Henry called after us.

I gave him a backward wave as Celeste and I hurried along. Although Home seemed to be a vast place, it never took more than a moment to arrive at any destination. No waiting for a streetcar, bus, train, or car to transport you. Simply wish to be there and you were.

I looked up at the beautiful, majestic building, a structure designed in an Egyptian style of architecture. This one was much smaller than the Great Hall of Records. It was made of white marble with two large, ornate pillars at the front entrance. There were only six steps up to the entryway. I took them two at a time, eager to get started, sure that my request would be granted. I stepped through the large wooden door, turned around, and tapped my foot as my spirit guide made her way at a more leisurely pace.

Once inside, Celeste took a deep, calming breath. "Are you sure this is what you want?" When I nodded, she clasped my hand, and together we walked solemnly down the hallway.

Our revered Supreme Council, made up of elders and spirits who have always been here and who are closest to The Source, sat in this building. The Council members were kind, caring, wise, but firm. In my rush I nearly forgot that.

A soul couldn't help but be awed in this magnificent place. The building's interior walls, floors and ceilings were all made of the finest marble, and by all rights our footsteps should echo, but instead there was total silence. We arrived at a closed, unmarked door at the end of the hall, which would look like an office if this were a building on Earth. Celeste rapped lightly.

"Come in, Celeste, Juliet," a voice called from inside the office.

Celeste turned the handle and motioned for me to go in ahead of her. Counselor Everman looked like one of those pictures of Moses you see in Bible story books on Earth. He appeared to be about fifty years old, although age is irrelevant here, and always wore a long gray beard. In this case the Earth clichés were correct. He and all the other Supreme Council members wore long white robes tied at the waist with a golden rope, and sandals made of the finest silver material, manufactured some way I didn't understand.

"Good day, Counselor," Celeste said.

"It is indeed a good day," he replied, motioning us in. I glanced around his office, in disarray as always, but Counselor Everman claims he knows where everything is, despite the clutter. Of course there was no dirt or dust, but the ornate wooden desk, which took up nearly the entire room, was completely covered with ancient scrolls, stacks of yellowing papers, Manila files, and a modern typewriter. Surrounding the desk on three sides were shelves of books that seemingly stretched forever, and a row of round metal containers which I knew from previous experience were film documentations of his clients' lives. Rom and I weren't his only clients. He had thousands of them, but since time was nonexistent here, he was always available when needed and always treated each and every one of us as if we were his only concern.

"I heard you were Home prematurely, Juliet." The

counselor embraced both me and Celeste and indicated two chairs in front of his desk.

I sat in one of the upholstered chairs with its tall, intricately carved wooden back. "Yes, Counselor, I made some mistakes." Embarrassed, I shifted in the seat, unable to relax.

Celeste plopped into the identical chair next to me. "Lettie has this wild notion..."

Counselor Everman held up his hand to stop her. He smiled at both of us as he walked around his desk and sat down in his wing-back chair. On Earth it would be called an antique, because the style dated to the eighteenth century, but here at Home, it was an original. The ones on Earth were the replicas.

He leaned his elbows on his desk, his beard dragging the floor, and looked me in the eye. "Tell me how I may help you, my child."

I squirmed under his gaze. "Um, well, sir, I was hoping to reincarnate immediately. If I do, by the time I'm nineteen years of age or so, it will be 1965 and Rom..."

"Will be in his forties and married to Rosemary."

I gulped. "Yes, but it won't be a happy marriage."

Celeste directed a stern glance my way. "I told her, Counselor, that she should wait till Romeo comes back Home, and together they can try again."

"But we've tried so many times," I whined. I knew I sounded like a petulant child, but I wasn't willing to let this opportunity slip away if I could help it.

The Counselor nodded. "Yes, indeed you have, Lettie. And yet you and Romeo are no closer to being united in life than you've been for the last few centuries. Do you even remember your purpose?"

"Yes." I looked down at my hands and fidgeted. "We were supposed to make amends. Help to reunite our quarreling families." The gap between our families had widened even more after our fourteenth century suicides and then was carried forward into future lives.

Everman lifted an eyebrow. "And have you accomplished any of that yet?"

I opened my mouth to speak, but no words came out. I sighed and shook my head.

Celeste, my ever-trusty friend and spirit guide, came to my rescue. "That's why we're here, Counselor. To see if there's any way to salvage this life."

He got up from his desk and perused the shelves behind him. He ran his fingers along the book bindings until he arrived at what he was looking for. Setting the large, worn book on his desk with a thud, he thumbed through the pages. I recognized that book, because it was a written history of all the lives Romeo and I had lived together.

The Counselor put his finger on a page. "Let's review, shall we?"

The last thing I wanted was a trip down memory lane, but Everman began reading from the book, so I had no choice but to listen.

He peered at me over the top of the book. "I believe we can skip over your initial failure. Mr. Shakespeare has documented it quite well."

I gulped and nodded. I'd like to forget that first life as well. Our families, the Capulets and the Montagues, had a centuries-old feud based on... Well, I never really knew. But despite that, Romeo and I fell in love, secretly married, and hoped our love would unite our families. "We were both new souls, just kids really, impetuous and in love. Neither Rom nor I understood the consequences of our suicides."

Counselor Everman glanced at me with pity. "After your deaths it seemed that the Capulets and Montagues might resolve their differences, but alas, it only exacerbated their feud."

Rom and I had been forced to watch the awful events unfold from Home, unable to intervene. It was a miserable feeling. "We knew we had to make it right, but we were so traumatized that we didn't try again until…"

"…1575," he finished for me. "I suppose you remember how that life ended."

My shoulders slumped. "My father said Lord Montaine had an unsavory reputation and sent me and my friend Norene to an isolated castle in the country. I was afraid to argue with my father, so Romeo—Lord Montaine—instead married wealthy Rose Covington. I died of influenza before my thirtieth birthday."

"And Rose is currently marrying Romeo as Nurse Rosemary Williams," Celeste reminded me.

"Why is she always inserting herself into our lives?"

Everman peered over his spectacles at me. "She's one of those aforementioned obstacles. Shall we continue?"

I held up my hand to stop him. "Romeo and I waited until the late seventeenth century to return. My sister and I lived in a small village outside of London. Our father was a retired clergyman, Romeo was the son of wealthy merchants, and…"

"Romeo's family, or should I say Mr. Ramon Morton," he said, looking up from the page, "put a stop to that friendship almost immediately."

"Well, at least that lifetime failure wasn't my fault," I said.

"Everyone has free will," the Counselor reminded me, "and Romeo could have exercised his. Instead, he allowed his family to hustle him off to law school. Not at Cambridge as everyone expected, but to Harvard, in Boston, Massachusetts, all the way across the ocean in America."

I slumped in my chair. "Where he met Roslyn—or Miss Bell—the daughter of one of his professors. They were married within the year."

"Well," Celeste said with a grin, "at least that lifetime convinced Rom that he preferred living in the United States rather than Europe."

"I suppose," I said.

"Let's continue." Counselor Everman turned the page. "The War Between the States."

I groaned as I remembered that life. It was not only our families but our ideologies keeping us apart. We lived in Louisville, Kentucky, a Union state that permitted slavery. I believed that slavery was wrong, despite owning Nancy, a gift from my father. Romeo, Romson in that life, fought for the Confederacy. "I gave up on Romson—Romeo—much too easily," I said.

"You most certainly did give up too soon," Counselor Everman reminded me. "Because Romson, or rather Romeo, had a change of heart later."

I nodded. "I know now, but as a young, impetuous woman, I didn't think we could overcome our differences. Our fathers quarreled and we drifted apart. When I saw him again thirty years later at the Chicago World's Fair, I realized my mistake." I put up a hand to stop further criticism from either Celeste or Counselor Everman. "I once again forgot what Rom and I set out to do in that life. My stubbornness kept us apart."

"Well, as long as you understand that..." the Counselor said as he closed the thick book with a whoosh.

"So can I go back? According to Henry, Mother is indisposed, but I can find another mother and be born by 1947, '48 at the latest."

"I would advise you against it," he said, "but we all have free will so I cannot stand in your way. Romeo may choose to honor his marriage vows with Rosemary. And with different parents, your mission can only be partially completed."

I gave his words serious thought. What if I outlived Rom? He would have to wait for me to return, as I was now forced to wait for him. I sighed and turned to face Counselor Everman. "I suppose I'll have to wait."

Celeste patted my arm. "As you know, Lettie, time is different here. Romeo will be home in the blink of an eye."

****

1992

Celeste and I applauded, along with the hundreds of thousands of other people listening to the concert. The outdoor amphitheater where musical performances were held here at Home was big enough to hold a million people, but even full, it never seemed crowded. It was surrounded by the most beautiful mountain scenery, the rocks glistening with hues of pink, green, blue, and silver. The guitarist slid off his stool, set aside his acoustic guitar, and stepped to the edge of the stage to modestly accept his applause.

"He's wonderful," I exclaimed over the applause. "I'm sorry I didn't live long enough to hear him perform on Earth. What did you say his name is?"

"John Lennon," Celeste replied.

Just then my wristwatch blinked with red flashing lights. Time here was irrelevant, of course, but the watch was a way of keeping track of Earth time. This was the signal I'd been waiting for. I glanced at over at Celeste, barely able to contain my excitement. "He's coming Home. Romeo's coming Home!"

Celeste gave me a quick hug. "Go."

I hurried out of the amphitheater, rushed through the lush gardens, and then stopped to envision the edge of the tunnel near the footbridge. And just like that I was there. It was a beautiful wooden bridge, the kind you would see in a landscaped park on Earth, or perhaps even in an idealized painting. Underneath it, the bright blue water bubbled with energy. I bounced up and down on my toes, eager to see my soulmate again after all this time.

And there he was. My Romeo. He walked slowly, hesitantly, out of the tunnel before pausing at the edge of the bridge. He reached out an arm to test the handrail, found it sturdy, then had to stop to catch his breath after only a few steps. His appearance reflected what it must have been as he drew his last breath: about seventy-four years of age, mostly bald with a few tufts of gray hair, a wrinkled forehead, hunched shoulders, and his cardigan sweater hanging limply on his thin arms. Rom took another tentative step and stopped to rest, then another step and another rest. But the closer he got to my side of the bridge, the quicker and steadier his steps became as his health and youth returned.

Rom jumped off the last step, completely restored to his youthful twenty-five years of age, if age mattered here. In place of the baldness was now thick blond hair, his thin frame replaced with a muscular build, and he had the twinkle in his eye I'd so admired all those centuries ago. "I was hoping you'd be here," he said with an infectious grin.

I ran to him and threw myself into his arms. "Oh, Rom, I'm so glad you're back." I held on tight, afraid if I let go he might disappear.

"It's good to be Home." He held me at arm's length for a better look at me.

His piercing gaze brought back all my guilt. "I know I messed up and I'm so sorry. I even consulted with Counselor Everman about coming back…"

He placed his fingers on my lips to silence me as he pulled me into the most wonderful, loving, electric embrace. I could feel every fiber of his energy pulsating, every cell more alive than it ever was on Earth.

"Never mind, Lettie," he whispered. "It wasn't all your fault. I should have worked harder to save you."

I pulled back and looked into his eyes. "I want us to try again right away."

"I'd advise against that," a male voice behind us said.

We both turned.

"And I'd have to agree," Celeste said.

Rom beamed and reached around me to offer his hand to shake. "Tio!" he exclaimed to his spirit guide. "It's great to see you again."

To become a spirit guide, one who looks after a soul as they make their way through the school of hard knocks known as Earth, one must train for centuries. Celeste would appear to be about forty years old if she were on Earth, and Tio was a bit younger, indicating their wisdom and maturity. He was short and stocky, wore thick framed glasses for fashion, not need, and his bright red hair was not easy to miss in any environment.

"Tough go this time, Rom," Tio said.

"I had the successful medical career I'd planned on," he said with a shrug, "but my personal life, my marriage…" He shook his head, turned to me, and brushed a lock of my auburn hair off my forehead. "We were cheated out of yet another life together."

"Which is why I want to try again."

Romeo shook his head. "I just got here. *Just.* I need time."

"And that's why I don't think going back now is a good idea," Tio told us.

"But I know we can get it right," I insisted.

Tio pointed us in the direction of the Great Hall of Records. Rom took my hand as we walked. "If I didn't know better, Romeo, I'd think Rose is your soulmate," he said. "You've spent more lifetimes with her than with Lettie."

I cringed as Rom and I exchanged glances.

"I don't love Rose, yet somehow she always forces her way into my life. Lives. How does that keep happening?"

"You knew the risks, Rom," Tio said. We paused in front of the enormous, heavy wooden doors of the Great Hall, and Tio indicated that Rom and I should go in ahead of him. "You forget everything once you incarnate, and it's only through experience and hard work that you're able to accomplish your goals. If souls remembered Home, no one would ever stay on Earth for long."

Tio and Celeste led us into a chamber, like a study room in a library on Earth. It was relatively small, surrounded with wooden shelves crammed with books from centuries past, and in a corner of the room was what looked like a microfiche machine. But it wasn't. It was the Scanner, used to replay the life a soul has just lived. But since this was Heaven, we were given a chance to learn from our mistakes, not be judged for them. I'd been forced to face mine, and now Rom must judge his own actions.

"Are you ready?" Tio asked him.

Romeo took a deep breath and nodded. He sat down at a stool in front of the Scanner, and his life began to unfold. Some of it included my life, too, up to the point where Dr. Raymond Montag was forced to pronounce me dead at the age of nineteen. I could see and feel his intense pain and guilt at my death. Somehow my premature death must have touched his soul, because his grief was beyond what an objective physician should feel.

I watched Rom as he smiled, winced, laughed, and cried. Rosemary Williams flirted and cajoled until Rom agreed to marry her. He didn't love her, but she'd announced their engagement to friends and family, and then planned a wedding, all before Raymond realized what was happening. And then the offer to practice medicine at Johns Hopkins in Baltimore came, and the two of them left Honolulu for a life on the East Coast. Raymond worked long hours, helping to cure countless patients with his skill and compassion. Rosemary, who left nursing, busied herself with volunteer and society work and paid little attention to her husband. He retired at the age of sixty-five, hoping for time with his wife. It wasn't to be, because shortly afterward he was diagnosed with cancer. The last few years of his life were spent fighting the disease, undergoing treatment, withering away.

Rom finished watching and sighed, a sad look on his face. "It turned out so differently than I'd expected."

I took his hand and squeezed it. "Which is why we have to go back."

Celeste lifted an eyebrow. "You remember what Counselor Everman said? That you and Romeo are star-crossed lovers. Another ten lifetimes might not accomplish your goals. You're better off staying Home and using your expertise to work with returning souls."

"Right now," Rom said, patting my hand, "I just want to rest and reflect, just unwind after that stressful life." He turned to Tio. "Is Mozart still here?"

"I'm afraid not," Tio told him. "He's on the verge of becoming a great twenty-first century composer, once he grows up, that is."

"See?" I said. "Another good reason to go back."

Rom stood, stretched, and pulled me close. "I'll think about it."

****

I glanced up from my book as the ocean waves quietly washed ashore. A breeze lifted the corners of my blanket and caused the palm trees to gently sway as I sat on the beach, the original Waikiki Beach from my last life. The one in Honolulu was the replica, similar to Home, but here we have all the beautiful, picturesque landscape without the bugs and risk of sunburn. Despite all the terrain from my previous lives, this was where I felt most at home. Rom and I have a small bungalow within walking distance of the beach, so I come here often. We don't need much space as long as we have each other.

Romeo told me about a book that brought him inspiration during his battle with cancer on Earth, so I went to the Great Hall Library and checked it out. *All I Really Need to Know I Learned in Kindergarten* was written by a minister. Clever title, and as I was discovering, an engaging collection of essays.

"Well, if it isn't little Julie Chinen."

Startled, I looked up into the eyes of a woman I have known for centuries, a woman whose scowl and angular features I'd recognize anywhere. "Rose!"

She dusted some powdery sand off her sandals. "Yes, I just got back."

I was quite surprised to see her on the beach, since I'd never known her to be anywhere but upscale urban environments, even here at Home. I glared at the interloper. "You know perfectly well my name is Lettie," I snapped.

I stopped, took a deep breath, and reminded myself that this was Heaven where love and respect were the only requirements. With effort I adjusted my attitude. "Good to see you Home, Rose."

She gave me a condescending smile. "I had a wonderful life, married to Raymond. I mean Romeo, of course. So sorry you had to depart early, but your death brought me together with the man I think of as my soulmate."

Okay, if this were Earth I'd stand up and challenge her on that, but it was our loving Home, so I swallowed my rage. "You and Rom have been thrown together by circumstances, but as you know, he and I are *true* soulmates."

She smirked. "I suppose we'll just have to disagree about that."

I took a few deep breaths and prayed for guidance before replying. "Have you seen him since you've been back?" Now it was my turn to smirk, because I knew perfectly well that she hadn't.

Rose shifted her stance, gazed out to sea, and once again focused on her sandy shoes. "Perhaps I'll just wait for our next life together." And with that, she turned and disappeared into the misty spray rising off the ocean water.

I tossed the book aside and lay down on my back to stare up at the sapphire blue sky with its muted sunlight. I needed a moment to think through what Rose had just said. In all fairness, I had to admit she was right, at least about the number of lives she and Romeo have shared. Some of it was beyond my control, but much of it was due to my own shortcomings.

"This ends now!" I shouted to the sky. "Next time, Romeo and I *will* be together."

****

1997

Counselor Everman faced the four of us—Celeste, Tio, Rom and me—seated in a semi-circle at a round conference table in The Great Hall, as he read through our new life plan. Once I was able to convince Romeo to return with me for one last time on Earth, we agonized, wrote, and rewrote the life plan over the course of five Earth years. Now the Counselor was studying every page with a furrowed brow, occasionally glancing up to eye us warily. I gripped the chair's luxuriously upholstered arms as if holding onto a life raft.

He set it aside. "Very ambitious."

"Perhaps *too* ambitious," Tio said with a stern glance at his client.

Celeste nodded, but nonetheless gave me a loving smile. "I'm afraid the two of you are taking on too much. If this life is lived as written, it will be very difficult."

"We know that," I said, "but I believe we've been on Earth enough times to understand the pitfalls. I'm sure this time we'll succeed."

"Are you certain you wish to try again so soon, Romeo?" Counselor Everman asked. "Rose will yet again be a factor in your relationship with Juliet." He thumbed through some pages before thumping one with his forefinger. "In fact, you've written her in right here."

Romeo nodded and clasped my hand. "We understand the risks, Counselor, but this is very important to Lettie."

"But what about you?" he asked. "Is this important to you as well?"

Romeo was silent a moment, and then he nodded. "I want us to finally succeed."

I held my breath. If we didn't begin right away, the opportunity to set things right and reunite our families would be lost. The Counselor just had to approve our life plan. The people who have been my parents throughout all these lifetimes, and those who have been Rom's, have already reincarnated. And my close friend Norene who was my nurse in that disastrous first life, then accompanied me in several other lives, and was

Norma in my most recent life, was being born right now. She willingly agreed to help me in this life as well. But first I have to be born.

Tio turned sideways in his seat to face the Counselor. "As you can see, I've decided to go into this life with Romeo to keep a closer watch on him."

The counselor lifted an eyebrow at him. "Mercutio, you haven't incarnated since the late fifteenth century, when you were stabbed to death by one of the Capulets. You vowed never to go back to Earth again. Are you certain you want to risk it?"

Tio winced and glanced at Romeo. "I know it'll be a big adjustment after all these centuries, but Romeo needs my help this time in human form."

"But then who will serve as his spirit guide?" The Counselor asked. "Romeo must have assistance from Home."

"Henry," Tio replied.

"The young soul who was my brother in my most recent life," I explained. Not that I needed to. Counselor Everman already had all the information in front of him. "Henry admitted to me that physical life was too hard for him, but he's been in training to be a Spirit Guide and feels he's ready."

The Counselor nodded and flipped through a few more pages. "I approve of your choice."

"So do we have your blessing?" I asked.

He peered at us over his glasses. "This will be the final attempt. And I will only give my approval on one condition."

Celeste and Tio exchanged surprised glances.

"Condition?" Celeste asked. "You never mentioned any such condition when we were drafting this plan."

The Counselor looked at the four of us with deep love and concern. "In order to prevent another wasted life, I have decided there must be a code word." He leveled a stern gaze at Rom and me. "Something implanted deep in your psyches, so that when confronted with it, the two of you will remember on some level who you really are and why you are on Earth." He turned to Celeste and Tio. "And it must only be used if the two of them are in danger of failing in this mission."

The four of us sat in an uncomfortable silence. I understood that Counselor Everman was only looking out for our best interests, but his word was final, and without his approval none of this planned life would happen. One by one we all nodded our agreement to his final condition.

"What will the code word be?" I asked.

"Everlasting," Everman said.

Chapter 3

Indianapolis, Indiana, 2020

"Are we about ready?"

I followed Nora's gaze, checking one more time to make sure I hadn't forgotten anything. If I messed this up, my father would kill me. Not literally, of course, but he'd be really disappointed, and I didn't need that kind of guilt.

"I think we're all set," I said. "Punch, cookies, red napkins, heart-shaped plates, candy hearts. Everything that goes with a Valentine's theme."

"And the shoes?" Nora walked over to the rectangle display table near the entrance that I'd been painstakingly arranging and rearranging all afternoon. The one I hoped would attract customers' attention as they walked in. She studied it from two different angles with a critical eye. "Are these going to bring people in?"

Would they? Maybe it was all wrong. Was the display too cluttered? Did I choose the wrong styles? I rushed over and moved the women's black pumps to the other side of the table, away from the brown leather, high-heeled boots.

Nora reached over and stilled my hand. "Julianne, relax. You've done a beautiful job here. I'm surprised you had time to do this much. Didn't you have classes this afternoon?"

I had so many balls in the air just then, I felt like a circus clown. "I was supposed to, but…" I sighed and tried to shrug off the guilt. "That English Comp class is a total waste of my time anyway. I learned about rhetorical analysis in high school."

Nora crossed her arms and tapped her toe. "Julianne, you can't be cutting classes. You know Samuel wants you to finish your degree in Marketing."

"Associate's degree." I groaned at her look of disapproval. "Don't worry, Nora, Dad doesn't know I missed one little class. Natalie's going to email me the notes so I'll be ready for the midterm."

Nora sighed. "Well, maybe if business picks up you can transfer to a university instead of Community College, which is obviously too easy for you."

"Part time schooling is the best I can do right now. Dad needs me here, and you work full time, and Mom…" I shook my head.

I stepped back and studied the display one last time, agonizing again over the arrangement of the shoes from our limited inventory of discount brands and designer knock-offs. Unlike that big chain store opening down the street that would cater to the couture crowd. I moved the ladies' ballet flats an inch to the right, back to the left, and then returned them to where I'd put them in the first place. I threw up my hands in surrender. "There. No worries. They should just fly off the sales rack and save this month's bottom line."

Nora crossed her arms and tapped a toe. "She said sarcastically, hoping to stave off financial ruin."

"Slight exaggeration, don't you think?"

Our open house was set to begin in an hour. I still

had to change out of my jeans and into my sweater and skirt, one that complemented the black knee-high lace-up boots I was planning to model. I was hoping some of our regular customers, many of whom had been shopping here or having their shoes repaired since Mr. Weinstein owned the store, would stop in and bring friends. Dad even made it a point to talk up this event to his shoe repair customers. Fingers crossed.

In addition to the flyers and social media posts, I'd put a big sign in the window and even put out one of those old-fashioned sandwich boards on the sidewalk. If buyers didn't stop in on their way to the Grand Opening at Montgomery International Footwear Emporium this evening, maybe the balloons and café string lighting would lure them down the street to our Shoe Lovers Sale afterward.

The big announcement that Montgomery's was buying an abandoned book store building in downtown Indianapolis got splashed all over the news and social media last year. Before we knew it, renovations were completed, and there it was, a high-end chain store a block and a half from our mom and pop store. How could we compete with something that size and with that kind of marketing clout? Customer loyalty could only go so far. I'd agonized for weeks over it, and then the idea for this event just popped into my head, almost as if someone had whispered it in my ear.

"Do you think this is going to work?" I asked Nora, sweeping my arms around the store to indicate all my hard work.

She gave my shoulders a squeeze. "Let's hope so."

****

Roman Montgomery was doing his final walk-through of the entire store before the Grand Opening. He checked his Rolex. One hour. Roman made sure that everything was in order on the second floor, which featured Men's Business and Casual Footwear, and Women's Business Footwear and Accessories with its large selection of handbags, gloves, and scarves. There was even a section for children's shoes. The main floor was mostly Women's Designer Shoes, but in the far corner near the street entrance were Men's and Women's Casual shoes and The Latest World Fashions.

Roman's employees were busy putting the finishing touches on eye-catching displays of footwear and setting out champagne and hors d'oeuvres for the shoppers, the media, and the expected local dignitaries. A four-piece chamber orchestra was tuning, ready to cue up the minute the doors opened.

In honor of the occasion, Roman was dressed impeccably in a dark gray Italian suit with a coordinating silk tie, its diamond clasp sparkling in the department store lighting. Tonight's event demanded that he showcase something from the designer collection, and the thousand-dollar black Italian leather monk-strap shoes fit like a second skin.

Instead of taking the stairs, Roman walked to the second-floor elevator bay. He pushed the Down button to go to the Main Floor and waited. And waited. Just as he was thinking he'd have to call the repairman before they'd even opened, the elevator doors parted and Roman was surprised to see his best friend inside the car, grinning at him.

Roman stepped inside. "I thought you said you weren't coming tonight." He pushed the button as he nodded silent approval of Mercer's attire. Tonight, his friend had traded in his usual frat boy look for jeans that were crisply starched and blessedly free of rips and had paired them with a white dress shirt and navy blazer. But then Roman caught sight of Mercer's worn sneakers and rolled his eyes.

Mercer shrugged and adjusted his black thick-framed eyeglasses. "Well, I don't have a date to impress, or a fiancée like some people," he said with a sideways glance at Roman. "I didn't want to embarrass you, just come out and offer support as you take on your first job." Mercer let out a low whistle. "General Manager. Wow."

"That's why Dad sent me to college," Roman said. "So I could take over the business one day." The elevator pinged as it opened one floor down. Roman stepped out with Mercer right behind him.

Roman gave the Main Floor a visual once-over. Everything on this floor, especially the women's upscale lines, had to be perfect. These designer brands were Montgomery's signature collection and brought in the high-end clientele. That had been proven repeatedly by his father's other stores all over the Midwest, as well as right here in Indiana at their anchor store up in well-to-do Hamilton County.

"Aren't you worried about that little place down the street?" Mercer asked. "That shoe repair store?"

Roman smirked and waved that idea away like he was swatting at a fly. "Caplan's will be out of business before the month is out."

"They're having an open house down there tonight, too. Something about a Shoe Lovers' Sale."

Roman stopped walking and turned to face Mercer. "Huh?"

Mercer shrugged. "I saw it on social media. Clever idea if you ask me. Valentine's Day and all."

"I didn't ask you," Roman said as he rearranged a table of women's dress pumps. Their retail price at other stores was about six hundred dollars, still pricey but not profitable. Even less if they went on sale. Montgomery's International Footwear Emporium took pride in never having markdowns, so the pumps were listed at eight-hundred and fifty dollars, a retail value usually found in places like New York or Chicago. And Roman was confident that not only would they sell, they'd soon be on backorder.

"Well, I think I might walk down there," Mercer said. "To the mom and pop store, I mean." Mercer picked up a pair of wedges from the carefully arranged display and examined them closely. "Thought I'd check out the competition for you." He tossed the shoes back down on the table.

"Caplan's is hardly competition." Roman moved the wedges back to their original spot. "But I expected some loyalty from my oldest friend." He gave Mercer the side-eye. "Besides, it's freezing outside and that place is bound to be Deadsville. All the shoe shoppers will be here."

"Just because your lady-love Rosaline will be gracing your arm tonight doesn't mean I want to spend my Valentine's night all alone. I hear there are some cute college girls who work at Caplan's."

"Where did you hear that?" Roman took a step back to assess a display of spring shoes with a critical eye.

"One hears things," Mercer said with an exaggerated wink of the eye. When Roman glanced at him skeptically, Mercer added, "Yeah, okay, I've been in there." He threw up his hands in surrender. "Hey, my favorite boots had a hole in them and the guy does great repair work. So what do you say? Go with me?"

"Count me out." Roman peered out the large glass entryway doors at the growing crowd of eager shoe shoppers waiting for the doors to open at seven p.m. He could feel the excitement like electricity crackling in the air. *Too bad the weather's not as nice this February as it was in 2012. Those people in line must be freezing.*

Back in 2012 Roman was fifteen and, with his parents rarely around, he'd long since figured out how to manipulate the nanny du jour and get out of the house whenever he wanted. And that year he'd wanted to go to downtown Indianapolis to take part in the pre-Super Bowl activities. He'd texted Mercer, told the nanny they were going to a movie, and gave the chauffeur a sizable tip to keep quiet. Then the two of them spent several hours enjoying the zip line, food booths, and celebratory activities, all set up for the thousands of people who had descended on Indianapolis for Super Bowl Forty-Six at Lucas Oil Stadium.

That year the outdoor temperatures were in the fifties and sixties, highly unusual for early February in Indiana. Hopefully when potential customers walked inside the new store tonight, they'd forget about the ten-degree wind chill, peruse the displays of spring and summer footwear, envision warmer weather, and then make sizable purchases. Roman was determined to prove to his father that his trust was well-placed.

Roman's Executive Assistant waved at him from across the room and hurried over. Ben Voss was short, skinny, and sported a bad haircut that made his face seem lopsided. His dark blue business suit was off-the-rack, but Roman had insisted that Ben at least wear a pair of decent business shoes. The knock-offs Ben had chosen, probably from a store like Caplan's, were at least unobtrusive.

"Everything's ready, Mr. Montgomery," Ben said as he shifted back and forth in his new loafers, "just waiting for you to give the word to open the doors."

Roman gave Ben a nod and a half-smile. He glanced up at the digital clock projected on the wall over the main entrance. "Okay, let's get this party started."

Ben gave a nod to the two doormen, who moved in sync as they unlocked the glass doors. With a blast of cold air, the shoppers streamed in, laughing, chatting, blowing on their hands and stomping their feet, and headed straight for the displays. The orchestra broke into an energetic classical piece, designed to get customers excited and moving. Waiters with trays of hors d'oeuvres circulated while others poured champagne for the adults and cider for the kids, with chilled water available as well. Roman didn't want his guests distracted by hunger or thirst while they shopped.

"Go mingle," Ben whispered in Roman's ear.

This was the part that Roman liked the least. He much preferred the marketing and financial strategies he'd studied in school, the ones that kept a large business like theirs at the top of the stock exchange. Schmoozing with customers wasn't his thing. That was why his parents insisted he needed Rosaline Vandenberg at his side. The daughter of his parents' dearest friends, she was older than Roman by a couple of years and already a pro at social events and mingling with high rollers.

But Ben was right, interacting with these people was expected of him, so Roman smiled at the throngs of buyers and gawkers, offering a nod here or a handshake there. "Has my fiancée arrived?" he asked Ben.

"I'll check, sir." Ben hurried off.

****

Dad studied my display with a critical eye. I held my breath, sure he would find fault with something, but instead he smiled and gave me a nod. "Julianne, you've outdone yourself. I have high hopes for this evening."

My father worked really hard to build this business. He bought the store in 1999 from original owner Mr. Weinstein, who retired after decades in this same location. The business had been successful for the most part—a few slumps here and there, like during the 2008 recession, but nothing as threatening as the possibility of a mega-chain store pushing us out. Dad spent a lot of money on the flyers we sent out to residences and nearby businesses to drum up interest in tonight's event, while I posted notices on our social media pages.

Dad used to be the face of Caplan's, busy greeting and waiting on customers, but as I got older and took on more responsibility, he seemed happier working solo in his shoe repair shop. He called it his private sanctuary, where he played his music—some weird heavy metal stuff from the 1980s—and worked on saving customers' old shoes from the trash heap. If I was not in class or at the library I was here, and I usually didn't have any other help except Jon or Mom, who really wasn't much help at all. Nora occasionally pitched in, but she was a nurse at St. Stephen's Hospital, so her free time was limited.

"Where's Jon?" Dad asked me.

I bit my tongue to keep from groaning. "Haven't heard from him."

Dad decided back when I was in high school that I should be dating Jonathan Parris, like he was anyone I'd ever be interested in. My parents and Jon's parents were friends from Synagogue, but Jon just wasn't my type. He was a computer geek, which wasn't a bad thing in this age of technology, but he was always so focused on whatever program he was writing or game he was designing that he couldn't talk about anything else. I usually got bored and tuned him out whenever he started droning on about pixels or algorithms. I preferred the tall, handsome, intellectual types, the ones who could discuss literature or theatre. But now that I spent all my time either working at the store or going to school to learn how to run a business I already ran, I rarely had time for dating. Not that Dad would approve of anyone but Jon anyway.

"He should be here." Dad pulled out his phone and fired off a text.

I made a conscious effort not to roll my eyes and changed the subject. "Where's Mom? Fashionably late?" I was being charitable.

Dad put his phone back in his pocket. "I told her I expected her to be here as well."

It was pretty bold of me to even try this on Valentine's, much less a night when a store like Montgomery's was having its much-publicized Grand Opening. But I was proud of the unique idea I'd come up with, and I was counting on it to work. I'd placed a stack of blank nametags on the checkout counter, and some red and black magic markers next to a large printed sign with these instructions:

How to Find Your "Sole" Mate!
Fill Out Your Nametag As Follows:
First Name Only
Favorite Type of Shoe
Ideal Place to Wear Those Shoes
Then:
Mingle and find like-minded shoe enthusiasts

Since it was Valentine's Day, the nametag idea seemed like a good way to get people moving around the store and talking to each other, hopefully making a connection with a new friend or, better yet, a new pair of shoes. And to my delight, customers or curiosity-seekers—it was hard to tell which—were starting to trickle in.

"Welcome to Caplan's Shoe Lovers Event," I told them. "Make yourself a nametag and help yourself to refreshments." I pointed to a table at the far end of the store with a bowl of chilled bottled water, a coffee urn next to small Valentine's Day-themed paper cups, and boxes of pink sugar cookies from a nearby mom-and-pop bakery. I had festively decorated the table with a red tablecloth, sprinkled it with candy hearts, and tied on red and white balloons. I just hoped it wasn't too cheesy.

"Put on your nametag," Nora whispered in my ear.

Hers, stuck to her scrubs shirt, read, "Nora, Nine West, black dress heels, dinner at La Bella Italiano." I filled out my nametag: "Julianne, flip flops, Waikiki Beach." I stuck it on my pink scoop-neck sweater.

"Why Waikiki Beach?" Nora asked.

"Why La Bella?" I shot back. When she just looked at me with that *duh* expression, I sighed. "Hawaii is on my bucket list, just like that fancy Italian place where everyone gets engaged is on yours."

"Well, don't book your reservations yet. Judging by this crowd," Nora said, scouting out the store, "a few pair of cross-trainers is about all you're going to sell."

I studied the clientele we were attracting, and she was right. Probably not big spenders. I didn't recognize anyone, so they weren't our regular customers, which was good because we needed to attract new shoppers if we were going to hold our own against Montgomery's. Other than the exercise enthusiasts, though, the rest were twenty-somethings wearing jeans, faux-fur lined boots, fleece jackets with trendy scarfs, and clinging tightly to their pocketbooks as they nibbled the free cookies.

"I can only imagine the kind of crowd they've got down the street," I whispered.

"Wealthy," Nora whispered back. "Oh, hi there, may I help you?" she asked as a woman picked up a pair of heavy-duty boots and examined them closely. Nora glanced at the woman's nametag. "It looks like you're into snow boots, Nancy. Planning a ski trip?"

****

"Roman, darling, this party is everything we hoped it would be." Rosaline gave him a peck on his cheek, clinging tightly to his arm and smiling benevolently at the store's customers.

Roman winced at the "we" part as he glanced at his fiancée. This whole event was his baby, but he had to admit Rosaline played her part well. Since she routinely socialized with Indianapolis's movers and shakers, lunched with Her Honor the Mayor, and was often seen dining with sports figures and local celebrities, Rosaline was constantly in the public eye and all over social media. Frequently her fiancé's new business venture was mentioned as well, which is precisely what Charles Montgomery had counted on when he insisted on their engagement before giving his son the job as general manager.

As the unofficial hostess for this evening's gathering, Rosaline displayed both good taste and high fashion. Her black sleeveless lace cocktail dress showed off her long legs and accentuated her short, dark hair, and she had on a pair of very expensive, suede, high-back pumps with a matching clutch. Roman estimated that the whole outfit must have cost nearly four thousand dollars, but her father could easily afford it.

"So far so good," Roman told her. "We probably have five hundred people here, and they're being free with their credit cards."

"Champagne, sir?" A waiter with a tray of flutes filled with bubbly stopped next to them.

Roman shook his head.

Rosaline accepted a glass. "Roman, darling," she said as she sipped from the glass, "don't be a bore. This is a celebration. Have some champagne."

He reluctantly selected a glass off the tray, toasted his fiancée, but only took one tiny sip before surreptitiously setting it down nearby. He wanted to remain clear-headed this evening.

"Dude, great party!" Mercer came up behind them, stopped the waiter and switched out his empty champagne glass for a full one off the tray. He toasted first Rosaline and then Roman before downing it in one gulp.

Roman waved the waiter away. "Mercer..." He eyed his friend warily. "You didn't drive tonight, did you?"

Mercer waggled a finger in Roman's face. "I did not." He turned to Rosaline and looked her up and down, then let out a low whistle. "Damn, girl, you look scrumptious." He tried to put his arm around her but staggered and completely missed.

Rosaline made a face as she shoved him away. "Honestly, Mercer, you're drunk and disgusting."

Mercer gave her a silly grin. "Just having fun." He glanced around the store and then fake-whispered, "On the prowl for pretty girls."

Rosaline lifted her nose as if she detected an unpleasant odor, then looked him up and down. "Why any woman would go out with you I can't imagine. You've got no job, no future, no style, nothing."

Roman narrowed his eyes. "Rosaline, that's enough. Mercer's my friend."

"I have job prospects," Mercer retorted as he teetered backward. "And the ladies love me. If it weren't for my influence, lover-boy here would have had no social life in high school or college."

Rosaline's eyes shot daggers at Mercer. "Well, you're not schoolboys anymore. You need to grow up." Before Mercer could answer, she caught sight of the mayor, broke into a smile, and waved over Roman's head. "Yoohoo, Carolina!"

Roman acknowledged the mayor with a tilt of his head, patted Rosaline's arm, and off she went.

As soon as Rosaline was gone, Mercer stood up straight and looked his friend in the eye. "Roman, why do you let that woman drag you around by the nose?"

Roman took a step back in surprise. "You aren't drunk, are you?"

"Nope. I've got a plan, but first I had to get rid of her royal snootiness."

Roman blew out a puff of air and patted his foot on the hardwood floor. "That's my fiancée you're slandering."

Mercer groaned. "It's an arranged match, dude. You don't know anything about real love."

Roman winced. Mercer was right; he'd never had a serious girlfriend, never had deep feelings for any woman, his fiancée included. "Rosaline's father is Dad's oldest friend," Roman shot back.

Mercer smirked. "I can see the headlines in The Indianapolis Star now." He drew his hand across an imaginary headline. " 'Billionaire real estate heir merges with designer footwear Golden Boy.' "

"Marries," Roman corrected.

"I didn't stutter. Come on, Roman, let's get outta here, go down to Caplan's and check out the Shoe Lovers' Sale."

Roman scowled. "I'm working."

Mercer pointed out all the employees hovering around customers. "They don't need you. If anyone has a question, there's Ben over there, running the whole show. Come on. Let's go have some fun."

True, Roman thought, the Grand Opening was on automatic pilot. But he had huge responsibilities and his father's high expectations to consider, which made just taking off seem irresponsible. And of course there was his fiancée. She'd be furious. "What about Rosaline?"

"She's not invited." Mercer pointed to a far corner

near the designer handbags where Rosaline was schmoozing with the mayor and some professional football players' wives. "You'll be back before she even knows you're gone." He gave Roman a shove toward the exit.

Roman's eyes darted around to see if anyone was watching before they stepped outside, and then he sucked in his breath, stomped his feet, and blew on his hands. "Man, it's cold out here." He thought about going back inside to retrieve his overcoat, but suddenly he liked the idea of this little adventure, and returning to the building would force him back to work.

Heads ducked against the wind, the two of them scurried to the corner and pushed the crosswalk light, jumping up and down while they waited for it to turn over. When it did, Roman pulled up the collar on his suit jacket and hurried across Maryland Street to the opposite side. Together they practically ran the block and a half to Caplan's.

"This is it?" Roman stopped to catch his breath as he stared skeptically at the structure. He'd been told there was a mom-and-pop shoe store near Montgomery's, but this was the first he'd seen of it. The building was all brick and not in good repair, judging by the roof tiles sticking up and a broken gutter pipe hanging from a corner. Caplan's Shoes and Repair was the only full-time business in the four-plex building, probably built in the 1940s, Roman conjectured. Caplan's was on the far corner. The storefront next to it was empty, and next to that was the former Kramer Florist with an old, rusted-out sign that had never been taken down. According to the banner inside the window, the shop was now one of those seasonal businesses called Holidays, featuring Valentine's gifts at the moment. The opposite end unit, whatever it had been before, was temporarily being used as a political campaign office. *Carpenter Smythe for Governor* signs were plastered to the windows and propped against the walls inside. "It's a wonder Caplan's is still in business," Roman said.

"Yeah," Mercer said, following Roman's gaze. "The place has seen better days." He shrugged.

Roman thought the owners were trying a little too hard to attract business. Next to their painted window sign they had strung café lights over a big banner announcing their Valentine's event, and even had one of those tacky sandwich boards right in front of the door. "Cheesy," Roman said as he kicked it out of his way.

Once inside, Roman had to admit that Caplan's was laid out in a functional manner and appeared to be neat and clean. Straight ahead were about a half dozen racks of shoes labeled Men's, Women's, Children's, and then off to the right and toward the back was an old wooden sign with a faded red arrow that read "Shoe Repair." To the left of the entryway door was the wooden check-out counter, with a computer balanced atop a strong box in lieu of a cash register.

"Welcome, gentlemen," a young woman said. "Make yourself a nametag, help yourself to refreshments, and feel free to mingle." She gestured to a stack of peel-and-stick tags next to the computer.

Roman watched as Mercer scoped her out. She appeared to be about their age, medium height and a bit plump, with short reddish-blond hair tucked behind her ears, revealing plain silver ear studs. She was wearing nursing scrubs and of all things in a shoe store, a pair of generic white nurse's slip-ons.

"Have a nice evening," the woman said.

Roman shuddered. "Thanks."

"Come on, play along," Mercer whispered. "There are some cute girls in here." He tilted his head in the direction of the refreshment table where a couple of twentysomethings in tight yoga pants had their heads together, giggling and nibbling cookies.

Roman sighed as they went to the counter to fill out nametags. "I can't believe you talked me into this," he muttered, filling out his tag and then handing the pen to Mercer.

Mercer wrote his first name, Nikes, and Lucas Oil Stadium, and then stuck his nametag on his lapel.

****

About an hour into the Valentine's event, we'd had a better turnout than I'd expected. Many of the shoppers were probably coming or going from the big opening down the street, but they did seem interested in the game of Find Your Sole Mate, and the free cookies from the popular downtown bakery didn't hurt, either. A few took Dad's Shoe Repair business cards which I'd prominently displayed next to the cash register. Dad, who was watching all the activity from the back of the store, looked pleased.

My friend Natalie from school popped in, still dressed in her Pilates workout gear.

"Thanks for coming," I said from behind the counter.

She smiled. "I said I would. Besides, this Find Your"—Natalie put up air quotes—" 'Sole' Mate thing sounds like fun!" She filled out her nametag, and then

50

scouted out the crowd. "Maybe I'll hit on him."

I followed Natalie's gaze to the door as family friend and Nora's work colleague Dr. Ty Bolton strolled in. Ty's a little scary-looking, if you ask me, short and stocky, over-developed quads, and his huge biceps are covered in tattoos. Not someone I'd want hovering over me in an ER. Even on a cold night like tonight he was wearing scrubs with a long-sleeve shirt underneath, no jacket, and sporting his perpetual scowl.

"Good luck with that," I told Natalie.

Natalie and I both watched as Ty made a beeline for Nora, who was pointing a customer toward the women's athletic shoes. Ty put his arm around Nora's shoulder, but she shrugged him off and shot him a dirty look. He winked at her as she turned her back on him to speak to the girl wanting workout shoes. He shrugged and sought out my dad.

"I see what you mean," Natalie said. "But I don't see a ring on his finger, so..." She grabbed the nearest pair of shoes, ones I doubted she'd ever wear because they were clunky brown pumps when all I'd ever seen her wear were ballet flats, and sidled up next to Ty and my father.

I shook my head.

As predicted, Mom was fashionably late from who-knows-where. She certainly didn't have any kind of a job. Lydia Coleman-Caplan strolled in the door dressed like a school girl in a way-too-short plaid skirt, a white cashmere sweater with a too low scooped neckline, and a pair of platform pumps that had her towering over Jonathan Parris, whom she dragged in with her. For all the pushing Mom and Dad did to get Jon and me together, Mom seemed to spend more time with him than I did. Mom used to occasionally help out here in the store, but she claimed that finances and cash registers weren't her thing, so now she spent her days lunching with friends, shopping, or attending yoga classes. Mostly spending Dad's hard-earned cash.

"Julianne, you look…" Mom left the rest unsaid as she gave my cheek a peck and my attire an obvious once-over. "Wearing pink I see."

"Mom," I groaned. I self-consciously swiped at my pink sweater and reached up to smooth down my curly auburn hair. My mother constantly harped on the fact that redheads should never wear pink.

She frowned as she studied my face. "And…"

I hurriedly pulled my glasses off. Mom hated those, too. She said they made my Jewish nose look even bigger and had insisted on buying me contacts when I was twelve.

"Nice to see you, Jules," Jon said with a big grin. "Did your mom tell you about the video game I'm developing?"

I hated that nickname. "Um, no." I did a quick visual search of the store, looking for a means of escape or customers needing assistance, anything to keep me from having a boring conversation with Jon. I spotted Nora trying to get my attention, waving her arms like she was hailing a cab.

"Mom, Jon, fill out nametags." I crossed the room to join Nora and said, "Thanks for the save."

Nora shook her head and lowered her voice. "Did you see the two hotties who just came in?"

She pointed to two very good-looking men who were filling out nametags. One of them was already eyeing some of the twentysomethings across the room, but the other one seemed nervous, his eyes darting between the door and his friend. I figured they were refugees from the high end party, judging by their appearance.

The nervous one was wearing a suit that must have cost a couple thousand bucks, not to mention his shoes, which had to be another eight hundred or more. He was over six feet tall, slender, with sandy blond hair that kept falling out of place onto his forehead, and he shoved it back in a way that I found quite sexy. The other guy, shorter, wiry build, with reddish-brown hair pulled back in a man bun, was dressed more casually, or maybe just less expensively, and rocking a pair of attractive eyeglasses. His shoes weren't nearly as expensive as his friend's, either, but of course I'd taken my glasses off, so I couldn't be sure.

I was surprised they weren't frozen to death, since neither of them had on a winter coat. They probably decided to come here on a lark. That made me a little angry, that Caplan's was their idea of a joke, but despite their chutzpah I decided I could be welcoming and professional.

Nora giggled. "Must have taken a wrong turn at the society party and ended up here. And don't look now, but Ty and Samuel have eyes on them."

I followed Nora's gaze and sure enough, Ty Bolton, his steely jaw set, was standing next to my father near the entrance to the repair shop and both were glaring at the two newcomers. *Oh now what,* I wondered. Ty always had his knickers in a twist about something, but Dad looked a little angry himself. The event was going well, so I decided to ignore them and refocus my attention on the hot guys as they moved toward the Men's shoe section and started browsing.

I felt a tap on my shoulder and turned in time to see Natalie pointing to the door. "Bald guy didn't bite, so I'm gonna go hit the books."

"See ya tomorrow," I said, my eyes and mind still on the cute guys.

"Unlike today?" Natalie grinned and left.

"Forget them," a voice behind us said, so close I could feel hot breath on my neck.

Nora and I turned around to see Ty standing behind us. I scowled at him. "Don't sneak up on people like that."

He managed a half smile and put a protective arm around Nora. "Sorry," he said. "Nice event."

She took a step back and his arm fell limp. "What are you even doing here? I thought you had the graveyard shift."

"Lunch break. Or whatever you call a meal you eat at nine p.m.," Ty said. To Nora's impatient toe tap, he added, "Julianne's dad invited me."

Yep, that sounded about right. Just like Dad was convinced I belonged with Jon, he kept pushing the Jewish doctor and my mom's younger half-sister together, thinking they were a match made in whatever passed for Jewish heaven.

"I was hoping you'd join me for a quick bite," Ty said.

"Well, I'm busy," Nora huffed. "If you're staying, go fill out a nametag." Hands on hips, she tilted her head in the direction of the checkout counter.

"Fine. But I'll be back."

"Now, where were we?" Nora asked with a conspiratorial giggle. We craned our necks to catch sight of the two cute guys, who had disappeared into the Men's shoe racks. "Maybe they need help with something. Go talk to them."

"Are you kidding me?" I frowned. "A guy dressed like that isn't seriously shopping here."

After a couple of minutes, they emerged from the Men's footwear aisle. I followed them to the counter, where they were eyeing the door and probably planning a hasty retreat. Of course Nora was right behind me.

"You guys look cold," I said. "Could I offer you some coffee?"

I spotted the nametag the tall guy had slapped on his expensive suit lapel, making me cringe at the thought of it leaving a mark, but I couldn't quite make out what he'd written. I really wished I'd put in my contacts.

"Yeah," cute guy Number Two said, "that would be great, if you have any." He gave his friend a smirk, grinned, and ambled alongside Nora to the refreshment table with the coffee urn.

That left me and the tall guy there alone, staring at each other. Yes, he was handsome, Ohmigod was he handsome, but there was something else about him...
"Um, you look really familiar. Have we met?" I bit my tongue when I realized that sounded like a lame pickup line.

"I don't think so," he said, a warm smile spreading across his face, "but I'm glad we're meeting now."

I melted right into my knock-off boots.

This advertising gimmick I'd thought up was working better than I'd imagined. I caught myself staring into his eyes, but then realized that was rude so I glanced down at his nametag. But because I didn't have on my glasses, all I saw was black chicken-scratches on a white nametag with a fuzzy red border. Fuzzy to me anyway. I took a step back, closed one eye, and forced the letters to come into focus. "Roman, flip flops, a beach in Hawaii," I read aloud. My eyes opened wide as I realized he and I had practically written the same thing.

He scrutinized my nametag and chuckled. "Hi, Julianne, nice to meet you." He extended his hand.

I reached for his outstretched hand and suddenly a tingle went down my spine. Like one of those déjà vu moments. "Uh…" I was rarely ever tongue-tied, but for some reason this guy was having a weird effect on me. I swallowed and tried again. "Thanks. Me, too. I mean, glad to meet you." I told myself to calm down, but my heart was racing a mile a minute. I wracked my brain trying to figure out why the guy looked so familiar. Handsome, well-dressed guys didn't usually just wander into Caplan's. School maybe? No, he didn't seem the type for Community College.

"I guess you work here, huh?" Roman said.

I nodded. "It's my family's business. Were you and your friend at that other party?" I glanced in the direction of the street.

He followed my gaze. "Yeah, Mercer—that's my friend—thought it would be fun to check this place out, too."

He hasn't let go of my hand yet. And I don't want him to. "So. Do you live around here?"

He had long lashes that framed blue-green eyes, and he was smiling at me. Me. Plain, plump, frizzy-haired, far-sighted, middle-class me. And he was still holding my hand.

"Um, yes, in Meridian Hills. I graduated from Butler University a couple of years ago, and..." His voice trailed off.

And what? I wondered. But I didn't really care what, because this was the most gorgeous man I'd ever laid eyes on. He was a little older than me, probably about twenty-three or twenty-four, with a college degree from a pricy private school in a ritzy neighborhood, while I was nineteen and still struggling to earn my Associate's Degree at community college. But right now, I couldn't care less about all that. What I cared about was the electricity that was flowing from his hand to mine.

Nora was back, juggling a Valentines-themed Styrofoam cup of hot coffee, her other arm linked in Mercer's, who was sipping from his own cup. "I didn't bring you one..." she said to Roman. She blushed, but whether from having forgotten his coffee or from the guy standing next to her, I couldn't tell.

Suddenly Nora's expression changed. She gave me the look, a signal we have between us when there was about to be trouble. I casually turned and followed her gaze to see my father and Ty in what looked like a heated discussion with frequent arm gestures and glances at me and Roman.

Roman saw them, too. "We'd better go," he said.

Mercer followed Roman's gaze and stared for a moment. "Roman, doesn't that guy in scrubs look kinda familiar?"

Roman shrugged. "Never saw him before."

Mercer shivered and set the nearly-full coffee cup on the counter. "I don't know, it's just something..." He shook it off. "Nice meeting you, Nora. Maybe we could get together for a drink some time."

Nora's eyes lit up. "Sure. I'd like that." She turned her back to Ty and Dad so she could sneak her phone out of her pocket. She gave it to Mercer, who inputted his numbers and handed it back.

"It was a pleasure meeting you, Julianne," Roman said. "Perhaps we can get together again, too."

I saw the look Mercer exchanged with Roman, probably meaning there was some reason I wouldn't actually see him again. Or maybe it was Roman's very polite way of saying *I'll call you,* with the full meaning of the brush-off. "Yeah, okay. Nice meeting you, too. I guess I'd better get back to work."

The two of them disappeared into the cold night air, as mysteriously as they'd arrived, and I was so disappointed I could cry. In defiance, I slipped my glasses back on. There was no one else here I cared to impress, and Mom seemed to have disappeared upstairs. I busied myself straightening up the nametags in disarray on the counter and looking around for any customers who might need assistance. But unfortunately the store had emptied out while I was busy flirting with Roman, and now there were only a couple of stragglers left. And pretty soon they were gone, too.

"Julianne, a word." My father had that look on his face, the one that said I'd disappointed him again.

Ty, hot on my Dad's heels, pulled Nora aside.

I rolled my eyes but only Nora could see. I put on my game face and attempted to sound light-hearted. "Great turnout, huh, Dad? A few sales and lots of good PR. I'm just sure we…"

"Yes, yes, it went well. However, that's not what I

want to talk about."

My shoulders slumped. "The guy I was talking to, right?"

"He's not our type."

And by "our type," Dad meant Jewish. "It was just a little harmless flirting." I sneaked a peek at my father, trying to judge whether or not I was convincing him. Didn't look like it. "I was just being a good hostess, hoping for a sale."

"Nonetheless, I expect you to stay away from him. You're practically engaged to Jonathan Parris…"

"Dad!" I said with a foot stomp. If I could see myself in a mirror I'd bet the expression on my face was pure horror. "Jon and I are friends. I'm only nineteen, for God's sake."

"Don't take the Lord's name in vain, young lady. And as far as your mother and I are concerned, Jonathan is the logical candidate to be your life partner."

I quit listening sometime around "life partner." Seriously, what was Dad thinking? I knew he and Mom got married really young, but there was no way I'd be making that same mistake.

I finished straightening up the counter in silence, restacking the unused nametags and tossing the used ones and the waxed backing into the trash bin, giving my father time to climb down off his high horse.

"You know I'm just looking out for your best interests, Julianne."

"I know, Dad." I faked a smile and let him hug me goodnight. I finished straightening the counter and ran the final sales report as Nora practically shoved Dr. Bolton out the door, locking it behind him.

"You okay?" Nora asked when we were finally alone.

I groaned. "Yeah, just Dad being Dad. He's all up in my face about Roman. Not like it's going anywhere anyway."

Nora gave me a conspiratorial grin and playfully punched my shoulder. "Yeah, but you two looked like you were hitting it off, so who knows?" She grabbed her coat from under the counter, put it on and buttoned it up, although I didn't know why she bothered. It wasn't like she had a long walk home. The four of us lived in the apartment over the store.

I shrugged. "I guess it wasn't meant to be. He gave me the old 'I'll call you' line."

"Don't write him off just yet," Nora said. She put up her hand to stop the inevitable *but*. "I'm off." She tossed her handbag over her shoulder. "If Ty asks, I went to bed because I have an early shift tomorrow."

"Do you?"

She winked at me. "What Ty doesn't know won't hurt him."

I snickered and started closing out the register.

"Oh, and by the way," Nora said, sticking her head back through the door. "About Roman. It took me a while but I finally figured out why he looked so familiar."

My heart started racing again at the mere mention of Roman. "Why?"

"He's Roman Montgomery, heir apparent to the Montgomery Designer Footwear fortune."

I stifled a gasp. "Are you kidding me?" But she looked as serious as a heart attack. I was pretty sure all the blood just drained out of my face. "How do you know?"

"I thought I recognized him from one of those celebrity gossip rags, so I Googled him." She wiggled her phone in my face. "He and his fiancée are all over the Internet." She waved over her head and closed the door behind her.

Seriously? I'd been flirting with a famous person who was a threat to my family's livelihood. The one guy on this planet I had no business crushing on. A soon-to-be-married man.

I groaned and pounded my head against the counter.

Chapter 4

Roman turned up the collar on his suit coat, shoved his hands in his pockets, and took off down the sidewalk.

"Hey, wait up!" Mercer called.

Roman wouldn't have chosen to slow his pace, but he was forced to wait for the crosswalk light at the intersection. Mercer caught up, panting, and leaned his hands on his knees to catch his breath.

"Why'd you take off like that?" Mercer gasped.

"That girl I was talking to," Roman said. The light indicated Walk, so he hurried into the street and onto the opposite curb. Mercer trotted along behind him.

"What about her?" Mercer asked, still breathing hard.

Roman stopped walking long enough to turn around and face his friend. "She's Julianne Caplan. Get it?"

Mercer's eyes widened. "Oh." He considered that a moment, and then shrugged. "So you flirted a little."

Roman finally took a deep breath and said, "It was more than that. Way more. Something just felt…" He fumbled for the right words. "Like I was supposed to meet her."

"What? Like karma or something?"

Roman didn't answer as he pushed through his store's glass entryway doors and into the building. It was blessedly warm inside, but for some reason he couldn't stop shivering. He blew on his hands several times.

"So you were talking to the daughter of the bug you're about to squash. No big deal."

Roman frowned. "It *is* a big deal." He looked straight ahead and muttered, "I like her."

Mercer guffawed. "That's ridiculous. You talked to her maybe ten minutes, and hello? Remember Rosaline? This was just supposed to be a little adventure."

"Mr. Montgomery, I've been looking all over for you." Ben Voss's face relaxed as he hurried to Roman's side, but then his expression changed to surprise as he surveyed Roman and Mercer's wind-blown appearance. "Have you been outside?"

"We went for some air," Roman told him. "What is it you need?"

"The musicians need to be paid, and the caterers wonder if it's time to start cleaning up or if you'd like them to stay. The champagne and hors d'oeuvres are nearly gone. Oh, and Miss Vandenberg is..." He tapped his foot as he gazed up at the ceiling, "...unhappy. She left with the mayor but told me to contact her when you reappeared."

Roman rolled his eyes. "Pay the musicians whatever we agreed on, tell the caterers they can finish up and go, and as for what to tell Rosaline..." His voice trailed off.

"Tell her...?" Ben prompted.

Roman pointed to the elevator. "Tell her nothing. I'll call her myself." Roman waved him away.

Ben opened his mouth, closed it, and then nodded

as he walked away. Once he and Mercer were alone, Roman reached for the elevator button.

Mercer jumped in front of Roman and prevented him from pushing the button. "You'd better call Rosaline right now. You know how she gets."

He knew. "Want me to call you an Uber?"

"Eager to get rid of me?" Mercer grinned. "Well, as a matter of fact, I'm meeting someone for a drink."

Roman started to reach around Mercer for the elevator button, but his phone pinged with a text. He glanced at it, saw it was from Rosaline, and pushed *ignore* before elbowing Mercer out of the way. "I'm not going back outside without a coat, but I *am* going. I've got to talk to that girl one more time." The elevator doors opened and he stepped in.

"Your funeral," Mercer called out as the elevator doors closed.

Roman almost agreed with Mercer as he rode up to his office, the executive suite, which was located in a private hallway behind the Men's Business Footwear department. He wasn't usually so impulsive, but this need to go back and see a girl he had no business seeing was as bewildering as it was overwhelming. He shook his head. *What's wrong with you?* But he knew the answer to that question. He wasn't in love with Rosaline, and he'd just met a very intriguing young woman.

Roman had known Rosaline Vandenberg all his life. Outside of their parents' friendship, he and Rosaline had little in common, since she was older and preferred a more sophisticated crowd. She'd never bothered with a job after receiving her marketing degree from Notre Dame, preferring her charity work and socializing.

Then six months ago Vandenberg Commercial Realty Company acquired a number of unoccupied buildings in downtown Indianapolis and brokered a sale of a former bookstore to Montgomery International Footwear Emporium. Charles named his son Roman as General Manager, moved some employees around from other stores, including Ben who had been at the Hamilton County store, and insisted Roman attend society and charity events to help promote the store's upcoming grand opening. Rosaline offered to introduce him to VIPs, and soon she was hanging on his arm as if they were a couple and hinting at getting married. His parents were all for it.

Before Roman knew it, his father's private jeweler had provided him with an engagement ring. He felt like he was on one of those reality TV shows, being rushed into an engagement to a woman he barely knew. At an art gallery opening two months ago, Roman handed Rosaline the jewelry box. Without a word she slipped the ring on her finger and that was that.

Roman unlocked his office and took his overcoat off the standing coat rack next to the door. He slid into it, tied the Burberry scarf around his neck, and started for the elevator. No, that wouldn't work. He'd be spotted if he tried to go out through the front doors again. So he went down the hall the other way, toward the freight elevator. That would take him to the back loading dock, out onto Maryland Street and completely out of sight of the front entrance.

There was something about that girl, Julianne Caplan. She wasn't what anyone would call beautiful, with a distinctly Jewish nose and long, curly auburn hair that seemed to have a mind of its own. Unlike Rosaline, who looked like a walking hanger, Julianne was average height with a build like a real woman, curves and all. And there was that sparkle in her hazel eyes that just reeled him in. He couldn't let it go.

Roman had to do something to get her attention. He sent Ben a text detailing what he needed and told him to meet him at the loading dock.

****

I kicked some boxes out of my way in the storage room behind the checkout counter. The delivery of new merchandise arrived a couple of days ago and I still hadn't gotten around to unpacking the boxes. I'd been too busy planning the Shoe Lovers Sale and pinning all my hopes on the outcome.

The sale and the evening had been going pretty well until those two cute guys came in, and wouldn't you know it, one of them was Roman Montgomery. What did they think they were doing? Spying? Hardly. Nothing in Caplan's came close to being competition for a place like Montgomery's. My original theory that they were playing hooky made more sense.

I glanced up at the institution wall clock, the one Mr. Weinstein installed back in the day. It was past midnight, but I wasn't the least bit tired. I was too wound up and had too many conflicting thoughts racing through my mind. *Start unpacking those boxes,* I told myself. Anything to get my thoughts back on business and off Roman Montgomery.

At least the shoe sale went okay. When I closed out the register and ran the final report, I was surprised to learn that we actually made a little money. But I'd bet the tally at Montgomery's tonight was in the thousands.

Lots of thousands.

I couldn't find a box cutter. I opened and closed the desk drawers, looked under shelving, and shoved aside the clutter near the overflowing trash bin. Which reminded me I needed to take it to the dumpster before I went upstairs to bed. I gathered up the bag and pulled its drawstring closed.

Our apartment over the store was a throwback to the 1940s, when families worked and lived in the same space. Mr. Weinstein's family lived in the suburbs, so he just used the upstairs apartment for storage. But when Dad bought the store and found out the living space came with it for free, he moved in with Mom. It had four small rooms, an efficiency kitchen, and one bathroom. The two of them were fine till I came along, and when Nora moved in several years later, it got really crowded.

A couple of years ago, Mom decided to do something about our tiny living quarters. She hired a construction crew to gut the old kitchen and turn it into a modern kitchen with marble countertops, stainless steel appliances, and custom cabinets. And Mom doesn't even cook. Then she put the crew to work on their bedroom, adding a bigger closet and small bathroom. It all cost a fortune and Dad wasn't happy, especially since Mom didn't have a job. Dad told her she was not to do any more redecorating until our finances improved, so Mom spruced up the twenty-year-old furniture with colorful throw pillows and bought new fluffy towels for the bathrooms.

I knew I should just go upstairs to bed, but I was still angry at myself for developing an instant crush on a cute guy who turned out to be the last guy on Earth I should ever crush on. "Damn it, Roman Montgomery," I shouted.

I reached for the door to the alley where the dumpsters were located, trash bag in hand. Before I could open it, someone knocked. Who could be here at this hour? It wasn't Nora, because she had a key. Jon Parris? Probably. I groaned and yanked open the door.

"Hi, Julianne. Mind if I come in?"

My jaw dropped because I was staring up into the handsome face of Roman Montgomery himself. And then I blushed when I realized I was holding a bulging trash bag, and realized he'd probably heard my outburst. I should tell him to take a hike, one practical joke per night, whatever, but I couldn't make my mouth work. Frigid air wafted in through the open door, so I tossed the bag aside and motioned him in as I shivered from cold, or maybe shock, I wasn't sure which.

I folded my arms across my chest and glared at him. "Slumming again?"

He seemed remarkably upbeat as he gazed around the cluttered stockroom. "I never was. Slumming, that is." He smiled at me. "I let Mercer talk me into coming down here on a lark, but if I hadn't come I wouldn't have met you. Here. I brought you this." He handed me a beautiful long-stem red rose.

I was stunned. I took the unwrapped rose, mindful of the thorns, and breathed in its divine fragrance. "Where did you get this in the middle of the night on Val...February fifteenth?"

He winked. "I have my ways."

He was so cute, and I was really tempted to play along with whatever this was, but he shouldn't be here. I shouldn't have let him in. What if Dad came down the stairs? I shook my head as I gazed at the floor, and then got embarrassed all over again because the floor clearly needed sweeping. "What do you want?" I asked as I kicked at a particularly egregious dust bunny.

"I want to talk to you."

I lifted an eyebrow. It wasn't that simple. It couldn't be. "Look, Roman, you're a competitor, sort of, and my dad already had a meltdown when he saw you talking to me earlier tonight."

Roman ignored my concerns and took a step closer to me. I would have backed up but there was no place to go without tumbling over unpacked boxes, so I just stood there. And when he reached for my hand, like earlier, I got the same tingle as before.

"I hope I didn't get you in trouble, but I really enjoyed talking to you."

Gulp. "Me, too." I shook my head. "But this is crazy." Whatever "this" was. And then I remembered what Nora told me about seeing him all over social media and jerked my hand back. "Aren't you engaged? To some rich heiress?"

Roman didn't blink. "Rosaline Vandenberg. Our parents are old friends and practically shoved us together." He glanced down at me, a sort of smirk on his face. "Would it help if I said I don't love her?"

"Help what?"

Roman took both of my hands this time and clasped them tightly. "Help me get a chance to know you?"

The guy's got a fiancée. And yet there I stood, unable or unwilling to move. We stayed in that position, hands together, staring into each other's eyes, for what seemed like an eternity, when suddenly he leaned in and kissed me lightly on the lips. I kissed him back, and just as we were really getting into it, the back door opened.

"Julianne!" Nora was standing there, her mouth agape.

I quickly withdrew my hands and lips and moved away from Roman. "Nora. I thought you...uh... Did you have a nice time?"

She shut the door, put her fists on her hips and glared at us. "What the hell are you two doing? Julianne, didn't you hear Samuel tell you not to associate with..." she jerked her thumb at Roman.

"Who's Samuel?" Roman asked.

"My dad," I told him, and then to Nora I said, "Roman and I were just talking."

"Talking. Right."

"Nora, please don't tell Dad. Or Mom. Roman's leaving anyway." I gave him a pleading look.

Roman looked me in the eye. "Not until you promise to see me again. Tomorrow?"

My eyes widened. "No way. I can't. I've got classes, work..."

"Fine. Then I'll meet you before your classes at that coffee shop on Illinois Street. Pop's? See you there at nine." He tipped an imaginary cap to Nora and left.

"Julianne..." Nora groaned after she closed the door behind him.

I'd just accepted a date with a guy I wasn't even supposed to talk to. Dad would disown me if he knew I was contemplating going out with a gentile, let alone that gentile. All perfectly logical reasons not to go, but still... "It's just coffee. I'll go and get it out of my system. Okay?" She didn't look convinced. "I promise

I'll go straight to class from there and not give Roman Montgomery another thought."

"Uh-huh."

****

"Where are you going this early?" It wasn't so much idle curiosity as it was an accusation. My father was at the breakfast table in his bathrobe, drinking coffee and reading the morning paper, something he did every morning. Except he usually did it an hour later.

I adopted my best *duh* face and replied, "Class."

Dad scrutinized me over the top of his newspaper. "Your first class isn't until ten-thirty." He squinted at the digital clock on the stove. "It's barely eight-thirty."

I had to do some fast thinking and even faster talking. "I'm meeting Natalie for coffee in the Student Union so we can go over notes for the quiz." I hoped I sounded convincing, and I reminded myself to fire off a text to Natalie as soon as I was out the door, just in case. "Why are you up so early?"

He returned to his newspaper. "Because it's just me in the store till you get there, since your mother..." His voice trailed off.

"I promised Nora I'd stop at the hospital and have lunch with her in the cafeteria." That much was true.

"Just don't forget you've got a job here in addition to your studies," Dad said. Coffee mug in hand, he stood and headed for his bedroom.

As soon as I was out on the street, I sent that text to Natalie. I've only known her a few months, but except for Nora, she was my only real friend. We were both studying business and struck up a conversation the first day of classes. And sometimes we did actually study, but more often we just grabbed a coffee or a bite of lunch.

Natalie replied to my text:

—*No problem*—

I'd never been to the coffee shop where I was meeting Roman, never even heard of it, but when I got there I figured out why. Pop's Bakery was tiny, tucked between a national brewery-style restaurant and a repertory theatre with a huge marquis outside. Pop's didn't have much of a sign, either, just the one stenciled on the window, but from what I could see from the sidewalk, the place had a following. Through the window I saw a line at the counter, men and women in business attire buying their lattes and muffins or bagels. I stood there shivering on the sidewalk, unsure if I was cold or nervous.

Should I really have coffee with a guy I just met a few hours ago, whose mega-store might force my family's business into bankruptcy? Aside from qualms about meeting Roman, I was also feeling guilty about blatantly lying to my father. But I couldn't solve either problem on the sidewalk in twenty-degree weather, so I opened the door and went in.

The place smelled heavenly. The scent of freshly baked goods and aromatic coffee wafted toward me, even though I was barely inside the door. Losing my nerve, I was about to bail, but was forced to jump out of the way to avoid being mowed down by a woman juggling hot coffee and a briefcase as she blew by me out the door. I took a deep breath. I did promise Roman I'd be here, and I was not one to stand up a date. Anyway it was cold and I could use a coffee before I went to class. I got in the back of the line.

"Ever tried Pop's famous blend?" someone behind

me asked.

I turned around and it was Roman. I smiled back as I drank in his twinkling eyes, his cute smile. "I usually just stop at the Student Union and pick up the ninety-nine cent special."

Roman grimaced. "Coffee's supposed to cost four dollars," he said in true rich-guy fashion. Then he winked at me and the cuteness was back. "Go have a seat and I'll bring you a cup."

"Cream and sugar," I told him as I scouted around the tiny shop for a place to sit. The few tables and chairs were already taken. "Have a seat where?"

"At the bar in front of the picture window."

There were three unoccupied barstools pulled up to a small countertop by the window that looked out onto the street. I was headed that way when I was hit with more anxiety. What if someone walked by and saw me in here with Roman? *That's stupid,* I chided myself. *You didn't know this place was here, so no one you know does, either.* I hurried over and claimed one of the stools, staring down a guy in jeans and corduroy blazer who'd tried to beat me to it. I was about to remove my coat and place it on the stool next to me, to make sure Mr. Metrosexual didn't try again, but Roman appeared just in time. He was juggling two steaming cups of coffee plus two very large blueberry muffins that looked and smelled yummy.

"Did you...?" I craned my neck and saw lots of people still in the queue, tapping their toes and checking their phones while they waited. Just because Roman was rich and famous didn't mean he should jump the line.

"Oh, Pop and I go way back," Roman said. "I

called ahead and he had my order ready." He handed me my beverage and muffin and sat down on the stool next to me.

I took a nibble of the muffin, which was still warm and practically melted in my mouth. Then I tried the coffee. I could taste hazelnut, but there was definitely chocolate in there, too, and a hint of mint, topped off with what I was sure was real cream whipped to a frothy peak. I moaned a little as I swallowed and let the steam circle around my still-cold nose.

"Pretty good, huh?"

"Understatement." I said. "So, why exactly are we doing this?"

Roman looked puzzled. "Drinking coffee?"

"This," I said, waving my arms around the coffee shop. "Meeting up?"

Roman shrugged and took a tentative sip of his still-steaming coffee, gasped, waved his hand in front of his mouth, and set it on the counter in front of him. "I told you last night," he said between coughs. "I like you."

I liked him, too, but that didn't get us anywhere except right back where we were before. I took another sip of the caffeinated ambrosia while I rationalized. Roman and I were just having a friendly cup of coffee, and he'd introduced me to a place I'd definitely come back to. If nothing else, that made it worth the trip.

But the truth was, Roman made my heart flutter in a way it never had before, so I decided to forget about my father's disapproval and enjoy the moment. "How did your Grand Opening go last night?"

Roman's eyes glazed over. "Great. We kicked butt. Do you really want to talk about work?"

No, but... "I don't know what else we can talk about. We barely know each other and shoes is the only thing we have in common."

Roman swiveled around on his barstool to face me. "So let's get to know each other. Tell me about yourself, your family. That woman, Nora. Is she your sister?"

I turned my stool to face him, too, bringing us so close that our knees were touching. But I was wearing black knee-high faux fur-lined boots, and he still had on his unbuttoned London Fog overcoat over his business suit, so there was a lot of fabric between us. Still, my spine tingled, and I didn't think it was the caffeine. "My parents married young and my dad bought the store from a guy who was retiring. I've lived in the apartment over our store my entire life. Went to an urban high school. Now I go to Community College part time and run the shoe store part time. And Nora Coleman is my aunt. What about you?"

"Raised by wolves." At my surprised look, he laughed. "Okay, nannies. My parents weren't exactly hands-on. Catholic schools all the way. Just got my MBA last spring. Now what about...she's your aunt?"

This was a story I didn't tell very often, especially to strangers, but somehow I trusted Roman. "Most people think we're sisters, and we don't usually correct them since that's how we were raised. She's my mom's half-sister. Grandma died pretty young and my grandpa soon married himself a trophy wife. She turned out to not be such a prize because she ran off with the manny when Nora was ten."

"Manny?"

I smiled. "Male nanny."

Roman nodded. "I had one of those once. Lasted six months."

"Anyway, after that, Grandpa was heartbroken, dumped Nora on my parents and moved to Florida."

"Ah," Roman said with a nod. "And she's a nurse?"

"Yeah, ER nurse at St. Stephen's Memorial. That's where she met Ty. Dr. Bolton. The guy who was glaring at us from across the store last night. He thinks she's his girlfriend and Mercer was encroaching on his territory."

"He's right," Roman said. "I think Mercer and Nora met up last night."

"I think so, too." I giggled at the thought of Nora shafting Ty like that. "What about you? Any sibs?"

He shook his head and his brow furrowed almost imperceptibly. "In fact, I'm surprised my parents stopped making money and jet-setting long enough to have me."

I felt really bad for him. He must have been lonely growing up, raised by hired staff. I wasn't particularly close with my directionless mother or my overbearing father, but at least I had Nora. "What about Mercer?" I asked. "A cousin or something?"

"Nope. Alvarez and I met in elementary school. His parents are members of the same parish. He was always kind of a free spirit, a wild child, and the two of us got into lots of mischief."

My take away from that story was "parish." I didn't know much about Protestant churches, but... My thoughts were interrupted when Roman's phone pinged with a text.

"Do you mind? It's probably my assistant, Ben."

He has an assistant? Of course he does. I motioned for him to take it and occupied myself finishing the marvelous brew and muffin before they got cold. Roman read his text, punched in a reply, and stuffed the phone back in its holder at his waist, frowning. Scowling even.

"Not my assistant. It was my dad. Wants me come to Chicago this weekend." At my raised eyebrow, he added, "Where my parents live. Something about a working lunch with the Board of Directors, and of course Sunday morning mass." Roman averted his eyes as we both silently struggled to avoid the elephant in the room. He was Catholic. I was Jewish.

What the hell was I doing anyway? "I gotta go," I told him. "My first class is at ten-thirty and I've got a bus to catch." I started digging through my handbag looking for, well, pretending to look for something anyway, trying to hide my embarrassment. Then I remembered I did need change for the bus, so I dug down in earnest.

Roman reached out and stilled my hands. I could feel him staring at me, just like he did last night right before we kissed. "Julianne, look at me."

I lifted my eyes to his.

"I know we come from different backgrounds, but we can figure it out."

"Figure what out? You've got a fiancée, and according to any number of social media sites, an upcoming wedding." Yeah, I Googled him.

He chuckled. "So you read that, huh? You know you can't believe half of what's on those posts."

I tried to envision a world where a Jewish girl and a Catholic boy could be anything more than friends.

Furthermore, I was the daughter of the small business owner that his Goliath of a corporation was about to annihilate. But he was still touching me and I couldn't focus.

"Well, Roman, aren't you going to introduce me to your friend?"

We forced ourselves to take our eyes and hands off each other to acknowledge the man standing next to us, a man who looked familiar to me. He was probably in his sixties, gray hair, kindly face, and drying his hands on a white apron.

"Morning, Pop," Roman said. "This is Julianne Caplan. Her father owns…"

"Yes. Caplan's Shoe Sales and Repairs." He nodded at me. "Your father does fine work."

Oh, of course. I remembered seeing Pop in our store last fall. He had a pair of wingtip loafers that badly needed resoling, and Dad did a masterful job of saving them from the trash heap.

Pop crossed his arms and lifted an eyebrow at Roman. "Interesting choice of breakfast companion."

"Don't start, Pop," Roman said. "Julianne and I met last night and I asked her here for coffee. *Coffee.* That's it."

"Did I say anything?" Pop raised his hands in mock surrender as he looked me over. Not in a creepy kind of way, but more like he was trying to figure out what was going through my head. I was wondering the same thing. Finally he rubbed his hand across his thinning hair and grinned. "I guess it doesn't hurt for a Montgomery to get to know a Caplan. Spread a little goodwill around the neighborhood."

"Thank you?" I didn't mean for that to come out

sounding like a question, but it was an odd thing to say. Were our families' situations really that unusual?

"Don't worry about us, Father," Roman said.

I glanced up at Pop and then back to Roman. "Father?"

Pop offered his hand to shake. "Pleasure to meet you, Julianne. I'm Albert Lawrence, also known as Father Al."

I turned to Roman. "A priest runs a bakery?"

"Yes, I'm still a priest," Pop said. "Just retired from parish service. Oh, I still get a call now and then to say mass, perform a wedding, or counsel a student at Roman's old high school."

"Whenever St. Agnes Prep had a bake sale, Father Al's homemade baked goods got snapped up fast." Roman waved his arm around the shop. "Coffee and pastry-lovers win."

Pop winked. "Everyone around here just calls me Pop. You can, too."

"Nice to meet you, Pop," I said, shaking his hand. A priest turned baker and coffee gourmet. Who knew?

"Can I get you two anything else?" Pop asked. "I'm not trying to shoo you out, of course, but I'd like to get started on some baking. Folks come in all afternoon for my famous chocolate chip cookies." He winked at us.

I glanced around the shop. I'd been so caught up in the chemistry between me and Roman that I hadn't realized the bakery had cleared out. "Oh, no thanks. I've got to get going."

"Let me walk you out," Roman said. "We'll come back soon, Pop, count on it."

Pop nodded and started wiping down the counter

that we'd just vacated.

Once outside, I pulled my coat tightly around me and fished my gloves out of my pocket. "Thanks again for the..." Breakfast? Date? Biggest mistake ever? I turned to head toward my bus stop, but Roman grabbed my hand.

"I'm not letting you go till you promise to see me again."

I sighed. "Roman, we can't." There were just too many obstacles to overcome to let this continue.

Roman drew me in close and wrapped his arms around me, warming me to my toes and providing an unexpected sense of comfort. He waved at something over my head, then tilted my chin up and kissed me. "Can I drop you at school? My driver's here."

Sure enough, a limo appeared at the curb next to us. Now don't get me wrong, I'd have loved to avoid the crowded bus and let Roman's driver take me to school in that huge rolling (and I assumed warm) glorified lounge, but I couldn't afford to let anyone see me getting out of it. I'd get way too many questions I couldn't answer. "No, but thanks."

"Here." He handed me his phone and waited while I keyed in my contact information. Roman waved his phone at me. "I'll call you," he said with a peck on my forehead.

His chauffeur, a beefy-looking guy more suited to the role of bodyguard than chauffer, opened the back door for him. Roman waved at me one last time before stepping in, and they drove off into downtown traffic.

Please don't call me. I didn't need the temptation. Better to remember a few stolen kisses and leave things as they were.

****

The one truth I'd told Dad this morning was that I was going to meet Nora for lunch. Since I hadn't eaten since that mouth-watering muffin and coffee at Pop's, I was starved, so I went. The hospital was only about a mile from campus, but despite the cold, I decided to walk and save the bus fare. I told myself the brisk exercise would do me good. I buttoned up my coat, tightened my scarf, and ducked my head against the wind.

I arrived cold and windblown, and pushed through the big glass doors at the hospital's main entrance. I was later than I'd intended to be, but with any luck Nora wasn't busy with a patient and could still meet me for a quick meal. I sent her a text and then texted my bank for my balance. I winced when I saw the amount in my account as I hurried through the maze of corridors to the cafeteria.

"Okay, I'm here," Nora said, a little breathless, as she joined me in the food line.

I glanced behind me and exhaled with relief. "Good. I was afraid it was too late for you to take a break."

The soup of the day was broccoli cheese, and it smelled as good as it looked, so I helped myself to a heaping bowl plus a generous handful of plastic-wrapped saltines. Nora took a cup of the soup, no crackers, and a large cup of black coffee. When we got to the checkout, I looked at her wistfully.

"Here, allow me," she said with an exaggerated eye roll. She swiped her badge which automatically got us both the thirty percent discount, and then she paid for our meals with her credit card.

"I'll pay you back, I promise."

"If I had a nickel for every time you said that, yada yada yada."

I gave Nora my best pouty-sorry face, which she ignored, found us a table and we sat down. I got a good look at her as I was crushing the crackers into my soup.

"Bad day?" I asked, tilting my head at her appearance. She was wearing wrinkled generic blue scrubs with a white long-sleeved shirt underneath, and the same generic slip-on nurse's shoes she'd had on last night. Her nametag, which read Nora Coleman, R.N., was sitting a bit crooked on her shirt.

"Yeah, an uncooperative GSW."

My eyes widened. "Someone got shot?"

She shrugged. "Never mind my day." She leaned in with a conspiratorial grin. "How was your morning?"

I tucked in to my food, mostly because I was hungry, but also because I was avoiding eye contact with her. "Got those English notes from Natalie."

She glared at me. "You know what I mean. Breakfast with Richie Rich."

I sighed and tossed the spoon into the half-empty bowl. "Did you know he's Catholic?"

"Shocker." Nora spooned up a bite of soup and let the rich, melted cheese ooze off her spoon and into her mouth.

I leaned back against the chair and stared at the ceiling. "Nora, what was I thinking? There's no way. Even if he wasn't engaged."

"Well, it's not like it was a real date. I mean, you know, coffee…" She shrugged, lifted her mug of coffee in a mock toast and took a sip.

A shadow darkened our table and Nora and I

glanced up at the same time. It was Ty, also wearing scrubs but with a white lab coat indicating his superior status. He sort of reminded me of a bull dog, all square shoulders and muscle. And he was scowling at both of us. I was glad I was just a family friend and not his patient.

"Date?" he asked.

I gave him a steely-eyed glare. "This is a private conversation."

He pulled up a chair next to Nora and helped himself to a sip from her coffee mug. "Not that Montgomery guy from last night? Don't tell me you're seeing him."

"If it's any of your business, which it's not," I said, "I ran into Roman this morning and he bought me a coffee."

Ty tossed back the rest of Nora's coffee, snagged one of my packages of crackers, and stood up. "Jewish girls don't date married Catholics."

"Roman's not married, and Julianne's not dating him," Nora growled at him. "And you owe me another cup of coffee."

Ty winked at Nora, lifted an eyebrow at me, and pointed to the coffee machine. "I'd better not hear that she is."

"You're not the boss of me," I said in true adolescent fashion.

He ignored me and left to get either Nora's refill or more coffee for himself, hard to say which.

Nora looked as exasperated as I felt. "I need to get to the store." I put my coat back on. "Any chance you can help out this evening?"

"Nope, I've got a double shift. Besides, now that

Montgomery's is open, I doubt you'll need two people on the floor."

She was probably right. "Thanks for lunch." I got up and started for the exit. "Give my regards to Dr. Buttinsky."

Chapter 5

Roman read his text message from Mercer.

—*Noon. Metro Community Center. No excuses!*—

Roman replied,

—*I'm working. Can it wait?*—

He waited for Mercer's reply, which made him smile:

—*The place is crawling with hotties. Need a wingman.*—

Typical.

His finger was poised on the keypad, ready to reply that he was too busy to go work out in the middle of the day. But after thinking it through, he buzzed Ben on the office intercom. "What does my afternoon look like?"

"You've got that meeting with the buyers at four," Ben replied, "and then you're free till the Altruistic Society dinner this evening. You're supposed to pick up Miss Vandenberg at seven."

Roman sighed. Another command performance with his fiancée. All the more reason to go work out some stress. "I'm going to the gym for a couple of hours," he told Ben. "But I'll be back for the buyers' meeting."

"No problem," Ben replied.

Roman put on his coat, closed his office door and rang for the private elevator that led directly to his parking space in the basement garage. Today he'd driven his own car, a BMW Limited Edition hot off the assembly line. He loved the luxurious feel of the leather seats and steering wheel, the five-speed gearshift, and the new color, a shade of royal blue the manufacturer called cobalt. Tonight, he'd have to let his chauffeur do the driving, but today he wanted to enjoy the freedom of being in the driver's seat.

Roman allowed himself to imagine seeing Julianne on his way to the gym. It wasn't such a far-fetched idea, really. Metro Community Center was located on the west side of Indianapolis near the community college and within walking distance of the medical corridor, both places he knew she frequented. He pictured her walking toward him, smiling, auburn hair flying in the breeze. But he sighed and let that fantasy go. He didn't know anything about what sort of schedule she kept, and he didn't even know if she'd ever agree to see him again. She hadn't exactly been answering his texts, and it had been days since their coffee at Pop's. So to take his mind off Julianne, he plugged his phone into the port and queued up a new classical piece, written by a young composer the media was calling the new Mozart.

Roman parked his Beemer in the lot adjacent to the sprawling one-story concrete building with the futuristic architecture. Metro Community Center was a fairly new facility, offering weight-lifting, indoor swimming, fitness classes attended mostly by women, and social and community information courses open to the public. He could have joined any number of private clubs with workout facilities, or just used The Skyline Club where his father had a membership, but he chose this one. He liked its lack of pretentiousness.

He beeped his car locked, walked into the building,

and swiped his membership card at the entry turnstile. Another perk of this place was his almost complete anonymity. Some of the members knew his first name, but with the exception of the office staff, who had his application on file, he was just another guy who liked to lift weights, use the Stairmaster, and occasionally relax in the sauna.

Mercer was leaning against the wall just inside the lobby, hands shoved in his jeans pockets, one foot propped on the wall, his gym bag slung over one shoulder with his cross-trainers peeking out.

Roman looked him up and down. "Trying out for our summer catalog?"

Mercer put both feet on the floor. "Huh?"

Roman shrugged. "You look like one of those male models we hire." He pointed to Mercer's bag. "Except for the lack of decent athletic shoes."

"Mine are decent," Mercer protested. "Comfortable, broken in, just the way I like them."

"Spend some money and buy yourself a pair of high quality cross-trainers, like I told you, and you won't get blisters."

"You forget my last name's not Montgomery." Mercer adjusted his gym bag and followed as Roman strode down the corridor adjacent to the free weights, and went into the men's locker room.

Inside were lockers all along two walls with benches, a weight scale like the kind found in doctors' offices, urinals and sinks off to the right, and the sauna at the far end. Like any gym, it smelled of damp towels, sweaty bodies and dirty socks. Roman wrinkled his nose as he spun the lock on his assigned rented locker, and drew out his blue polyester knee-length training shorts, Indiana Pacers t-shirt, and of course his high-end cross-trainers.

"All that griping about fashion and you're wearing an old basketball t-shirt?" Mercer looked askance at Roman's attire as he laced up his athletic shoes, tucked his sleeveless shirt made of moisture-wicking fabric into the matching shorts, and shoved his gym bag into the locker.

Roman glanced at his friend, who was obviously dressed for more than just a good workout. "I'm here to exercise, not fraternize," Roman replied. But he had to admit his clothes could use a wash. He crammed his bag into his own locker and slammed it shut.

The weight room wasn't crowded in the middle of the day. Roman started for the treadmills but Mercer tapped his shoulder and redirected him to the stationary bikes, conveniently located next to the stair climbers, which were occupied by a couple of attractive young women in neon-colored sports bras paired with coordinating yoga pants. Roman lifted an eyebrow at Mercer, but climbed onto a bike and programmed it.

Mercer gave the women his most seductive smile. "You ladies come here often?" He swung one leg over the bike and sat down, eyeing one of the girls.

Roman groaned inwardly and could almost hear the women groan, too. "Don't mind my friend," he told them. "He's harmless."

One of the girls giggled and slowed her pace on the Stairmaster. "I've heard worse pickup lines," she said.

Mercer grinned back, and then scrutinized her. "Say, didn't I see you back on Valentine's Day? At Caplan's Shoe Store, that Shoe Lovers thing?"

Roman took a quick peek, but he couldn't tell if

she was one of the women Mercer had been hitting on that night or not.

"Actually, we were," the woman said, smiling at Mercer. "Did you buy those loafers you were admiring?"

"Nah, I went to Montgomery's. Better quality."

Roman ducked his head and kept on pedaling. Since when did Mercer care about quality footwear? Apparently the girl was annoyed, too, because she upped the speed on her machine, placed her earbuds firmly in her ears, and went back to stair climbing,

"Was it something I said?" Mercer glanced at the other girl, but like her friend, she poked her earbuds in and stared straight ahead at the television attached to her machine.

"Smooth," Roman said.

They pedaled in silence for a while, and then Roman slid off the bike and headed to the free weights, Mercer at his heels. Just as Roman picked up a twenty-five pound barbell and started bicep curls, he caught sight of someone he thought he recognized. "Mercer, isn't that Ty Bolton? The surgeon at St. Stephen's?"

Mercer followed Roman's gaze. "Who?"

"The guy who dates Julianne Caplan's aunt, Nora Coleman. You know, the nurse you went out with that night?"

"Nora's her aunt? Huh. Thought they were sisters." Mercer watched Ty for a minute, shrugged and picked up a fifteen pound free weight. "Dude looks like he works out a lot."

Roman nodded. No doubt about that. The doctor's loose-fitting shorts accentuated his overdeveloped quads, and a too-tight sleeveless t-shirt showed off his broad shoulders, biceps the size of grapefruits, and ripped abs. He was bench-pressing what looked to be over one hundred-fifty pounds, with some other bulked up gym rat spotting for him. He finished the series, dropped the barbell onto the rack with a clanging thud, and sat up to wipe his brow with a towel. Ty glanced at his reflection in the mirror and scowled when he caught sight of Roman and Mercer gawking at him from across the room.

Roman quickly turned his attention back to his own workout, but the motivation drained out of him. The night he met Julianne, Dr. Bolton kept giving him the evil eye. Roman couldn't blame the guy for being overprotective, though, since his engagement to Rosaline was splashed all over social media and the gossip magazines. Still, being in such close proximity to a guy that size who was a Caplan family friend made Roman start to sweat more than the workout warranted. He replaced the free weight on the rack and breathed heavily, willing his pulse to slow.

"Mercer," Roman said without making eye contact, "we gotta go before trouble finds us."

"I hear you. That guy still gives me the creeps. Just something about him…"

Ty got up, stretched his arms in front of his chest, said something to his friend, and the two of them ambled over, a grim set to their jaws.

"Don't you rich boys ever have to work?"

"Lunch break," Roman mumbled. "And I could ask the same about ER doctors."

"I was on duty all night, saving lives and making a difference," Ty said with a curl of his lip, "and Greg here—"

"Works out a lot," Roman finished. "Yeah, I get that." His breathing under control, Roman picked up his towel and motioned to Mercer to do the same. "Nice seeing you again, Doc."

"Is this the guy that's been sniffing around Jules?" Greg asked. "And this one," he said with a head tilt toward Mercer, "was hitting on your lady?"

In response, Ty picked up a fifty pound free weight and started doing bicep curls as easily as if it was a five pounder. "Can't say I'm glad to see you, Montgomery. In fact, I don't want to see you ever again. Stay away from Julianne and Caplan's Shoes."

Mercer smirked. "And just as I was about to ask Nora out. Again. Right, Roman?"

Roman cringed.

Ty's face got all red, his eyes narrowed as his anger mounted. "Stay away from my girlfriend."

"From what I could tell," Mercer said with a look of amusement on his face, "Nora's got you firmly in the Friend zone."

Ty dropped the weight on the floor. Roman jumped sideways to avoid it landing on his foot. With a menacing look, Ty got up in Mercer's face and growled, "You don't know anything about it, so back off."

Greg stepped in closer, ready to jump to Ty's defense.

Mercer took a step back, his hands in the air. "I'm just saying!"

Roman wasn't about to let anyone bully his best friend, even if Mercer's mouth had started this altercation. "You're about three times his size, Ty," Roman warned. "You and your workout buddy need to go back to what you were doing and..."

"Is there a problem here, gentlemen?"

All four of them turned to see a stern-faced employee in khaki pants, navy blue golf shirt with the MCC logo on it, and a nametag that read Sylvester Prinze, Club Manager. The African American guy had the build of a pro line-backer, tall and beefy, not someone even Ty and Greg would want to mess with.

Roman grabbed Mercer's arm, gently pulling his best friend back and out of the line of fire. "No problem, Mr. Prinze," Roman said. "We were just chatting with the good doctor here about a mutual acquaintance."

"Well, you gents need to keep it civil. This is a family place, not the 'hood," Prinze said. "If this happens again, we'll have to ask you to leave."

"Sorry for the disturbance." Ty shot Roman a warning glare that said he wasn't the least bit sorry, and he and Greg ambled back to the other side of the room.

Prinze crossed his arms but stood his ground. "And you, Mr. Montgomery?"

Roman realized this was one of the people on staff who actually knew who he was. "I apologize," he said.

Prinze harrumphed and walked off.

Mercer's gaze traveled back to the cardio area where he'd seen the two women earlier, but they were gone. "Damn. I was hoping to get their attention again."

"You never had their attention. Why don't you call Nora? Have some fun and stick it to the meathead doctor."

Mercer shrugged. "Maybe. I'm free tonight. What are you doing?"

Roman blew out a puff of air. "I've got to make it

through another one of those interminable charity dinners."

Mercer playfully poked Roman's arm. "Enjoy the evening with the lovely Rosaline." He gave an exaggerated wink and headed for the locker room.

Ty was still glaring at them from across the room. Although Roman was tempted to scowl back at him, he decided to take the high road. He waved in the doctor's direction and followed Mercer to the locker room.

****

"Roman, darling, you're late. As usual." Rosaline stepped aside to allow him inside her downtown luxury penthouse that overlooked the White River Canal.

"Something came up at work," he told her. No, it didn't, but he couldn't exactly tell her that he'd stalled in his office till the absolute last minute, dreading this evening.

"Well, your chauffeur better step on it, because otherwise we'll completely miss the cocktail hour at the country club." Rosaline kissed him lightly on his cheek as he helped her on with her winter-white, wraparound coat, the five carat diamond engagement ring twinkling in the light of the chandelier. He waited while she tied the coat and retrieved her black designer clutch bag off the entry hall table. The private elevator took them down to the well-appointed lobby and out to where his driver was standing beside the limo, ready to open the back door for them.

Once inside, seatbelts fastened, Rosaline took Roman's hand. He didn't pull it away, but try as he might he couldn't think of anything to say to this woman. So he stared out the window. Eventually she laid her head on his shoulder, an intimacy that made him squirm. In fact, there was no intimacy between them at all. He kept coming up with excuses—long work day, migraine, coming down with something—whatever it took to avoid the issue. He even tried the trite "Let's wait till our honeymoon," but Rosaline wasn't buying it. Roman always felt this relationship was doomed, and now that he'd met Julianne, he was sure of it. He wanted out of this engagement.

Roman imagined how he would break it off with Rosaline, in a way that would let them both save face and move on. The two of them had nothing in common, he'd tell her, except the size of their trust funds, their parents' long-standing friendship, and their Catholic faith. No friends, no mutual interests, no shared hobbies. No common ground that engaged couples usually established long before getting to the altar. Surely Rosaline would agree.

"It's a lovely evening," she said. "Not quite as cold."

Roman didn't answer. He was lost in thought about Julianne Caplan, causing his heart to beat faster. Maybe it was the forbidden element, but he cared more for her after a couple of short meetings than he had ever cared for Rosaline.

She took Roman's chin and turned it to face her. "Darling, if you can't be bothered with small talk, can we at least agree that you'll be pleasant to the committee members this evening? No ducking out early."

Roman forced himself to smile. "I'll try to be charming."

She patted his hand and they rode on in silence. Roman sighed and vowed right then to make some changes in his life. Soon. Their wedding was only three months away and he felt trapped, both by Rosaline and his parents' expectations.

Chapter 6

Roman paced back and forth in front of his office window. He hadn't heard from Julianne in days, other than a cursory text or two, and then only in reply to ones he'd sent her. Nothing that was a brush off, but nothing encouraging either.

His desk phone buzzed and he jumped to answer it. "Hello? Jul…"

"Roman," Rosaline cut in, "I've been trying to reach you for days. Where on earth have you been? Why haven't you returned any of my calls?"

He rolled his eyes and sank listlessly into his high-backed desk chair. "I'm in my office right now, and I'm expected in a meeting," he lied. "I sent you a couple of texts."

"I know you're in your office. I called you there, and I told Ben to put me right through."

Roman tapped a pencil on the edge of his desk. "I'll have to call you back." He didn't wait for a response before disconnecting.

He had to come up with a plan, one that gracefully extricated him from Rosaline and helped him advance his cause with Julianne. Suddenly an idea came to him, just as his office phone rang again. He reached for his overcoat on the antique rack near the door and hurried to his assistant's desk, his office phone still ringing.

"Ben," he said, "tell Miss Vandenberg I was late to

my meeting and I'll call her tonight."

"Meeting? But..." Ben stopped, blinked, and picked up the ringing phone. "Mr. Montgomery's office. No, ma'am, I'm sorry..."

****

I glanced once more at the institution clock on the wall behind the professor's head and groaned when I realized we still had over an hour of class time left. I watched Natalie furiously typing notes into her tablet, somehow keeping up with the professor despite how fast he was speaking in that monotone. I was too distracted to concentrate anyway, so I pulled up a game of solitaire on my laptop and just hoped she'd email me her notes after class.

My urban high school wasn't exactly known for outstanding academics, but despite my inferior education, I'd always excelled in my writing classes. Community College's freshman English Comp was an entry level course for students who needed remediation. My advisor enrolled me based on my high school's reputation, and it irked me that I was paying good money to essentially repeat high school course work. And for all her suburban education, Natalie hadn't done well in English because she didn't like writing all those papers, so she needed what the college called a refresher course.

Dr. Knoll had returned our most recent assignment at the beginning of class, a bright red A circled at the top of my cover page. I was proud of myself, but I flashed back to a weird reaction I'd had last week when the teacher gave us the assignment. He told us to dissect Shakespeare's use of alliteration in the Prologue to Act One of *Romeo and Juliet,* "From forth the fatal loins of

97

these two foes; A pair of star-cross'd lovers take their life." Out of nowhere I'd envisioned a young girl in medieval dress, kissing a handsome older boy, and then saw their dead bodies lying in coffins side-by-side. Then suddenly it was me in that dress, making a fatal choice, and the boy...

Since I've never done any Shakespearean acting, I sighed and shook off the unsettling vision and tried to focus. Dr. Knoll was droning on about rhetorical analysis again, pointing out the mistakes other students had made in their essays. A boring lecture was what I needed to bring me back to reality, but I couldn't bring myself to type any notes into the laptop.

Finally class dismissed. I gathered my belongings, pulled on my coat, and put on my best "poor me" face for Natalie. "Any chance you could..."

She narrowed her eyes at me. "You were sitting right there the whole time."

My shoulders slumped. "I know, but I couldn't concentrate. Please?"

She blew out a puff of air and took off down the hall. "I'll shoot you an email."

I flew out the door and rushed off campus to the bus stop. Most days I was finished by lunch time, but on Fridays my classes didn't end till late afternoon. With any luck, the bus would be on time and I'd arrive at home or our store, however you wanted to look at it, in time to assist Dad with the Friday after-work rush. In the past, Caplan's was able to capitalize on the fact that people preferred to stick around downtown to shop or eat dinner rather than tackle the rush-hour traffic home to the burbs. We'd always been able to draw in customers wanting new shoes for the weekend or needing to drop off or pick up shoe repairs. Lately, though, business had been pretty slow. I blamed Montgomery's.

Today was March first, and with any luck that meant spring was on the way. The sun was beaming in the sky, creating a bit of warmth, and I wasn't quite as cold as I walked the six blocks from the bus stop to our store.

"Dad!" I called out as I hurried inside. "I'm here."

"In the back!" Dad shouted.

Sadly, the storeroom floor was empty of customers. "Where's Mom?" I called back. She usually covered for me on Friday afternoons, but there was no sign of her.

"She's not here." Jon Parris peeked around from behind the computer atop the cash box on the counter. "I'm filling in for her."

"Perfect." I hoped that didn't sound sarcastic, but all Jon ever did was stare at me like a lovesick puppy-dog, and it was completely unnerving. Ever since I attended his Bar Mitzvah years ago, when he was thirteen and I was eleven, my parents had this idea that he and I were boyfriend and girlfriend. Yes, he's a nice, smart, Jewish boy, but we have nothing in common other than religion.

Besides, I didn't find him the least bit attractive. He was tall with unkempt dark brown hair, way too thin, and he still dressed like he did back in seventh grade—faded jeans, a worn Black Sabbath t-shirt, and a gray unzipped hoodie sweatshirt. And don't get me started on those worn-out athletic shoes. When I compared him to Roman Montgomery, whom poets must have been thinking of when they described male beauty, and who had the most sophisticated wardrobe and killer designer shoes… Well, there was no comparison.

Wait. *Stop it, Julianne! You can't be thinking about Roman. He's off limits.* I let out a huge sigh. "Thanks for helping out today, Jon."

He came out from behind the counter and gave me that crooked grin of his. "No prob. I had some free time because the deadline on that computer program I'm writing isn't till Monday, so when your mom called and said something about lunch with a friend…" He shrugged.

I needed to be nicer to Jon, because he was doing us a favor. He earned a pretty good living doing freelance computer work, writing code, and (I suspected but had no proof) hacking into corporate computer systems for some of his clients. Mom said I could do worse financially, and Dad went on and on about him being "our kind." I'd rather be single for the rest of my life because no way would I ever consider a future with Jon Parris.

I walked behind the counter, glanced at the computer screen, took a second look and gasped. "What did you do?"

"I updated your files. Really, Jules, that program you've been using is a dinosaur."

I cringed at the nickname but brushed it aside as I punched in a few keys and looked at the new program in dismay. "I had a system in place—all my spreadsheets and data bases exactly where I wanted them."

Jon tried to put an arm around me but I stepped back. "Don't worry," he said, his arm falling limp to his side, "it's easy. See, just…"

I watched closely as he showed me how the new program worked.

But Jon must have misunderstood my attentiveness and the fact that we were standing side-by-side staring at the same computer screen, because he made another move, this time reaching for my hand. "Anything else you need me to do?"

I gently withdrew my hand and put both hands on the keyboard, trying not to be overtly rude to him. Our parents were old friends, Dad needed his occasional help in the store when Mom flaked out, and he never asked for pay that we couldn't afford to give him anyway. "I guess you could bring out those boxes of new merchandise from the storeroom. I'll need to shelve them before the evening rush."

Jon rolled his eyes because we both knew there wasn't going to be any rush, but he went to do as I asked.

In case someone did come in to shop, I wanted to look busy. I glanced around the store and noticed the display racks were in disarray. People trying on shoes seemed to put them back in the most random places, especially in the women's casual section. The display shoe in each section clearly marked what was in that row, arranged by shoe sizes in descending order. But today there were heels with sandals, boots with athletic shoes, and a pair of men's loafers from two aisles over. I guess the mess meant customers had been in today, a good thing, but Jon didn't tidy up after them, so not so good. Too busy fiddling with my computer to notice anything else, I suppose.

After about an hour with no distractions from anything like customers, I'd finally restored order when

the door opened, ushering in some cold air and—
Omigod—Roman Montgomery.

"Hi?" Really, what could he want in this store?
Certainly not shoes.

"Hi yourself." He gave me a warm smile and
walked in like a man with a purpose. "I was hoping
you'd be here."

I took a step back to get some perspective, since I
had already told myself that Roman and I were a
nonstarter. My head understood, but my heart
apparently hadn't gotten the message. I tried to ignore
its rapid fluttering and did my best imitation of a
professional saleswoman. "How may I help you?" He
smiled at me, I melted, and all my resolve vanished.
"Seriously, what are you doing here?" I whispered.

He was holding a shoe box with the Montgomery's
logo on the outside. "I came in for shoe repair." He
opened the lid and pulled out one of the expensive
black penny loafers.

I took the shoe and turned it over to examine it.
Yes, there was a hole in the sole, but it wasn't from
wear, because these were brand new shoes. It was like
someone (Roman?) had taken a screwdriver and run it
through. If it was anybody else I'd wonder what got
into them, but I guess Roman could afford to throw
away that kind of money. The question was why.

I lifted an eyebrow. "What a shame." I poked my
index finger through the hole and wiggled it at him.

"Yeah, okay, you got me." Roman took the shoe
back from me and returned it to its box. "I wanted an
excuse to come see you, since you wouldn't return my
calls or texts."

"I texted you."

"A few half-hearted attempts to blow me off, and I don't give up that easily." Roman gave me a warm smile. "I was hoping you'd go out with me. On a real date."

A date? Was he serious? I remembered why I'd been ignoring his messages, and it wasn't because I wasn't attracted to him. I put a hand on my hip and glared at him. "Will your fiancée be joining us?" Not waiting for an answer, I went to the counter, got the feather duster from underneath the shelf and made a big show of dusting everything on top of the counter. Cash register receipts, flyers, discount coupons, a pen holder, and a few shoe horns went flying. I reached down to pick them up, but when I stood back up, Roman was leaning his elbows on the counter, right in my face, daring me to avoid him.

"Here's my idea, Julianne," he said, as if I'd never mentioned the ubiquitous Ms. Vandenberg. "We can go see that musical at the Indianapolis Theatre Company on Washington Street. It starts at eight, after it's already dark outside."

"But it's not dark *in*side."

"I've got it all figured out." His eyes twinkled. "I'll leave a ticket for you at Will Call, and then I'll meet you at our seats. No one will know we're not just two people randomly seated next to one another."

I let that rattle through my brain, along with all the scenarios of how things could go wrong. My heart overrode my head. "Okay, it might work, but what about after the play? Do I have to walk home alone in the dark?"

"Of course not. We'll duck out before they bring up the house lights for curtain calls. I'll have my driver pick us up and we can go to a quiet little restaurant I know of in Broad Ripple. No one will bother us."

Maybe they wouldn't bother *us*, but what about if they recognized *him*? That could create all sorts of problems, the kind that end up going viral on social media. I should have given him an unequivocal "no" but this offer was too tempting. An evening with Roman Montgomery. I opened my mouth to give him my answer, but before I could get a word out, I saw Dad standing behind him. And if looks could kill...

"Julianne, what's this man doing here?"

"Mr. Caplan." Roman turned to my father and offered his hand to shake. Dad just glared at him, so after an awkward moment, Roman self-consciously pulled his hand back. "Pop said—that is, my friend Father Al Lawrence—he told me you do excellent shoe repair." He thrust the box of penny loafers at my dad.

Dad was suspicious, just like I'd been. He took one of the shoes out of the box, turned it over in his hand, frowned and said through gritted teeth, "A hundred fifty. They'll be ready next week." He took the box but didn't take his eyes off either of us.

Roman didn't flinch, but I nearly died of embarrassment. Dad usually charged about forty to fifty dollars for sole repair, so he was deliberately gouging Roman. "Dad..."

"It's okay, Julianne," Roman said before noticing the menacing look from my father. "I mean Miss Caplan. I'm happy to pay a premium for quality work. I'll even pay in advance." He turned his back to my father as I printed out his work order, ran his credit card, and handed him the receipt. He winked at me while signing. "About that other question I asked you?"

My eyes got wide and my heart skipped a beat. I was hoping Dad thought it was work-related as well. "Yes, I can do that."

Roman grinned at me, stuffed his receipt in his pocket and left.

Dad was still standing there, the veins in his forehead popping out. "What was that all about? What question?" He tucked the shoe box under his arm.

"Uh..." I wracked my brain for some excuse. "Mr. Montgomery asked if I'd like to come over to his store someday for a tour." I watched Dad's face redden and I was pretty sure he was about to have a stroke. "You okay?" I put my hand on my phone ready to punch 9-1-1 if necessary.

Dad took a deep breath, exhaled and slowly his color returned to something more like normal. "You won't be doing any such thing." He opened the shoe box for another look at the shoes. "I'm sure you know these loafers have been deliberately damaged."

"I know, Dad," I said. "Maybe Roman's just trying to make nice. You know, be a good neighbor?"

Dad was incredulous. "Now it's Roman?"

"Mr. Montgomery."

Dad was starting to get red in the face again. "The man's either checking out the competition or checking out my daughter, and either way, I won't have it." He turned to head back to his shop. "Jon!" Dad called over his shoulder. "Come out here and keep Julianne company."

Dad disappeared down the hall into his shop as Jonathan poked his head out of the storeroom, a quizzical expression on his face.

"I'm fine, Jon, just a spat with my father." I waved

him away.

And then I was hit with something like a lightning bolt as I remembered why I was making lame excuses to my father about Roman Montgomery. I'd accepted a date with him for tomorrow night. Despite my misgivings, I got a tingly feeling all over, and butterflies in my stomach.

Chapter 7

I couldn't sleep last night. I kept going back and forth in my head about this covert plan to meet Roman tonight. So even though it wasn't even dawn yet, I got up, flipped open my laptop, and started making a list of pros and cons. The con side filled up pretty fast.

Then I started on the pro column, and I could only come up with one entry. I was seriously drawn to Roman Montgomery. Like a magnet.

So if I was going to pull off this subterfuge, I had to pretend that this was a normal Saturday and stick to my regular schedule so as not to tip off my parents. I always leave the house early to head to the public library, because that was the only time all week that I could really get schoolwork done and still be at the store when it opened at ten a.m.

I loved being in the library. It was so quiet at eight a.m., with no crying children or loud conversations among patrons. But mostly I just liked the alone time, something in short supply sharing a small apartment with three other people who also worked in the family business.

Every time I walked into the library, it stirred something inside me that felt familiar, something I couldn't explain, like I'd forgotten something important. Of course it *was* familiar, because I went there every week, but I was never able to put my finger on it. All I knew was that I felt at home there. The building's design was Greek architecture, really beautiful and really old, and just walking up the front steps was awe-inspiring.

I opened my backpack, took out books, pen and paper, and re-read my English assignment that I'd printed off Dr. Knoll's class website yesterday. "Write a seven hundred word essay examining the irony Jane Austen employs as Mr. Collins's proposal to Elizabeth Benet misses the mark in *Pride and Prejudice.*" I found the topic interesting because I love Jane Austen, but then as I reread the instructions, I had a reaction similar to the one I'd had with the *Romeo and Juliet* essay. A vision flashed across my mind, this time me in Regency dress, dancing with a man who could give Colin Firth a run for his money. I closed my eyes and the vision melted, leaving me with only one thing on my mind: whether or not I should go to the theatre tonight to meet Roman. And how I'd explain myself if anyone found out, or how I'd apologize to Roman if I bailed.

I decided to text Nora and see if she could offer any encouragement. I hit send, waited and waited, but got no reply. I sent another, and another, and yet another. Crickets. *She's probably still in bed,* I told myself. I fired off one last text, tossed the phone on the desk and slumped in my wooden chair at the study carrel, frustrated. I definitely couldn't concentrate on my work, so I got up and wandered around, perusing the stacks, not looking for anything in particular.

The big antique clock over the library's main entryway was going on ten a.m. and I hadn't gotten anything done. Even worse, I'd be late getting the store open and Dad wouldn't be happy. He was probably already there, working in his shop, ready to give me an earful when I walked in. I quickly gathered up my belongings, zipped the book bag closed, and darted out. I checked the bus schedule on the corner and realized the next arrival wasn't for half an hour. No time to wait. I ran the whole eight blocks.

Breathing hard from the exertion, I dug my keys out of the bottom of my book bag, unlocked the front door of Caplan's Shoe Store and Repair, and let myself in. The lights were already on, meaning my father was already down the hall in his shop. I turned on the computer and stashed my coat and book bag in the back room while I waited for it to boot. The time stamp at the bottom of the desktop page read fifteen minutes past the hour. Hopefully we didn't miss any customers while Dad was busy doing shoe repairs. These days we couldn't afford to turn anyone away.

I heard the back door open. Nora waltzed into the store through the storeroom, hands on her hips. "What's so freakin' important you have to wake me up on my day off?"

I'd almost forgotten about the texts I'd sent her. I gave her the once over, frowning at her gray hoodie, flannel pajama bottoms, and faux fur-lined bootie house slippers. "I guess you're not down here to help."

"I'm going back to bed once I find out why you had to text me five times in the space of an hour. I didn't get home from the hospital till the wee hours." Nora stifled a yawn. "So make it quick."

That yawn did its job. I felt guilty about waking her up for no other reason than I was having a crisis of conscience, especially because her work was so important and my current angst could wait. I shook my head and gave her a gentle shove toward the back door. "It's nothing. I'll figure it out. Sorry I disturbed you."

She didn't argue. Once Nora was gone and I ascertained there were no customers in sight, I decided it was best to keep busy and do inventory. At least if someone came in, it would appear I had actual work to do. Besides, I'd been putting off inventory for days now. I had no idea if we should order merchandise that we may or may not be able to sell. But while I tried to run through my usual orders, I found myself unable to think about anything but Roman... *Stop it, Julianne!* I slapped my forehead and forced myself to focus.

By six p.m. closing time, I'd taken inventory, re-straightened the display racks I'd just tidied up a day earlier, rearranged the merchandise in hopes of attracting shoppers' attention, and dusted and swept every inch of the store. The only customers I had all day were a mother with her pre-teen daughter, looking for athletic shoes to wear when she tried out for the school's basketball team. They shopped around, finally settled on a pair of inexpensive cross-trainers, and left. If business didn't pick up soon, we might as well go ahead and shut our doors.

With the lack of customers, I had lots of time to think. I had about decided to bail when Roman sent me a text confirming that he'd left my ticket at the theatre's Will Call booth. I hated to break my promise so I decided to go. I told myself it was because I really wanted to see the play, and I further justified it by asking myself *what could it hurt?* Sit next to a great-looking guy for a couple of hours in a dark theatre, maybe have some dinner afterward, and then offer him best wishes on his upcoming marriage. All perfectly innocent.

Nora knocked on the door of the tiny bathroom we share and poked her head in. "You decent?"

I waved her in. I was all nervous and fidgety, feeling like I was about to jump out of my skin, and my hand shook when I tried to comb my hair. I was getting ready for either the best or worst night of my life. I had to confide in Nora.

"Can I trust you?" I checked out my look in the mirror one last time.

"Always." She opened the drawer that contained her makeup and started touching up her mascara, blush and lipstick. She gave me a sideways glance. "You look nice. Got a date with Jon?"

I gulped. "Date yes, Jon, no." She shrugged and finished applying her makeup. "What about you?" I asked, more as a stalling tactic. "You're a little overdressed for a night of channel surfing."

"You're deflecting," she said.

I caught her eye in the mirror. "So are you."

"I've got a date, too, sort of," she said, twisting shut her tube of mascara and tossing it back in the drawer. "I agreed to go out with Ty." She paused mid blush-stroke to give me that *Don't start* look. "It's no big deal. We're meeting up with a bunch of other hospital people at some comedy club in Broad Ripple, someplace Ty happened on to one night while mingling down there."

"Mingling? Is that what he calls it?"

Broad Ripple was an eclectic dining and entertainment area in mid-town Indianapolis that attracted the twentysomething crowd. For all his insistence that he and Nora were a couple, I was pretty sure Ty and his coworkers went there to meet women.

"You look nice, too, but I doubt you're dressed in those tight jeans and that new black V-neck sweater for Ty's sake. What about Mercer?"

"Him?" She sniffed. "Haven't heard from him since Valentine's."

"Oh." I glanced at her reflection, which said she was disappointed. "Well, I know Ty isn't your first choice of a date, but maybe you'll meet someone else while you're out tonight."

She shrugged. "Maybe." She gave my outfit a critical once-over. "So, my dear niece, if it's not Jon, who's the lucky guy?"

I did a slow turn, checking my dress from all angles as best I could in the short bathroom mirror. I was wearing a long-sleeved black sweater dress that I liberated from Mom's closet. It was a little tighter on me than it was on her because I was bustier, but the hemline was just right. She always wore her dresses way too short for a forty-year-old wife and mother, but that meant her dress hit me just at the top of my knee-high faux leather boots. I'd found my grandmother's retro silver watch-on-a-chain in Mom's jewelry box, and it looked nice against the dress. I let my reddish-brown hair—crazy curls and all—hang loose around my shoulders. I planned to wear my wine-colored winter coat with a hood, so that if necessary, I could use it to hide my face from prying eyes. Wearing my glasses was also a good disguise.

I turned to face Nora. "I know they say to always tell someone where you'll be and with whom, so..." I glanced in the mirror and the look on my face was somewhere between glee and panic. "I'm meeting

Roman Montgomery at Indianapolis Theatre Company." I offered up my hand for the high-five we'd done since kids.

Nora gasped like I'd just sucker-punched her. She wouldn't even high-five me. Instead, she turned back to the bathroom mirror, picked up her comb and started frantically swiping at her short, brown hair. "No, you're not."

"Yes, I am, Nora. I've thought about this a lot. A lot a lot. I'm only telling you for safety purposes. It's not up for negotiation."

She threw the comb on the countertop and glared at me. "No good can come of this, Julianne. The man's engaged, for cryin' out loud. What if someone sees you?"

"Roman has everything all worked out."

She didn't let up on her glare. "You've known him all of ten minutes."

"Yeah, I know. But we'll be in public the whole time." I sighed. "Nora, I just can't seem to stay away from him."

She stood completely still for a moment, her eyes closed, her breathing uneven, and then her shoulders relaxed and she gave me a big hug. "Are you sure? You could go out with Ty and me tonight. I've already told him we're just going as friends, so you're welcome to hang with us."

"You know I'm too young to go clubbing." I pulled back from her embrace.

Nora cocked her head to one side. "Text me if you change your mind. Or if things with Roman go sideways."

I hurried out of the bathroom, darted into my

bedroom for my coat and handbag, and once I was bundled up, left the apartment. Dad took Mom out to dinner, nothing fancy, just a Chinese restaurant they like, but I told them I was meeting some friends from school and going to a movie. I even researched movies, just in case they asked, so my official story was we were seeing the new Julia Roberts film, a romantic comedy. I told my parents we'd probably go out for a burger afterward, so I'd be late. The prospect of spending time with Roman, even if it was just for one evening, helped alleviate any guilt I had about lying to my parents.

I let myself out of the apartment and started the half mile trek to the theatre. The streets of downtown Indy were well-lit and already filled with people headed to dinner, a sporting event, or an entertainment venue, so I could easily blend in with the crowds on the sidewalk. I wound my way around Monument Circle and onto Washington Street.

There it was. The Indianapolis Theatre Company. The marquee lights were blazing, announcing their production of *West Side Story*. I loved that musical, but then I laughed at the irony, given the circumstances between Roman and me. I stopped and reminded myself there *was* no Roman and me. Just two people about to enjoy a play and then go their separate ways. I walked in and went to the Will Call booth, just inside the main entrance.

"Roman Montgomery," I told the attendant.

She thumbed through the box in front of her, looked again, and shook her head. "Sorry, Miss, no ticket with that name."

Oh, great. After all this angst, maybe something

came up and he couldn't make it. Or maybe his fiancée found out. But he sent me that text, right? "Try Julianne Caplan," I said, fingers crossed.

She nodded, dug through the box again, and this time pulled out the ticket envelope. "Enjoy your evening."

It was as simple as that. And as complicated.

I looked at the seat assignment and we were in the Mezzanine, front row. Roman could easily have afforded orchestra seats, but as I walked up the stairs and had a look around, I realized he'd made a good choice. It was much less crowded up here in the cheap seats. In other words, folks not likely to run in Montgomery or Vandenberg circles.

I took the Playbill from the usher and made my way down the short aisle to seat AA 102, expecting to see Roman waiting for me in AA 101. But that chair was empty. I wondered if he was running late, had gone out for some air, or maybe wasn't coming at all. I wiggled out of my coat and checked the time on my phone. 8:02 p.m. I drummed my fingers on the arm rest, kept a close watch on my text messages, and craned my neck to watch late-comers filing in and taking their seats.

Maybe it was for the best. As long as I was already here, I might as well enjoy the play at Roman's expense. I pulled my glasses out of my bag and thumbed through my program, making a point to avoid eye contact with any curious or pitying audience members. Finally, ten minutes past the advertised curtain time, the orchestra leader walked onto the stage to loud applause, bowed, took his place, and the overture began as the house lights went down. I hoped the play was worth being stood up. I groaned inwardly because I could already hear Nora's *I told you so*.

The curtain opened, actors took the stage, and out of nowhere someone quietly sat down next to me. Roman. Relief and dread got equal time in my emotions.

"Fashionably late?" I whispered.

"Just playing it safe," he replied. He wasn't wearing an overcoat, just a dark business suit with an expensive-looking tie. I couldn't help but notice the high quality of his shoes when he propped his feet on the wall in front of us.

I self-consciously pulled my glasses off my face, but Roman stopped me.

"Leave them on. I like them."

That was something I'd never heard before, so I put them back on. I tucked my boots as far up under my seat as possible to hide them from Roman's discerning eye, since they were not only faux leather but outdated by at least two seasons. But Roman wasn't looking at my feet. He reached for my hand just as The Jets and The Sharks burst into song to display their rivalry and hatred of one another. When I glanced over at Roman, he was looking at me, not the actors onstage. Again I got chills, like I was having another déjà vu. I directed my attention back to the stage, but instead of actors dressed in 1960s garb, an image of men in medieval clothing flashed through my mind. What was this recent fascination with the 1400s?

During intermission, Roman released my hand and we stood up and stretched. "Do you want a snack or something?"

I looked around at all the strangers, but it was

possible there was someone here, somewhere, that knew one of us. Besides, if I got a drink, eventually I'd need to go to the ladies' room in the lobby. "No, I'm fine."

He looked relieved. "Probably not a good idea anyway. Rosaline's parents have season tickets, although they usually come on opening night."

We sat back down and I got the chance to revel in the heady feeling of being on a date with this fascinating guy. It wasn't just his Italian suit and silk tie that captured my attention, it was his enticing cologne, his neatly combed sandy-blond hair, his winning smile, and the way his hand fit around mine like a glove.

Roman did a quick look around the mezzanine. "I think we pulled it off." Then he gave me a very fast but light kiss on the lips.

My eyes widened, because they hadn't lowered the house lights yet.

"Ashamed to be seen with me?"

I blushed. "Of course not. But you're the one engaged to be married."

He blew out a puff of air. "I made myself a promise recently. To end that relationship. It's not fair to Rosaline." He turned to look directly in my eyes. "Not when I'm falling for another woman."

Gulp. What was the correct response to a man who just told you he was dumping his high-profile fiancée for you, the other woman? I opened my mouth to reply at the same moment the house lights flickered on and off, letting everyone know to take their seats. I squeezed Roman's hand, relieved to have another hour to think this through.

The play was wonderful. I'd seen the movie

version before, back when I was in high school and the English teacher was comparing *Romeo and Juliet* with this twentieth century take on the story. I knew the whole plot, how the play started out with nothing more than a rivalry between two gangs, proceeded to the love story of Tony and Maria from opposite sides, and ended in his death and her near-suicide. Something about the story touched me deeply. I was blinking back tears when the final curtain went down.

"Ready to go?" Roman whispered as thunderous applause broke out.

Even though he'd told me this part of the plan, part of me expected we'd just say goodbye right here and go our separate ways. "So we're doing this?"

"We are," he whispered as he helped me on with my coat.

It was raining outside, coming down in a soft mist that seemed to hang in the air, but the dampness made the cold air feel colder. I shivered, but as planned, there was a black limo with tinted windows idling in front of the theatre's main entrance. Roman did a quick look around, opened the back door for me and we both slid inside the warm vehicle.

"Remember where we're going, Phil?" Roman said to his driver.

"Yes sir," Phil replied. He glanced in his rearview mirror, turned on his signal, and pulled out onto Washington Street.

Roman and I exchanged nervous glances as we held tight to each other's hands, like we were high school kids going to the prom. But this wasn't high school, and there was a whole lot more at stake.

"Did you like the play?" Roman asked at the same

time I asked him, "Should we really be doing this?"

We both laughed nervously, then Roman said, "You first."

"It was great. Very sad how two people can fall in love so quickly and then it's over so fast."

"Sort of like us?"

My jaw dropped. "Falling in love?"

Roman shrugged and grinned. "Speaking for myself, of course."

I carefully withdrew my hand. "We barely know each other, and you didn't answer my question. Should we even be here?"

Roman turned sideways to face me and reached out to push an escaped lock of my hair behind my ear. "What we should do is go with our guts, the rest of the world be damned."

Go with our guts. My gut was telling me that, although I was extremely attracted to this guy, trying to be together would be an uphill battle. "It sounds romantic and all, but in the real world, we've got tons of obstacles." Like my father. And his father. And his fiancée.

Roman took my chin and pulled me in for a kiss. It started as a sweet, soft kiss, and then grew more passionate as I kissed him back. He released me with a peck on my nose and smiled. "Why don't we just enjoy the moment? Forget the problems, just for tonight."

I smiled back at him. "Deal."

Phil drove through some suburban neighborhoods and up to Broad Ripple, a fifteen minute drive from downtown. He pulled the limo up in front of La Bella Italiano, Nora's dream restaurant where many a romance began, situated in the middle of strip stores and clubs.

It was raining pretty hard now. I watched out the window as umbrella-less women in spike heels, and guys in their best jeans and loafers, ducked their heads or held a coat over themselves, running to get out of the rain. To my great relief, no one had time to pay any attention to the two people stepping out of the stretch limo.

Roman handed me out, but he did have an umbrella, so we arrived at the covered entrance to La Bella Italiano relatively dry. "Reservations for Montgomery," he told the hostess, as he set the dripping umbrella in the tall black bucket just inside the door.

"Welcome, Mr. Montgomery." She picked up two menus and led us to a table at the back of the restaurant.

The room was dim-lit with votive candles and low-wattage lamps, so it was a good choice for people like us wanting privacy. The restaurant was beautiful, quaint, and breathtaking, sort of a throwback to another time. The tables looked like antiques and were all set with white lace tablecloths, mismatched plates, and silverware wrapped in red linen napkins. On the walls were old black and white photos of families back in the twentieth century in what was probably the Italian countryside. Religious icons were sprinkled throughout the space, and the Italian flag hung proudly over the bar. In one corner was a small fountain with a statue of Mother Mary, and behind the hostess stand were colorful café lights strung around a fake garden setting.

"What do you think?" Roman asked me as he held my seat at the corner table.

"Nice," is what popped out of my mouth.

Understatement for sure. I could feel romance oozing out of every corner of the room.

"Red wine for me, and sparkling cider for the lady," Roman told the hostess.

She nodded and handed us our menus. My stomach was rumbling. I'd skipped lunch because I got busy at the store, although I doubt I could have eaten anyway because I was too nervous, and now it was after ten o'clock. I opened the menu and perused the variety of choices, all in Italian of course.

The waitress appeared with our drinks. "Have you decided what you'd like?"

I looked up at Roman and fervently hoped he knew what to order.

"How about the veal marsala?" Roman asked me as he handed his menu back to the waitress.

The color probably drained out of my face because the idea of eating a baby calf was nauseating. "I'm a vegetarian."

"You are?"

I guess Catholics didn't have any dietary restrictions. Except that fish on Fridays thing, if that was still a thing. I sighed. "Even secular Jews have way too many dietary restrictions. Nora and I figured out years ago that it was just easier to be vegetarian." Poor Roman looked bewildered, retrieved his menu from the waitress and perused it again. "I do eat fish," I told him.

Roman returned the menu to the waitress. "Salmon filet with linguine Alfredo."

She nodded, took our menus, and left.

It looked like the difference in our family heritages was widening the gap between us. "I'm sorry, Roman, I didn't mean…"

He took a big gulp of wine and set his glass down. "No, I should have asked. I really don't know much about your religion, but I'm willing to learn."

"Says the guy headed to Catholic Mass first thing in the morning."

Roman silently swirled the red wine around in his glass, watching the color as if he were a wine connoisseur. For all I knew, he was.

"So let me ask you a question." He pointed to my fake leather knock-off boots. "Since you don't eat meat, is that why you don't wear real leather?"

I glanced down at my feet. "Real leather's expensive, but yes, it also used to be a cow."

He got the weirdest puzzled look on his face. "But you're wearing a wool coat."

That made me giggle. The guy knew shoes but not much about textiles. "Roman, you don't have to kill the sheep to get the wool off."

He blushed and then reached across the table to put his hand on top of mine. He lifted up his glass with what was left of his wine and offered a proper toast. "To getting to know you, and to not making an ass of myself doing it."

We clinked our glasses and I took a sip of my sparkling cider, which was very good. Just as we kissed, I saw something out of the corner of my eye. I tensed up and turned around.

"What?" Roman asked, following my gaze.

"I thought I just saw a camera flash." We both glanced around the darkened restaurant, which was filled with people eating their meals or concentrating on their dinner companions. No one was paying any attention to the two of us. "I probably just imagined it."

"Yeah, probably." Roman didn't look convinced as he visually swept the restaurant.

He and I both knew that well into the twenty-first century, expectations of privacy were nil. I tried to squash the fear that we actually did end up in someone's selfie and would find ourselves on social media in a matter of minutes. *Don't be so paranoid* I chided myself. People were going to take pictures no matter what, but there were so many photos posted on social media every minute of every day, who could keep up with it?

Roman reached across the table for my hand. "Forget about the outside world for now. We're in a romantic restaurant, and all I want to do is enjoy my time with you."

I'd already agreed to put our problems aside, so I nodded just as the waiter brought our food. It smelled delicious and tasted even better.

So what if someone caught us in a photo? Chances of anyone I knew seeing it were slim. I glanced up at Roman and I was in heaven.

Chapter 8

I rolled over and looked at the bedside clock. Ten a.m. I yawned, stretched, and then closed my eyes as I replayed every minute of my date with Roman last night.

After leaving the restaurant, we hadn't been willing to risk a limo pulling up in front of Caplan's, so Roman's chauffeur dropped us off in the parking garage next to Montgomery's, and Roman walked me down the street to our apartment, claiming a gentleman must see his date safely home. He was careful to avoid the street lamps near the alley entrance to our apartment when he kissed me goodnight, and we didn't stop with just one kiss. My toes were still tingling. I held his hand until he had to pull out of reach, making eye contact before turning around, shoving his hands in his pockets, and walking out of my sight. I wasn't deluding myself that the two of us had any kind of future, but we sure did have chemistry.

Sundays were my day to sleep in and take it easy. No school, store closed, homework (mostly) done, no demands on my time. There was a delicious aroma still lingering in the air, which meant Nora had baked muffins. I crawled out from under the covers, stepped into my slippers and slid into my bathrobe hanging on the back of my bedroom door.

I poured myself a cup of coffee, took a sip but then

spit it out, because it was lukewarm and stale. I poured the rest of the pot down the sink and started fresh.

But the aroma of freshly-brewing coffee didn't distract me from the smell of Nora's oversized, bakery-quality muffins. I scouted out the small kitchen and pounced on the muffins sitting on a large china serving plate on top of the kitchen table. Even though the kitchen was all new, Dad put his foot down when Mom wanted new furniture to go with it. The space was just too small, as was Dad's bank account. As a result, the small, round, antique breakfast table with four mismatched chairs that belonged to Grandma were glaringly out of place. To hide the table's imperfections, Mom kept it covered with colorful placemats and napkins that she changed frequently. Today they were seafoam green.

There was a note from Nora propped up in front of the muffins.

I'm on the early shift but knew you'd want breakfast. Check your Facebook account.

Hmm. I wadded up the note and tossed it in the trash bin.

I plopped a muffin onto a plate, poured myself a cup of the freshly-brewed coffee, and scrolled around on my phone. The minute I logged into my social media account I nearly fainted. Natalie had re-posted a picture on my news feed that had already been re-posted hundreds of times, and she tagged me in it. There it was, staring back at me, my worst nightmare. Roman and me kissing last night at La Bella Italiano.

I had no idea who actually took the photo, but that didn't matter anyway because the comments were horrifying:

"Montgomery heir and unknown girl out on the town,"

"Cozy date night—wrong girl,"

"Wait till Rosaline Vandenberg sees this!" among others. Natalie left me a message asking how on earth I'd managed a date with such a rich and handsome guy, and why I hadn't told her about it, but I couldn't take time to answer.

I sent Nora a text.

—Is it posted anyplace else?—

Her reply was disheartening.

—Every Place.—

I groaned and started to text Roman, but then I remembered he was going to Mass and wouldn't have his phone on. Plus it was possible he'd already seen the photo.

"Good morning, Julianne." Dad was wearing his faded blue chenille bathrobe over gray sweatpants with Indianapolis written down one leg and Colts down the other. He squeezed by me at the table and got his favorite coffee mug out of the cabinet, the one that said:

Guns Don't Kill People
Dads with Pretty Daughters Do

Mom gave it to him three years ago at Hanukkah, just as I was turning sixteen and Nora was twenty-one. Mom thought it was funny. I never did.

I quickly stuffed my phone in the pocket of my bathrobe. "Nora made muffins."

"Is that who you were texting?" Dad asked as he sat down across from me.

"Yes." I took a too-big bite of muffin to avoid saying anything else. Dad wasn't too savvy about social media, so with any luck he wouldn't see the posts.

He sliced his muffin in half and liberally applied butter to both sides. Sometimes I worried about his health because he sat all day behind his workbench repairing shoes, never exercised, and lived on a diet of mostly deli or Chinese carryout.

"How was your movie last night?"

"Good," I said, taking my time swallowing. I preferred not to get deeper into the lie if possible. Just then there was a loud knock at our door. Make that pounding. "I'll get it."

I walked down the stairs to the alley door and stood on tiptoe for a look through the peephole. Great. Ty Bolton. I opened it up and put on my best fake smile. "Hi, Ty. Looking for Nora?"

Ty was dressed in hospital scrubs, light jean jacket despite the morning chill, and his shaved head must be freezing because he wasn't wearing a hat. I imagine he'd just finished his hospital shift, but I wasn't about to ask him. I didn't want to start any kind of conversation with the scowling guy with a short fuse standing on our doorstep.

"Your dad here?" he growled.

I stepped aside to let him in, then blushed when he looked askance at my bathrobe. "Kitchen. If you'll excuse me." I darted up the stairs ahead of him and ducked into the bathroom. I could already hear their voices getting loud. My heart sank as I heard Ty say something about YouTube, Facebook, Instagram, Twitter, yada yada yada.

Dad banged on the bathroom door. "Julianne!"

I hurriedly turned on the water. "I'm in the shower, Dad!" I called out as cheerfully as I could manage. I needed to stall for time, but I already knew I was screwed.

How was I going to explain this?

****

Roman had gotten up and gone to early Mass, but it wasn't like he'd been sleeping anyway. He kept replaying his evening with Julianne, hoping to commit every single second of it to memory. She enchanted him, with her voluptuous figure—so unlike Rosaline's uber-thin frame—the curls that surrounded her face and bounced when she talked, that adorable oversized nose covered in freckles, and her lips, those kissable lips.

Back home from church, Roman trudged up the stairs in his parents' ninety-year-old, five-thousand square foot Meridian Hills home, and opened the door to his bedroom. It was a wreck and this was the housekeeper's day off. The rumpled, unmade bed reflected his restless night, and the bedside lamp was askew from when he'd fumbled for the light and hadn't bothered to set it upright. He'd carelessly tossed last night's Italian suit and silk tie on the chaise lounge in the corner, meaning they'd be wrinkled and have to be sent out for a press. His overcoat was draped over the desk chair, and his undershirt, socks and dress shirt had been tossed on, but not in, the hamper. He also noticed he'd tracked in mud from the rain and it was all over the white carpet. The maid would have her hands full tomorrow.

Reliving their evening together was one reason for his insomnia, but what had really kept him awake was what Julianne had said. Was she right? Was there really no future for the two of them? For sure, obstacles lay in their path. More like major roadblocks. He'd told Julianne he planned to break off his engagement to

Rosaline and had hoped Julianne would agree to keep seeing him till he did, but breaking up with Rosaline was easier said than done. His parents would have a meltdown and her parents would cry foul, especially after all the wedding expenses, which were mounting into the hundreds of thousands. And none of that addressed the problems with Julianne's family.

Roman changed out of his church clothes, added the dress pants and Polo sweater to the pile on the chaise lounge, and pulled on sweat pants and a red fleece. He kicked off his loafers and pulled on his joggers. Maybe going for a run would help him clear his head.

He was searching through the mess for his stocking cap when his phone pinged. A text from Mercer? Huh. His best friend never saw the early side of noon on the weekends, yet here he was texting before ten a.m. Curious, Roman opened it.

—*Check social media. You're screwed.*—

Roman did as Mercer suggested and his heart sank. The picture of him and Julianne in an intimate kiss was plastered all over every social media site he was on. And probably some he wasn't on. Roman felt nauseous. The quiet, romantic evening they'd shared had almost felt too good to be true anyway, but now it was no longer private.

He left the house for a run. A long run.

****

I stalled in the bathroom as long as I could, but just how long does a shower take? I could still hear Dad's and Ty's raised voices coming from the kitchen, so I slipped into my bedroom and quietly shut the door behind me. Of course that didn't fool them.

"Julianne! Come out here now!" Dad didn't sound too pleased.

"I'm getting dressed," I sang out.

"Julianne..." Dad warned.

"Fine," I called back with a groan. I pulled on a pair of worn jeans with an old, stretched-out sweater, didn't even bother with a bra, tossed the wet towel on the floor, and shook out my hair. "Brace yourself," I told my mirror reflection.

Barefoot, I stepped out of my bedroom and into the kitchen to find both Dad and Ty glaring at me. "You bellowed?"

"Don't be flip, young lady," Dad said.

"You've disrespected your parents enough as it is." Ty was leaning against the refrigerator, arms crossed.

"And I'm sure you couldn't wait to tell them all about it," I shot back.

"What's going on here?" Shocker. Mom was up before noon. She waltzed into the kitchen, elbowed Ty out of her way, and reached into the fridge for a bottle of orange juice. She lifted an eyebrow at all three of us. "It's too early for all this commotion."

"Sorry to wake you, Lydia," Dad said, never taking his eyes off me, "but we've got a situation here."

"It'd better be serious to get me out of bed at this hour." Mom pulled out a chair, scraping its legs across the hardwood floor, and settled herself into it. She absent-mindedly picked up my phone and started scrolling. I snatched it out of her hand.

Ty pointed to the phone. "Your daughter is all over social media."

Mom lifted her head. "Is that a bad thing? Some positive comments about Julianne, our store..."

"Lydia," Ty said, showing her a photo on his phone, "Julianne was kissing that Montgomery guy."

I sank into the chair next to Mom, hoping for moral support, even though I'd never had any from her in the past. It was obvious Dad and Ty weren't going to listen, so I pleaded my case to Mom. "It's not like we were in a hotel room. That's a perfectly respectable restaurant."

Ty scrolled through his phone for more social media posts and handed it to Mom. "If you're out in public with a guy in the media spotlight, Jules, expect to end up online somewhere."

Mom squinted at the photo of Roman and me mid-kiss. Like me, she was far-sighted, but unlike me, she refused to wear anything as unflattering as glasses. Obviously she hadn't put her contacts in yet.

"And another thing." Dad narrowed his eyes. "You lied to me. You said you were at a movie with your girlfriends."

I turned to my father. "Because I didn't want"—I waved my hands at them—"all this. We went to a theatre to see a play and then to that restaurant." I pointed to the photo. "No place else. And his chauffeur drove."

My mother choked on her juice. "Chauffeur?" she squeaked out. She took another gulp.

"You're missing the point, Julianne," Dad growled. "I expressly told you not to see him again, and you disobeyed me."

I stood up, put my hands on my hips and glared at both Dad and Ty. "No, you're missing the point. I'm nineteen. You can't keep treating me like a kid. I go to school…"

"…which I pay for," Dad interjected.

"...keep up my grades and run the store practically by myself. So if I want to spend a nice evening with a friend..."

"One whose family business might bankrupt ours," Dad said, talking over me.

"...then I should be allowed to make that choice, and not have to face an inquisition," I finished.

"Julianne." Mom put her hand on Dad's shoulder to stop his escalating tirade. His face was starting to turn red and the vein in his neck was bulging. "I thought we agreed that you'd date Jonathan Parris," she said.

I groaned, slumped in the chair and folded my arms across my chest. "You agreed. Other than Synagogue, Jon and I have nothing in common. Nothing."

Ty walked over and tried to put an arm around me, but I shoved him away and stood up. Why was he acting like he was my big brother? He wasn't even officially Nora's boyfriend. He shouldn't be here right now. This was a family matter.

Ty crossed his arms. "I agree with your parents, Jules. That Montgomery guy's trouble. He's got a bad temper, which I saw firsthand at the gym last week."

My mouth dropped open. From what I knew of Roman, admittedly on short acquaintance, he seemed like a gentle, easy-going guy. "What are you talking about, Ty?"

Ty shrugged and gave me his trademark steely-eyed glare. I was sure he was exaggerating about Roman just to make a point, but in his current self-righteous state I'd never get the whole story out of him.

"Just take my word for it, Jules. The man's trouble."

"Stop calling me 'Jules'!" Tears came to my eyes, but I wiped them away with the back of my hand to stop them from flowing down my cheeks. I didn't want Ty, or Dad, to know they'd gotten to me. "It doesn't matter anyway. He's engaged, not to mention Catholic."

"So that settles it," Dad said. "Spend more time with Jon, or find another nice Jewish boy to date. Forget about Roman Montgomery."

Chapter 9

"My God, Roman. I've never been so humiliated in my life!" Rosaline hissed.

Roman had spent days dodging Rosaline's calls and texts, even as their tone escalated from angst to fury, but he was at work now and truly didn't have time to get into it with her. Mornings were always busy with staff meetings, sales reports, appointments with vendors, and conferring with Ben to make sure their calendars were coordinated. So even if he'd been inclined to return Rosaline's calls, which he hadn't, there'd been no time. Unfortunately, when she rang his office line and barked orders at Ben, he'd put her straight through.

In order to keep this conversation private—if you could call it a conversation, since he'd barely gotten a word in—Roman took her off speaker and put his desk phone to his ear as she continued to rant. Of course she'd seen the pictures of him and Julianne at the restaurant. Half the world had. He didn't blame his fiancée for being mad, but perhaps this was just the conversation starter they needed. "Rosaline, I'm sorry you saw all that, but…"

"No buts. We need to talk."

Well, at least they agreed on that. Roman sighed and tapped a pencil on his desk. "Can we meet for lunch today?"

"I'm not sure I even want to be seen in public with you. I'm already the laughing stock of Indianapolis," Rosaline sniffed.

"I'm the one in the photos," Roman said.

"But I'm the one being cheated on!"

She had a point. He rolled his eyes but kept his tone even. "Okay then, dinner?"

"You'd better have a way to fix this, Roman!" Rosaline screamed before abruptly disconnecting.

He stared at the receiver a moment, trying to figure out his next move. A spark of an idea came to him. "Ben? I need to see you," he called out.

Ben stepped into the open doorway and tentatively peeked in. "Ready for our meeting?"

"Come in and close the door."

Ben quietly closed the door behind him and took a chair across from Roman's desk. "I take it you and Miss Vandenberg had a disagreement?" He was blushing and looking everywhere but at Roman.

Roman swiveled in his chair so he was facing the window. The streets were bustling with people, everyone in a hurry to get to their office and start their day. He stared out for a long while. "I guess you've been on social media."

"No offense, but I wouldn't be much of an assistant if I wasn't on top of that."

Roman turned the chair back around. "None taken. Can I ask your opinion?"

Ben's brow furrowed and he tapped the arms of the chair with nervous energy while shifting his weight from side to side. He crossed and uncrossed his legs, and then he, too, stared out the window.

Roman realized he'd put his assistant in an

awkward position. Even though Ben Voss was Roman's right-hand man, he'd been handpicked for the job by his father, Charles, which divided Ben's loyalties. "Julianne Caplan," Roman said, answering the question that was probably on the tip of Ben's tongue. "The girl in the photo. She's the daughter of the owner of that shoe store down the street."

Ben blew out a puff of air. "Well, that's awkward."

Awkward was an understatement. Roman's shoulders slumped. "Can I trust you, Ben?"

Ben's eyes widened. "Of course, sir."

"It's unfortunate that someone posted those photos online, but it might be for the best. I really like this girl, and I've been thinking of breaking up with Rosaline."

Ben blanched. "Oh, Mr. Montgomery, your father isn't going to like that. Not to mention how heart-broken Miss Vandenberg will be."

Somehow, he didn't think Rosaline would be so much heart-broken as humiliated in front of her peers. Roman fidgeted with the pencil holder filled with gold-embossed pens on his desk, arranging it every way he could think of and finally putting it back where it originally was. "I know I'm letting people down," Roman said, "but I just don't feel about Rosaline the way I should, and I'm falling in love with Julianne, so…"

"But you've only known Miss Caplan for a short time," Ben said. "Perhaps it's just a crush."

Roman inhaled, exhaled, and tapped his fingers together while staring at nothing on the ceiling. A crush? Something that would blow over in a week or two? No, when he examined his heart, he knew this was the real deal, something he'd never felt before and would never come close to with Rosaline. Maybe he and Julianne hadn't known each other very long, but he didn't think giving it more time would change his mind. He had to end his engagement.

Ben sat attentively on the edge of his chair. "Uh, sir, did you want to talk about your schedule for today?"

Roman grabbed his phone and hurriedly punched in a text as he glanced up at Ben. "My schedule? Not now. Please make dinner reservations for two at Carson's Steakhouse. Email Rosaline—no, call her personally, and ask her to meet me there tonight at seven. And send her two dozen red roses." He thought for a minute. "No, no flowers. She'll think I'm begging for forgiveness." His phone pinged with a reply to his text. He glanced at it and smiled. "I'm going out for coffee right now. Start the meeting without me. Sales are booming, so congratulate the staff or something."

He pulled on his overcoat and sailed out of the office, leaving Ben staring wide-eyed after him.

****

The text from Roman read:

—*Meet me at Pop's ASAP*—

I was on my way out of the store, off to catch the Metro to take me to my morning classes. If I didn't catch that bus, chances were good that I'd be really late for class or miss it altogether. Would Natalie be willing to lend me her notes—again? I wasn't sure, but even as I debated what to do, I knew I was going to meet Roman at Pop's. If nothing else, we needed closure after the internet fiasco.

Before leaving, I peeked into Dad's repair shop to make sure he wasn't in there. I flipped on the light and searched through the boxes and bags on the shelf marked Completed, lined up in alphabetical order by the owner's last name. I ran my finger along the packages until I came to Montgomery, took the box, and stuffed it in my backpack.

I wrapped my scarf tighter around my neck against the chill March wind and headed toward Washington Street. Roman was probably already there, dropped off by his driver or something. I picked up my pace.

Pop's Bakery looked as inviting as it did the first time I came here, only this time it wasn't as crowded. Peering in the front window, I could see only a couple of people in line at the register. That was a relief because I didn't want anyone recognizing me as the scarlet woman breaking up power-couple Roman Montgomery and Rosaline Vandenberg. At least that's what the social media posts were saying about me.

I knew Roman felt safe there with his old friend Father Al, and for some reason I had that same sense of security. I stopped to inhale the mingled aromas of coffee and baked goods as I walked inside and scouted around for Roman. Great. He hadn't gotten here yet. Well, at least I could order one of those delicious lattes while I waited.

Pop was busy waiting on a customer, but he waved over the head of the lawyer, or CEO, or accountant, or whatever she was, as he ran her credit card. "Ah, Julianne, nice to see you again. Be right with you."

He handed the woman her beverage and receipt, and I watched her wobble to the door on impossibly high heels. It was no doubt hard enough walking in that tight skirt, but why anyone would choose four inch heels for downtown business wear, I couldn't imagine.

Her feet must be killing her.

I had to do whatever it took to keep our store in customers, so I handed the woman one of Caplan's business cards as she reached for the door handle. "In case you want to rethink your footwear," I said.

She took the card and stuffed it in her bag without comment. Maybe she wouldn't come to our store, but she might leave the card where someone in her office might see it. Didn't hurt to try.

Pop smiled at me and crooked his finger. Curious, I followed him around the counter, through the kitchen, and into his private business office in back. It reminded me of Caplan's, another mid-twentieth century building with an attached office space next to a storage room. I had no idea why we were going to his private office, but Pop winked at me, opened the door and let me go in ahead of him. There was Roman, sitting in a metal chair with a worn gray leather seat and sipping a coffee.

"I'll just leave you two lovebirds alone," Pop said.

"Pop…" Roman whined.

But he was already gone. Roman indicated the chair next to him and handed me a coffee. "Pop's special brew, just like last time."

My mouth started watering at the aroma of chocolate, mint, and cinnamon. It was still hot, too, so I took a tentative sip and set the cup down on the edge of Pop's industrial-style metal desk. "So. We're going to have to stop meeting like this." I grinned and yes, I blushed.

But Roman didn't look happy. In fact, he had a serious expression on his face and I figured it had to do with us, or his fiancée, or our respective parents, or social media… The list of naysayers was endless.

"So Rosaline saw the photos."

I frowned and let out a big sigh. "I'm sorry."

"An unhappy Rosaline is a force to be reckoned with." Roman took a swallow of his coffee. "My assistant is arranging a dinner date for the two of us tonight."

Just as quickly as my heart had fluttered, it sank. What had I been thinking? Of course he was going to try to patch things up with her. Roman's claim that he didn't love her may or may not be true, but he was certainly committed to her, and their families had a lot riding on their marriage. I suppose it said a lot about his character that he was telling me in person before going ahead with a romantic evening with her.

But it still hurt. I was developing feelings for this guy, and I'd even gotten up the courage to argue with my father about him. Still, I knew this was an impossible situation and I'd said so repeatedly. I pretended to check the time on my phone while I got control of my emotions.

"I understand." If I left right now, I'd only be about fifteen minutes late to class. I stood up and reached for my coffee. No way was I leaving that behind, but as I hoisted my heavy book bag onto my shoulder, I remembered something. "Here." I pulled his repaired shoes out of my bag, the work he'd overpaid for on a pair of loafers he'd probably never wear.

Roman stood up, too, set the box aside, and pulled me toward him. "No, Julianne, you don't understand. I'm having dinner with Rosaline tonight so I can break it off with her. I meant what I said. I want the two of us to be together with nothing hanging over our heads."

Suddenly my heart was pounding so loud I was

sure he could hear it. I glanced up in surprise. "Really?" He nodded. "But we've still got lots of…"

Roman put his fingers to my lips. "Yes, I know. But I'm falling in love with you, so we can face the problems together. If you're willing."

I tried to speak but nothing came out, so I just nodded. Roman leaned down to kiss me just as the door opened.

Pop poked his head in the office and cleared his throat. "You two about finished? 'Cause this is a place of business."

"Yes, Pop, and thanks for the privacy," Roman said.

I blushed. "I've really got to go. If I hurry I can catch the next bus to campus."

Roman picked up the box of loafers, put his arm around me and steered me out of the small office. "I'll drive you." To my look of panic, he added, "In my car. No driver today."

Well, okay, arriving in a regular car wouldn't be as conspicuous as a limo, but then again, I doubted he drove anything that could be called regular. Despite my misgivings, I let him lead me out the door and onto the sidewalk.

"Why's Pop helping us?" I scouted around for which car might be Roman's. "Wouldn't he want you to marry the Catholic girl?"

Roman beeped open a late-model BMW parked at a meter by the curb. "Father Al, Pop, he's a hopeless romantic. But he also thinks the Catholic Church is too rigid about certain things, like inter-faith marriages. So it's his way of bucking the establishment I guess."

Whatever Pop's reasons, I was glad he was on our

side.

****

The rest of Roman's workday had been a waste. His time with Julianne this morning was on his mind, and he was eager to finally be able to move forward with an open, honest relationship with her. Roman physically sat through his meetings and appointments, but mentally he was planning a tactful end to his engagement and not paying attention. Hopefully Ben took good notes.

"Ben," he said as the meeting concluded, "did you get the dinner reservations?"

"Yes, dinner for two at Carson's, seven o'clock."

Roman marveled at Ben's efficiency and appreciated his discretion. He texted Mercer, telling him to meet him at Carson's at nine p.m. That would give him and Rosaline an hour for their meal, a few minutes for the uncomfortable discussion, and then he could escape with his best friend.

At six fifty-five, Roman was standing in front of Montgomery's waiting on his car. Usually Phil texted when he arrived and then waited till Roman came down to the street, so the surprised look on his driver's face was priceless.

Roman told him where they were headed. Phil shut the back door, went around to the driver's side, and pulled out into traffic. "You'll need to drive Miss Vandenberg home this evening. I'll catch a ride with Mercer."

Roman could see Phil's shocked expression in the rearview mirror, but Phil was too much of a professional to say anything. The uncomfortable silence only lasted a few minutes, though, as they drove the short distance from Montgomery's to the restaurant on Illinois Street. "I'll text you." Roman opened the door, waved at his driver, and went inside.

He didn't see Rosaline, so he gave his name to the hostess, who checked his reservation. "I'll be at the bar," he told her. "Let me know when the lady arrives." He glanced around and saw that the place was crowded, even though it was a weeknight. Carson's Steakhouse was where many a private business deal was brokered and conversations got drowned out by whatever game was on the big screen TV. Perfect for a breakup.

Roman sat down on a barstool at the ornate, antique wooden bar from the nineteenth century that stretched the length of the restaurant. He ordered a beer and slowly sipped it as he watched the basketball game on the overhead TV screen. *March Madness,* he reminded himself. Indiana University was in a near tie with The University of Oklahoma. Several people at the bar were rooting for IU, yelling and cheering every time they scored or got the ball back, while off in a corner a small cluster of women wearing maroon Sooners shirts cheered for the other team. Roman lost track of time as he got caught up in the game, too. He finished off his second beer and had nibbled his way through an entire bowl of peanuts by half time. Eight forty-five. He frowned. Rosaline was sometimes fashionably late, but not this late.

—*Where are you?*—he texted her.

No reply came, so he put his phone away. His stomach was growling and, even though good manners dictated that he wait for his date, he put in an order for a New York Strip, medium rare, and a large baked potato. Maybe she'd be here by the time it arrived.

But the waiter placed his food before him and still no Rosaline. Then his phone pinged with a text. "Finally," he muttered as he pulled it out. But it was from Mercer.

—*How's it going?*—

Roman cut off a bite of steak and shoved it in his mouth.

—*I think I've been stood up*—

—*On my way*—

A half hour later, Roman had finished his dinner and paid his tab just as Mercer walked up to the bar.

"So your girl stood you up, huh?"

Roman lifted an eyebrow as he put on his coat. He texted Phil that he didn't need his services tonight after all, and he and Mercer headed out of the restaurant. "I have no idea what happened. I've texted Rosaline but she's not answering, and when I call I get voice mail."

"Dude," Mercer said as they started walking to the adjacent mall parking garage, "the lady saw the handwriting on the wall and made a pre-emptive strike."

Roman stopped in the middle of the sidewalk and faced Mercer. "Pre-emptive how?"

Mercer shrugged. "My guess is she went crying to daddy."

Of course. Why hadn't he thought of that? It would be just like Rosaline to let her father fix things for her, and the idea of Justin Vandenberg getting in his business made Roman's blood boil. He took out his phone again, waited for her voice mail, and shouted, "Rosaline, quit playing games and call me."

"Yeah, that'll teach her," Mercer said with an exaggerated eye roll. "But if she did go to her parents' house, man, you are so screwed."

Roman groaned as Mercer rang for the elevator, but then he realized he didn't particularly want to go home, sensing or fearing the worst. "Say, how 'bout we stay and see a movie?"

"I hear there's a new DiCaprio film out," Mercer said. Instead of going down to the parking garage, he let the elevator close and pushed Up.

When they got to the movie theatre on the top floor of the mall, the DiCaprio adventure film was sold out and the only other one available was a sappy chick flick. Roman didn't care what they saw, since cinematic excellence was hardly the point, so he bought tickets, turned off his phone, and in they went.

It was after midnight when they emerged from the theatre into the deserted mall. Mercer dropped him off at home and Roman planned to go straight to bed. He'd just taken his phone out of his pocket to get undressed, when he realized he'd forgotten to turn it back on. Nine missed messages! That couldn't be good.

Rosaline:

—Roman, I stood you up tonight because I needed to think. I went to my parents' house in Carmel.—

Rosaline:

—It's me again and I'm still really angry with you. I told my parents everything, about the social media photos with that ridiculous Jewish girl. Daddy was very upset and called Charles. Your father will be getting in touch with you.—

Charles Montgomery:

—Son, I just spoke to Justin Vandenberg. Some nonsense about you wanting to break up with his daughter. I'm sure it's all a misunderstanding. Call

me.—

Charles Montgomery:

—I'm still waiting for your call.—

Charles Montgomery:

—Roman, if you're avoiding me, it must be because what Rosaline said is true, that you want to end your engagement. This is untenable.—

Rosaline:

—Your father is livid after he talked to Daddy. You'd better come out of hiding and talk to them.—

Charles Montgomery:

—Roman, Rosaline sent me the social media posts and I will not hear of you ending your engagement. Especially not because of some Jewish girl. The Vandenbergs are long-time friends and associates, and your marriage has been planned for a long time. I demand that you call me back immediately.—

Charles Montgomery:

—Since you are ignoring my messages, I will have to take matters into my own hands.—

Ben Voss:

—Uh, Roman, just to let you know, your father and your fiancée are, uh, upset. Mr. Montgomery called me at home and...well, give me a call.—

Roman shuddered. He lay down on his bed but spent most of the night staring up at the ceiling.

Chapter 10

It had been days and I'd never heard anything from Roman about his dinner with Rosaline. Maybe things didn't go as planned and they were still together. That thought made me miserable. So I decided to focus all my attention on school and the store.

But as much as I tried to put it out of my mind, Roman was all I could think about. I went to classes this morning and daydreamed my way through them. When I looked down at my notes, all I saw was his name and mine intertwined in doodles.

"Wanna get some lunch?" Natalie asked me after English Comp class. "Maybe we could look over the test review Dr. Knoll handed out."

I was still distracted, checking and rechecking my phone for messages. I looked up to see her standing in front of me, tapping her foot. "What?"

She shifted her book bag onto her left arm. "Lunch?"

"Oh, well, I was going to run over to the hospital cafeteria, maybe meet up with Nora."

Natalie brightened up. "Sounds good. Can I join you? There are some cute doctors over there."

I'd barely been paying attention in class and I wasn't even sure I'd gotten a copy of the test review that Natalie mentioned. "Okay, if you don't mind institution food."

She smirked. "What do you think we'd get if we ate on campus?"

True. I sent off a quick text to Nora and we started walking the mile from school to the hospital. It was a beautiful late-March day, one of those early spring days where the sun was shining, the buds were starting to appear on the trees, and the air temperature was warm enough that we didn't need several layers of clothing. Natalie and I were chatting away about nothing in particular when off in the distance, I spotted a black stretch limo driving slowly down the main street adjacent to campus.

"Look at that," Natalie commented with a tilt of her head in the limo's direction. "Must be some bigwig visiting campus."

"Maybe," I said, but the car looked awfully familiar. The closer we got, the slower it went, and then it pulled over to the curb into a clearly marked No Parking space and a man got out of the backseat. I gasped when I realized it was Roman.

"He's coming this way," Natalie whispered.

And indeed he was. I didn't know whether to run to him or hurry off in the opposite direction.

Natalie stared as Roman came ever closer. "Isn't that the guy you were kissing in that Italian restaurant?"

"Umm, yeah," I said. "But…"

"Julianne," Roman called out, "can we talk?"

Natalie pointed to an empty bench along the pathway, walked over, and sat down out of earshot. I hurried over to Roman.

"I've been searching all over this campus trying to find you," he said.

"You could have texted." I was pretty peeved that

I'd been worrying nonstop about him, and yet he hadn't sent a single message.

"I'm sorry." Roman was usually so polished, sophisticated, and well-spoken, but today something was off. His eyes were red and had dark circles under them like he hadn't slept, his hair was uncombed, and the most obvious indication that there was something wrong was his attire: torn jeans paired with a faded t-shirt, an unbuttoned pea coat, and worn athletic shoes. He looked like a lost little boy and my heart went out to him.

"The other night. I was going to talk to Rosaline…" His voice trailed off.

"Yeah, you told me. So…?"

He shook his head and let out a huge sigh. "She stood me up."

Well, that sucked. The woman wasn't stupid, though, so she probably figured out what he was going to say. But was all his angst the result of her not showing up for a date? That didn't bode well for me. "What happened?"

"Instead of meeting me, she ran crying to her daddy, who then talked to my father, and now my dad's on the warpath. It's been nonstop arguments with Dad, with him threatening my job or to move up the wedding if I don't do what he says, and fights with Rosaline, and my assistant stuck in the middle fielding calls from everyone. I've been so distracted and upset…" His voice trailed off.

I studied Roman's face and he did seem rattled. I could sympathize. I didn't know what sort of relationship he had with his father, but I knew how I felt when Dad was angry with me. Roman had a lot more at stake than I did. "Is there anything I can do?" I pretty much assumed the answer was say goodbye forever, but I guess I just wanted to hear Roman actually say it.

He wiped tears from his face as he leaned his back against a nearby tree. Maybe he was trying to find the words to tell me, but he was taking his sweet time and it was killing me. All I wanted to do was reach out and hold him, but I looked off in the distance and saw Natalie still sitting on the bench watching us. I also noticed other students on campus staring at Roman and me, and I watched as the campus police stopped by his illegally parked limo and spoke to Phil. All this while I was waiting for Roman to say something.

I had to break this unbearable silence. "Roman, I'm so sorry."

"For what? None of this is your fault."

"Some of it is," I told him. "I feel like I led you on, meeting you at Pop's, going to the theatre with you... You're engaged, and even though I'm not in a relationship, it wasn't fair."

"Julianne." Roman took both my hands, tears threatening to spill out of his eyes, his voice raspy. "Listen to me. I never believed in love at first sight, but that's what happened to me when I met you. I can't go back to Rosaline. I want you...need you, in my life." He took a deep breath. "Marry me."

Say what? My mouth dropped open. "Uh, I, uh..." Neither my mouth nor my brain would engage.

"I know I'm not making any sense, but I love you..."

I gasped. "You love me?" I went from total despair at the thought of losing him to total elation at hearing his words, and then to feeling like I couldn't catch my breath. "We've only known each other a few weeks. You can't know that yet."

He looked into my eyes. "Yes, I can. I do."

He leaned down to kiss me but I put up a hand to stop him. We had too many eyes on us for a PDA.

"And I know you feel it, too," Roman continued. "Like we were supposed to meet, supposed to be together."

Roman was right about that much. I'd felt that same bolt of lightning the moment we laid eyes on each other on Valentine's Day. I did want to be with him, forever I hoped, but for every reason why we belonged together there were a dozen more why it would never work. "Okay, yes, I do feel it, but…"

"I know it's rash and way too soon, but the only way to avoid marrying Rosaline is to marry the woman I really love."

I pulled away from him, crossed my arms and narrowed my eyes. "So I'm your get out of jail free card?" No way was I going to get used like that.

Roman shook his head. "That's not what I meant. I love you and I know we'd get married eventually, so why not just speed up the timetable? My parents don't believe in divorce, so…"

"…so they'd have to think long and hard about you leaving your wife." I blew out a puff of air.

That sort of made sense, but then it didn't. My head was spinning. This rich, handsome man, one I was falling in love with, just asked me to be his wife. That should be a dream come true, but I just kept picturing all the problems this would cause. Problems? Understatement. His church might not recognize an inter-faith marriage, and I didn't even want to think about the stink this would raise in my Synagogue.

"You didn't answer my question," he said.

I kicked at some dead leaves under the tree. "Roman, let's slow down a minute and think this through."

He lifted my chin. "No. If we overthink it we'll chicken out."

I didn't have time to do my usual list of pros and cons. Never mind that just a few weeks ago I insisted to Dad that at nineteen I was too young for marriage. All I had was my gut, and my gut instinct told me I couldn't live without this man. So... "I may be crazy, *we* may be crazy, but yes, I'll marry you."

Roman grinned, started to reach for me, glanced around at the onlookers, and instead began pacing. "I'm sorry I don't have a ring."

"It's okay," I said. "Do you at least have a plan?"

He nodded. "I did think that much through. Meet me at the county clerk's office in the courthouse at nine a.m. tomorrow. We'll need a marriage license, but then we can get married at Pop's."

I gulped. "We're getting married tomorrow? In a bakery? By a priest?" I wasn't sure if it was butterflies or pure fear, but I could feel my knees shaking.

Roman took my hand. "Pop—Father Al—can perform civil ceremonies."

"And what about flowers? Attendants? Music?" Like every other girl, I'd pictured my wedding, and I always saw myself in a white dress with all the trimmings. I might look back and have regrets if I didn't at least get some of those things.

"Don't worry, I'll take care of all that. Pop will

bake us a cake, I'm sure. I'll get Mercer to stand up for me, and you can get..." His gaze drifted over to Natalie, who was watching us intently.

"Not her," I said. "I'll ask Nora. She can be discreet."

We said goodbye and parted company, our hands and eyes lingering as we reluctantly went in opposite directions. By the time I rejoined Natalie, I was dancing on air.

"Girlfriend, you look like the cat who swallowed the canary."

I tried to be serious, but I couldn't wipe the grin off my face. "Yeah, well..." Then I remembered why she and I had been walking in the first place. "Lunch. You ready?"

Natalie stood up and shook her head. "You and lover boy took so much time over there that if I go now, I'll be late to class." She turned to go, but stopped and said, "Whatever you two have going on, I'm happy for you." She waved goodbye.

More than ever, I needed to talk to Nora. I sent a text pleading with her to meet me in the hospital cafeteria.

****

"Mercer, you've got to help me out here."

"Help you what, man? I don't know what kind of jewelry your fiancée likes. Aside from that ten-thousand dollar rock she's already wearing."

"Twenty thousand," Roman replied.

Mercer trailed alongside Roman, up and down the rows of diamond rings on display at Sullivan's Warehouse Jewelers. The store was huge, with aisle after aisle of rings for all occasions, with at least half the showroom devoted to engagement and wedding rings. "And why this big box store up here in the burbs? Why didn't you go to your family's private jeweler if you wanted an apology gift for Rosaline?"

Roman cleared his throat but avoided Mercer's gaze. He'd been deliberately vague when he'd pleaded with Mercer to meet him here. "I chose this store because of the anonymity."

A salesman on the other side of the row of glass counters kept pace as Roman perused the selection. He was looking for the perfect ring in what he hoped was Julianne's correct size, but he had to choose one in a hurry. "There, that one." He pointed to a two carat solitaire diamond in a platinum setting. "What do you think?"

The salesman smiled and nodded, but Mercer stared at it in dismay. "Rosaline won't accept your apology if you give her something like that."

Roman nodded to the salesman who took the ring out of the case and set it on the counter on a black velvet display pad. "But it's pretty, right?" he asked Mercer.

"It is, sir," the salesman replied, even though he hadn't been addressed. "Halo diamond solitaire engagement ring, on sale for twenty-two hundred dollars."

"Bro, you gotta be kidding," Mercer scoffed.

Roman shot his friend a withering look and picked up the ring for closer inspection. The band was wide enough to serve as both an engagement ring and wedding band, and because they were short on time, he hoped Julianne would be happy with just the one ring instead of a matched set. "I'll take it," Roman told the salesman, setting it back on the velvet display pad. "And that platinum groom's ring next to it, wrap that up, too." He took out his wallet and almost withdrew his corporate business card, but instead pulled out his personal debit card.

Mercer waited till the salesman was busy ringing up the sale and out of earshot. "What the hell is going on?"

Roman lowered his voice. "It isn't for Rosaline, it's for Julianne. We're getting married tomorrow. I need a ring, and…" he cast a sideways glance at his friend, "a best man." Roman watched Mercer's jaw drop. "I told you I needed your help."

Mercer swallowed hard and took a step back. "Are you nuts?" he hissed. "You can't marry one woman while you're engaged to another!"

Roman shrugged, feeling almost giddy about the new life he was starting with Julianne. "I've tried repeatedly to end the relationship with Rosaline and no one will listen to me. No one except Julianne. We're in love and we're getting married tomorrow morning at Pop's. Are you with me?"

Mercer's face contorted into a myriad of emotions, ranging from shock to disbelief. But before he could answer, the salesman returned to the counter with the engagement ring and groom's ring in two separate boxes, which he set on the display counter next to the credit card receipt. Roman scribbled a signature and stuffed his copy in his pants pocket.

"Congratulations, sir," the salesman said. "Your lady will be very happy." He put the boxes in a carry bag and handed it to Roman.

"Thanks." Roman accepted the bag and started for

the door. "So, you in or out?" He hustled out of the store and into the suburban mall parking lot before turning for his friend's answer.

"In," Mercer said with a grin. "I never liked Rosaline's snobby attitude, and I kinda like sticking it to her."

Roman beeped his car's horn with the remote to locate his Beemer parked a few rows over in the crowded lot. "Great. Meet me at Pop's tomorrow morning. I've still got to arrange for flowers and talk Pop into conducting the ceremony." He started walking backward as he called out, "And wear a suit. I want this to be a special day for the woman I love."

****

—Stuck in the ER with an emergency appendectomy. Waiting for an OR to open up—

Nora had replied to my earlier text.

So I sat drumming my fingers on the table in the hospital cafeteria, unable to concentrate on the nonfiction essay I was reading for English Comp, while I waited for Nora to join me. I sipped my ginger ale and took a few bites of my tuna salad, but despite my growling stomach, I eventually gave up and tossed the fork down. It was already an hour past the time I'd told Dad I'd be at the store. If Nora didn't get here soon I'd have to leave.

But then she sailed in, looking frazzled and a little breathless, scouted out the busy cafeteria till she spotted me, and hurried over. She crossed her arms and tapped her foot. "Whatever this is, make it quick. We're seriously understaffed today."

I nodded and blew out a puff of air. This was a subject that would require a certain amount of finesse, and I hoped the few minutes she seemed willing to allot me was enough. "I need your help," I said. "Tomorrow. And maybe today. Tonight. I need a dress…"

She looked puzzled. "What kind of dress?"

I couldn't look her in the eye. I didn't know if that meant I was ashamed of what I was planning to do, or nervous, or getting cold feet, or … All I knew for sure was that Nora wouldn't like it. "A white dress. It's for…"

"For what?"

Nora and I both turned to see Ty glaring at us. "Don't you have some guts to cut open somewhere?" I asked him.

"Soon," he said. "What do you need a white dress for?"

I scrambled around for a logical answer. Other than the truth, that is. "My friend Natalie. From school? She invited me to her younger sister's confirmation. Not that it's any of your business."

Ty scowled. "Shouldn't the sister be the one in white?"

I shrugged and did my best to appear nonchalant. "Well, maybe I misunderstood. I've never been to a Catholic Quincenera."

Ty's gaze wandered as he lost interest in the topic of dresses, and without another word he left and went to the buffet line. Nora slid into the booth across from me.

"What do you really need a white dress for?"

"I'm getting married tomorrow."

Nora gasped. "Julianne! What the…"

"Shhh." I looked around to see who might have overheard, but the cafeteria was crowded with people eating, checking their phones, or talking with table-mates, and no one, not even Ty, was paying attention to us. Still, I leaned in for privacy. "Roman's family won't let him out of his engagement to Rosaline, so he asked me to marry him."

"Have you lost your mind?" She checked herself and lowered her voice. "You must have. He's using you. You get that, right?"

"I'm not stupid, Nora. I asked him the same thing. But he told me loves me, and I know I love him, so I guess we'll deal with the fallout later."

Nora leaned back against the booth's cushions and stared at the institutional light fixture overhead. "Fallout. That's putting it mildly."

"Please help me, Nora. Help us. You're the only one I can turn to."

Nora seemed conflicted as she considered what I was suggesting, as well as her potential role in the subterfuge. Finally, she sat up and shook her head. "Julianne, you can't do this. Samuel and Lydia will have a meltdown. And Roman's family..." Just then her pager went off. She glanced at it quickly and slid out of the booth. "Can we talk about this later?"

I stood up, too. "No, because you can't change my mind. All I is need a dress, and a decent pair of shoes." Nora scowled, her skepticism written all over her face. Make that horror. "Please, Nora, just meet me at Consigning Ladies this evening after work."

"Let it be known I highly disapprove," Nora groaned, and then called to me over her shoulder before she hurried out. "I'll be there."

****

Consigning Ladies carried an eclectic assortment of clothing. Some things were definitely second-hand

and priced accordingly, some were what their salespeople liked to call "gently used," and occasionally you could find outfits that had never been worn and still had the original store tags on them. I was hoping to score one of those, thereby getting a new dress at a bargain basement price.

I browsed through the color-coordinated dresses, starting at the all-white selection and slowly pawing my way through off-white, shell, light beige, and eventually into the pale pastels. Nothing. I sighed as I scouted around for other display racks.

"Are you looking for something in particular?" the saleswoman asked me.

Well, I couldn't very well tell her that I wanted something to wear to my own wedding, tomorrow. "I'm looking for something dressy." That didn't exactly narrow it down. "To wear to a, uh…"

"We've gotten in a few prom dresses," she said. She crooked her finger and I followed her to a rack in the back corner of the store.

"Thanks," I said, hoping for some privacy. But she just stood behind me watching as I perused the few formal gowns. And I still couldn't find anything or even concentrate with her hovering over me like that.

The bell over the door tinkled and I glanced up to see Nora coming in, still in her nurse's uniform, and looking about as frazzled as she did at lunch. I waved her over.

"I'm so glad you're here." I went back to the rack of dresses, still hoping to get rid of the saleswoman. She was probably working on commission, so I felt a twinge of guilt about that, but not enough to encourage her to stay.

Nora gave me a steely-eyed glare. "You're determined to do this?"

I glanced at the saleswoman, not wanting her in my business, but also not wanting to argue with Nora in public. "Yes," I whispered.

"Let me know if you ladies need help." The saleswoman finally took the hint and stepped back, giving us some breathing room.

"Have you found anything?" Nora asked. She began picking through the white and off-white prom dresses that I'd just gone through.

I shook my head. "It's too early in the spring so there aren't many formal dresses to choose from."

"What about this one?" Nora pulled out a long white strapless empire dress with a rhinestone belt and held it up to her.

I stepped back and studied it a moment, and then saw its price tag. Seventy-five dollars. "Too prom-y. And too expensive."

She nodded and put it back, but then something caught her eye. "Look at this!"

I hadn't seen that one. It was a tea-length dress that had been squished between two long evening gowns. I took it from her and held it up in front of the mirror. It was white lace, sleeveless with a rounded collar embellished in silver sequins, and a fitted waist.

"We've had that one a while, which is why it's marked down," the saleswoman said, rejoining Nora and me. "Most girls looking for prom dresses want sizes zero or two, so we don't get much interest in size eight. But it's a lovely dress."

I nodded. Size eight may have been considered full-figured these days, but it was just what I needed. It had been marked down twice, from one hundred to seventy-five, and then down to forty-five. "Can I try it on?" I asked the saleswoman.

Once in the dressing room, I found that the dress zipped up the back, so I poked my head out of the curtains and motioned for Nora. She stepped in behind me, the zipper slipped right up, and we both stood there in awe, gazing at the beautiful dress I'd be getting married in. "It's perfect."

"Let it be known I'm still opposed to this, but it's lovely on you," Nora said with a warm smile." Now what about shoes?"

"I'm gonna snag that pair of sling back pumps we just got in at the store."

"The ones in ivory?"

I nodded. "Hopefully Dad won't notice them missing. I'll put them back later."

Nora gazed at my reflection in the full-length mirror. "You look beautiful, Julianne." She smiled and gave me a hug before unzipping the back of the dress. "My sweet, well-behaved niece is getting married on the sly." She chuckled. "I wouldn't miss it for the world."

I put the dress back on its hanger, admiring its lace and curved neckline one more time. "What are you going to wear?"

"Scrubs." When I looked at her askance, she winked at me. "Lydia never notices anything about me, but Samuel would wonder why I was going to work all dressed up. I'll put your dress in my car and bring it in late tonight when I get home. I'll stuff a change of clothes for myself in my bag before I leave in the morning." She smiled. "But you may have to accept me in white hospital sneakers."

I laughed. "I don't mind, but Roman might object."

Neither Nora nor I said another word as I took my wedding dress to the cash register. This was surreal.

Chapter 11

Roman stood outside Pop's Bakery before seven a.m., tapping his foot impatiently. Finally Pop appeared, unlocked the door from the inside, and flipped on the electronic Open sign. "Pop, I need your help," Roman said as he burst through the door.

Pop craned his neck to see around him. "You seem to be the first one here," he said. "And it's early, even for you."

"Yeah, I know, but…"

"Right. You need my help. What can I do for you, Roman? More clandestine coffee dates?" Pop chuckled as he closed the door after Roman. He stepped behind his bakery counter, retrieved a large tray of just out-of-the-oven baked donuts, and slid them into the display case, the smell of cinnamon and orange glaze wafting through the store. Next, he checked to make sure the coffee machines were ready to brew, and picked up the half-empty sugar dispenser to refill. "Speak up, son. How can I help you?"

Roman gathered his courage. "You can perform a marriage ceremony."

Pop nearly dropped the sugar dispenser, got control of it, and set it down safely on the counter before raising an eyebrow. "I could have sworn you said 'marriage ceremony.' "

Roman nodded. "You're still licensed to perform

weddings, right?" Pop leaned his elbows on the counter, listening intently. "Because Julianne and I are getting married today. Here, we hope."

Eyes closed, Pop slowly stood up, probably praying if Roman had to guess, but then Pop rubbed his ear and scratched his balding head. "You said Julianne, right? Not Rosaline?" He crossed his arms and glared like a disapproving parent.

"I said Julianne and that's what I meant." Roman let out a sigh. "I don't love Rosaline and my family still insists I marry her, so…"

"So you want to outsmart them?" Pop let out a low whistle. "Roman…" He stared up at the ceiling and shook his head.

"I've heard all the objections and I—we—don't care. We're getting a marriage license this morning, and then I'm hoping you'll let us have the wedding here. With witnesses, flowers, music from my phone, and…" Roman winced. "A cake?"

Instead of an answer, Pop got back to work prepping for customers. Roman had known Pop for many years and he knew Pop couldn't be rushed into a decision. So Roman waited. After several minutes of feigned busyness, Pop turned to face Roman.

"You sure about this, son?"

"I love her," Roman said.

Pop shook his head in disbelief. "Ordinarily I'd say no outright, insisting you have your family's blessing, but I can't condone anyone forcing you to marry a woman you don't love." He did more gazing at the ceiling, and after a while, Roman looked up to see what Pop was staring at. All Roman saw was a few cobwebs around the industrial light fixture.

Eventually Pop lowered his eyes and grinned. "So according to my sources..."

"Sources?"

Pop pointed upward. "...your marriage to a Caplan will bring some much-needed diversity to the Montgomery family. It might even help Samuel Caplan's business by having you as a son-in-law." Pop sighed. "So yes, I'll perform the ceremony."

Roman grabbed Pop's right hand and shook it vigorously. "Thanks, Father. I owe you!"

Pop withdrew his hand. "You certainly do. Closing unexpectedly for a private event will cost me a lot of business."

Roman reached into his pocket and pulled out his credit card. "I'm happy to pay for renting out your facility, for your services as officiant, and for the cake. Here. Run it for whatever you think all that's worth."

"I think it's worth a great deal." Pop took the credit card and rang up a large sale.

****

"Are we really doing this?" I asked Roman. We were standing in front of Pop's at ten a.m., fresh from the Marion County courthouse, marriage license in hand.

Roman turned to face me. "I know it's fast. Hell, it's a huge risk, but I'm ready to do this." He stroked my cheek with his finger and brushed a stray lock of hair away. "If you are."

I took a deep breath as I glanced at the Closed for Private Event sign hanging from the door. "I'm as ready as I'll ever be."

Roman held the door open and we went inside. Pop's Bakery not only smelled as wonderful as always, it looked amazing. As I surveyed the transformation, my eyes started to mist over. "This is…it's…"

"I hope you like it," Roman said with a squeeze of my hand.

"It's beautiful." I concentrated on the surroundings to keep myself from crying. The tables and chairs had been pushed aside to make way for a makeshift altar—a speaker's podium covered in a white tablecloth placed next to the carryout counter. On top of the display case, covered with another white tablecloth and festooned with confetti, sat a small, round cake with white icing and pink flowers, which read Congratulations Roman and Julianne. Next to the cake was a silver serving knife tied with a blue ribbon. Off to the side were plates, champagne glasses, and a bucket of ice with a bottle of something cooling inside.

"How did you do all this"—I waved my arms around the shop—"so fast?"

Roman pulled me into an embrace. "It's amazing what you can do with a few apps and a lot of cash."

"Hello?" Pop came out from the kitchen. He'd traded in his baker's whites for clerical black with a cleric's collar. "Ah, here's the happy couple." He beamed as he embraced us both.

The three of us were the only ones here, and just as I was about to text Nora, the door opened to admit her and Mercer, walking in side-by-side like they'd planned it. But I knew they couldn't have since Nora left for work before six this morning. I guess their choreographed arrival was a coincidence.

Roman gave his best man a visual once-over and grinned. "Dress shirt and pants with a blazer. Nice."

I had no idea what clothes Nora would be able to

sneak into her work bag before she left home, but she'd pulled it off with understated beige linen pants paired with a blue crepe blouse tucked into her tiny waist, her short hair curling around her face. I couldn't help but notice Mercer's obvious admiration of her.

Nora seemed a little breathless. "Hope we're not late."

"No," I said, "we just got here."

Mercer slowly turned his attention from Nora to whistle at me. "You look gorgeous."

I got up really early this morning and completely dressed in the bathroom. I took extra care with my makeup and pulled my hair back with an oversized rhinestone clip. Then I put on the white dress from the consignment store, my winter coat on top of it despite the warming weather, and a pair of sneakers for walking. I'd stuffed the sling backs I borrowed from our inventory in my school bag to change into at the courthouse. I didn't want to scuff them up, since I planned to put them back on the shelf later.

I'd hoped to get out of the house before either of my parents woke up. I almost made it, too, but Dad called after me from his bedroom doorway. "Where are you headed this early? And isn't it a little warm for that coat?"

I didn't even turn to face him, sure he'd notice the care I'd taken with my hair and makeup. I reached for the front door while pretending to adjust my school bag. "The library to cram for a test," I lied, "and they keep it really cold in there." And with that, out I went. Here I was eloping with a man he disapproved of, a Catholic and a business rival, and yet a little part of me wished my father could be here to give me away.

I blushed at Mercer's compliment. "Thanks. And thanks for agreeing to come today."

My handsome fiancé—could I call him that?—had on an expensive suit, probably Italian if I had to guess. It was navy, but the material almost seemed to shimmer, catching the light and making the material appear to have flecks of green and pink. And of course Roman chose top-of-the-line dress shoes.

Mercer shrugged as he playfully punched Roman's shoulder. "You've pulled off quite a coup."

Nora gave me a big hug and whispered, "I hope you two know what you're doing."

"So, Roman, looks like you've thought of everything. Except maybe flowers," Mercer said as he glanced around the shop.

Roman's eyes widened. "Pop…?"

"Over there." Pop tilted his head toward the counter.

Roman reached behind the counter and pulled out a white florist's box. He parted the green tissue paper, removed a white carnation boutonniere for himself and handed the other one to Mercer. He then pulled out a bouquet of white calla lilies for me and a wrist corsage of white roses for Nora. Roman had indeed thought of everything, and as I took in the beauty of his last-minute decorations, it seemed like a fairy tale come true.

"Shall we?" Pop said. He planted himself in front of the podium and, facing us, indicated where Roman and I should stand. Roman set his phone on the display counter, pushed a button, and the first strains of Pachelbel's *Canon in D* drifted through the room, accompanying me as I took a few short steps to the makeshift altar. I took my place next to my about-to-be-husband, Nora found her place at my right side, and Mercer stepped to Roman's left. I should have been nervous, shaking even, considering the huge step we were taking, but I was surprisingly calm.

"Dearly beloved," Pop said with a warm, paternal smile as he tossed a glance at Roman, who nodded and paused the music. "Today we're not only joining two people in holy wedlock, we're merging two cultures." He winked at us. "So I'll dispense with the religious ceremony and get right to the good stuff."

I giggled nervously. I had to admit I'd been worried about being married by a Catholic priest, but I should have known Pop would make things okay for both of us.

"Do you, Roman Montgomery, take this woman to be your lawfully wedded wife?"

Roman smiled down at me. "I do."

"And do you, Julianne Caplan, take this man to be your lawfully wedded husband?"

I had a moment of panic, my stomach doing unexpected flip-flops, but then Roman reached out and took my hand. A sense of peace washed over me as I looked him in the eye. "Yes, I do."

"Do you two have vows to recite?" Pop asked. We glanced nervously at each other and then back at Pop.

"I didn't really plan anything," Roman said, "but I'll give it a try." He took a deep breath and looked into my eyes as he spoke. "I love you, Julianne. I feel like I've always loved you, and I will cherish every minute we spend together. If we get sick, go broke, fight about stuff, whatever, I promise to never give up on us. No one and nothing is more important than this."

I swallowed a big lump in my throat. That was the most heartfelt thing anyone had ever said to me, ad lib no less. Could I match that? I had to try. "Roman, I agree that from the moment we met, it was as if our souls recognized each other. I want to make you as happy as you make me, so I'll cook for you—once I learn how—support you in all your endeavors, and stand with you as we take each day as it comes. And if I get sick, scared, or frustrated, I'll always turn to you for love and support. For me, this is forever."

Roman leaned over to kiss me, but Pop gently pressed us apart. "Rings?" Pop asked.

Roman turned to Mercer, who reached into his pocket and pulled out a black box from Sullivan's Warehouse Jewelers. I gasped when Roman opened the box, because inside was the most beautiful solitaire diamond ring I'd ever seen.

Roman glanced at Pop, who nodded approval. "With this ring, I marry you." He slipped the ring on my left hand. I couldn't take my eyes off its sparkle and beauty. It must have cost a fortune.

But then it hit me. Nora and I exchanged glances, because of all the things I'd thought about, a ring for Roman wasn't one of them. "Uh, I..."

"Oh, I forgot," Mercer said. He reached back into his pocket and withdrew a man's platinum wedding band. "Roman figured you wouldn't have time for ring shopping." He placed the ring in the palm of my hand.

Embarrassed, I turned to Roman and whispered, "I'm sorry you had to buy your own wedding ring."

Roman grinned and shrugged. "In case you hadn't noticed, I'm pretty picky about what I wear. That includes jewelry."

I laughed. "Okay," I said as I placed it on his left hand, "then with the ring you specially chose for yourself, I marry you."

Pop nodded to Roman, who hit play on his phone, sending the wedding march resounding through the bakery. "Then by the power vested in me by God and the state of Indiana, I now pronounce you husband and wife. You may kiss the bride."

****

After they sealed their vows with a kiss, neither one moved or spoke. Roman was mesmerized.

"Okay you two," Mercer said. "Save it for the honeymoon."

Nora nodded. "Cut the cake and pour the cider, because some of us have to get back to work."

"Oh, right." Roman took his new wife by the hand and led her to the counter. With their hands intertwined, they made the first slice.

"I'll take it from here." Pop tied a white apron around his black clerical garb and accepted the knife from Roman. "And no shoving cake in each other's faces," he said. "You two have enough problems without starting out with a pastry fight."

The music playing in the background was an instrumental version of "My Funny Valentine." Pop cut five pieces of the chocolate cake with white icing and emptied out the bottle of sparkling cider into five champagne flutes.

Mercer raised his glass in a toast. "To Mr. and Mrs. Roman Christopher Montgomery. I wish you lots of luck. You're going to need it."

"Gee thanks, man." Roman rolled his eyes as he took a sip. "That's the kind of toast any best man should offer up."

Julianne turned to her new husband. "Christopher?"

It wasn't the first time Roman had realized how little the two of them knew about each other, but it had never occurred to him to mention his full name. Come to think of it, he didn't know Julianne's middle name. Or if she had one. Maybe tonight they could talk and... His mind wandered as he looked at his bride. He definitely didn't want to spend their wedding night talking.

Nora took a couple of bites of cake and then set her plate and mostly-full glass on the counter. "I've got to get back to the hospital." She turned to Julianne. "Don't you have class?"

Julianne shrugged. "I think I missed it. Hopefully I can get the notes. I'll just change into my jeans and hit the library till it's time to go to the store." She retrieved her bulging school bag from where she'd dropped it near the front door.

"Oh, wait, I almost forgot." Julianne turned and tossed her wedding bouquet to Nora, who caught it with a surprised look on her face. "I didn't want to miss out on any traditions," Julianne said with a grin. She hoisted the bag onto her shoulder.

"Ladies, feel free to use my office." Pop crooked his finger and led the two of them back.

"So what's your plan?" Mercer asked.

Roman forced his attention back to Mercer after watching Julianne walk away. He shrugged. "I don't know that I have one."

"You mean you didn't plan a wedding night? You two gotta consummate this thing before your families

172

find out."

Roman choked on his cider. Mercer gave him a slap on the back as Roman could feel himself blushing deeply. "Thanks for pointing that out. But for now I'm gonna check in with Ben and maybe get some work done. If I can concentrate."

"How about a workout?" Mercer suggested. "Meet me at the gym in two hours." He pointed to Roman's left hand. "And you'd better hide that ring for the time being."

Roman nodded, but he didn't want to take it off till he'd talked to Julianne about it. "Okay, see you at the MCC."

Julianne and Nora emerged from the back of the shop. Now his wife was wearing jeans and a pale pink turtle neck sweater, with a pair of ballet flats and no socks. Nora had changed back into her scrubs and had Julianne's dress bag folded over one arm. She waved at Roman and gave Julianne one last shoulder squeeze before hurrying out the door, which Mercer was holding for her.

Roman took Julianne's left hand and studied her ring. It certainly wasn't the size, cut and clarity of the one he'd bought Rosaline, but it suited her. "We can't wear these for a while, you know."

Julianne nodded. "I planned for that." She pulled a silver chain from underneath her turtleneck, strung the diamond ring on it and then tucked the chain and ring back inside her sweater.

Roman reluctantly took off his own wedding band and stuffed it in his pocket. "This is just temporary," he assured her. "We're going to tell our families. Soon." He pulled her into an embrace.

"When?" she asked. "Not that I'm in any hurry to listen to all that yelling."

Roman groaned. "Me neither. Maybe this weekend. But for tonight…" He lifted her chin and gently kissed her. "…for our wedding night, come to my house."

Julianne opened her mouth, closed it, and blinked. "I don't even know where you live. Just like I didn't know your middle name."

Roman winced. "Oh, yeah." He thought for a moment. "Can you get out of your house tonight? I can have my driver pick you up."

Julianne nodded. "I'll think of some excuse. Tell him I'll be in front of the public library at seven."

They kissed goodbye. It was hard for Roman to let her go, but he held the door and watched as his wife got on a city bus. As soon as they could announce their marriage, he promised himself she wouldn't have to do that anymore. "Pop?" He called out.

Pop appeared from the back of his shop. He had removed his clerical collar and pushed up the sleeves of his black shirt, still wearing his baker's apron. "Yes?"

Roman couldn't stop grinning. "I just wanted to say thanks."

"You're welcome. Of course I didn't do it for free. Check your credit card statement."

It was a mild day, so Roman decided to walk to the store. In fact, he practically danced his way to work. Instead of the elevator that went to his private office suite, he jumped on the escalator and rode impatiently for a moment before bounding the rest of the way up. He smiled at his employees who were busy waiting on customers or rearranging displays, waved at the janitor who looked surprised, and burst into his office.

Ben was hard at work on his laptop. "Good morning, sir. Or should I say afternoon?"

Roman glanced at the time on Ben's computer and saw that it was past twelve. He'd have to hurry if he was going to meet Mercer at the gym. "Ben, can you cancel my two p.m. meeting?"

Ben turned around in surprise. "That distributor is in from New York."

Roman sighed. "Okay, then reschedule it for four. I'm going to the gym."

Ben clenched his jaw but scrolled through his phone and sent off a text. He nodded when it pinged back. "Four o'clock is confirmed."

"And I want you to order an elaborate dinner, uh, vegetarian I guess, some sparkling champ...cider, two dozen red roses, and have it all sent to my house by seven thirty. I'm entertaining my wife." Roman stopped in his tracks when he realized what he'd just said. He could feel the heat and fear rising up, prickling the back of his neck.

Ben bobbled his phone and nearly dropped it. He swiveled around in his chair, his eyes wide. "You and Miss Vandenberg got married?"

Roman forced himself to calm down. He'd already blurted it out, and Ben had never been anything but loyal, so he decided to take the risk. "This is between you and me." Ben blinked. "I got married today to Julianne Caplan. We eloped, obviously. We're planning to tell our families in a few days, but tonight..."

The color drained out of Ben's face. "Yes, I understand."

"And text Phil. Tell him to pick up my wife in front of the public library at seven p.m."

Chapter 12

Gym bag slung over one shoulder, Roman walked through the lobby of the Metro Community Center. He scanned his membership card at the check-in desk where Club Manager Sylvester Prinze was seated. "Good afternoon," Roman said.

Prinze didn't answer, didn't even look up from his phone. But Roman was in too good a mood to care, so he shrugged and headed toward the locker room. As Roman passed through the array of cardio machines, he spotted Mercer already on a treadmill, flirting outrageously with the attractive blonde woman on the machine next to him. And she was flirting back. Roman briefly wondered about the spark he'd seen between Mercer and Nora, but he hoped that maybe this time his best friend was hitting on a woman who was actually interested in him.

Roman spun the lock on his locker and took his freshly washed shorts, t-shirt and new athletic shoes out of the bag. Before he stepped out of his trousers, he reached into his pocket to make sure his wedding ring was still there. He was tempted to put it on, but he didn't know who he might see, and besides, he didn't want the ring to get caught on any equipment. So he set it carefully on the top shelf of his locker, changed clothes, and gave the lock an extra spin to make sure it was secure before heading out to the exercise floor.

He didn't think it had taken him that long to change clothes, but when he returned to the workout area, Mercer was no longer on the treadmill. *Maybe he went off to the juice bar with that woman,* he thought. Great. Meeting here was Mercer's idea, a way to keep Roman distracted so he wouldn't have to dwell on the upcoming blowouts with both the Montgomery and Caplan families, and now Alvarez was AWOL. Roman sighed and got on a stationary bike, programmed it, and began pedaling. He plugged his earphones into the audio outlet to watch the Food Network on the attached TV screen. Roman didn't know anything about cooking, but he thought he might like to learn, especially now that he had someone to cook for. Julianne mentioned in her vows that she didn't know how to cook, either. Maybe they could learn together.

Completely absorbed in the cooking demonstration, Roman jumped when the club manager tapped him on the shoulder. He turned around and pulled one earbud out.

"Mr. Montgomery, you need to go rein in Mr. Alvarez," Prinze said.

"Rein him…what?" Roman did a visual search of the large room, expecting to see that poor woman trying to ditch Mercer, who could be pretty persistent when he wanted to be.

Sylvester tilted his head to the far corner of the room near the free weights. Roman followed his gaze and groaned. Mercer was there, all right, but the blonde woman was nowhere in sight. Instead, Mercer was scowling and waving his arms in what appeared to be a shouting match with Ty Bolton, of all people. And Ty's beefy friend Greg stood right behind him.

Roman put his earbud back in. "Isn't crowd control your job, Sylvester?"

Prinze didn't budge, just crossed his arms and glared at him. Roman sighed, paused his program and slid off the bike, draping his earbuds across the handle bars. He ambled across the gym, the club manager a few steps behind him.

"...you rich boys," Ty was saying, "using this gym like it was a pickup bar, bothering women trying to exercise."

"Who made you hall proctor?" Mercer asked, fists balled at his side.

"I've seen how you operate, Alvarez. Like with Nora Coleman." Ty's face was red and sweaty, a vein in his neck throbbing.

"What about her?" Mercer demanded. He inched closer to Ty.

"She's my girlfriend, that's what," Ty growled.

"Not according to her," Mercer said through gritted teeth.

Roman could see why Prinze needed his help. He'd known Mercer a long time, since middle school. He'd seen many displays of his friend's quick temper, and now saw the tell-tale signs of Mercer's escalating agitation. The balled fists, sweat forming on his brow, the gritted teeth. Roman had to talk him down, keep him from creating trouble with Nora's colleague. He reached over and put his hand on Mercer's shoulder, but Mercer brushed him away.

Ty got in Mercer's face. "When I was your age I was already in med school."

"And when I reach your age in a decade or so, I'll be killin' it on Wall Street."

"Leave my girlfriend alone. Leave all these women alone. Grow up and go find a job," Ty shouted, jerking his thumb toward the exit.

"Says the trauma surgeon slash gym rat," Mercer shot back.

The two of them were now toe-to-toe, but if it got physical, Mercer didn't have a prayer. Ty had at least fifty pounds on him, all muscle.

"All right, all right," Sylvester said, finally stepping between them, his well-developed arms outstretched. "I've warned you fellas before. This is a family place and we don't allow street fighting."

Roman wrapped an arm around Mercer's chest and tugged him back a couple of steps. "Come on, Mercer, let's go. I don't want to cause a scene. Especially not today."

Ty rounded on Roman. "Why not today? Did you hit the lottery and get even richer?"

That made Roman mad. Dr. Bolton was certainly being well paid for his services, so why did he look down his nose at people who were well off? Roman took a deep breath and forced himself to calm down. He didn't want to start off his association with the Caplans by getting into an altercation with a family friend.

"Back up, Ty," Roman said. "Let's all relax here, like Sylvester said." He tapped Mercer on the shoulder. "You okay, man?"

"Hell, no," Mercer said, still glaring at Bolton.

Before Roman could stop him, Mercer lunged at Ty, who wasn't ready for it and stumbled back, tripping over the bench press and crashing into the shelf of free weights. A few of the barbells rolled off the rack and onto the floor with loud thuds.

"Why you little—" Ty jumped to his feet and landed a punch on Mercer's jaw. Mercer reeled around, lost his balance and fell to the floor, hitting his head on a twenty pound free weight. He lay there motionless, blood dripping onto the floor from a gash in the side of his head.

"What is the matter with you, Bolton?" Roman shouted. He rushed to Mercer's side, frightened by his friend's appearance. "Ty, come on, Mercer's bleeding. Do something."

But Ty went from red in the face to completely pale. He sat down on the bench press and groaned as he reached to the back of his head. Ty must have hit his head when he fell against the free weights, because Roman could see blood on Ty's hand.

For a moment no one moved, but then Greg jumped into action. "Sylvester, call 9-1-1. Tell them there are two men with possible head injuries, and there's an EMT on site." He looked in Ty's eyes, checked his pulse, and then knelt by Mercer. "You," he said to Roman, "I need some towels to stop the bleeding."

Roman ran to the shelf along the wall for the towels, his pulse racing as adrenaline coursed through his veins. Greg said Mercer had a head injury, and Ty was bleeding, too. How badly was his friend hurt? For that matter, how much damage had Ty sustained? That guy was a pain in his butt, but he was a friend of Julianne's family, and he didn't see this ending well.

****

Since my wedding pre-empted my Business Accounting class, my plan was to go to the library, finish the homework that was due today, and then email it to the professor with some lame excuse. Sounded good, but unfortunately, I couldn't concentrate.

I just became Mrs. Roman Christopher Montgomery. Well, okay, I hadn't thought through the name situation, and I was pretty sure being Mrs. Somebody's First Name wasn't for me. But at the least, I'd gladly take Roman's last name. Maybe hyphenate it? I sat at a study carrel in the far back corner of the school library doodling various choices in my notebook. You'd think I was in high school again, swooning over some cute boy in math class and linking our names with hearts. I finally settled on Julianne Caplan Montgomery. Since I didn't have a middle name, I would take my maiden name as a middle name with no hyphen. I circled it and then added hearts and flowers.

I felt guilty for blowing off my class assignment. After all, Dad was paying for my schooling and he didn't deserve to lose his money if I flunked out. So even though my heart wasn't in it—because my heart was with my husband—I finally got to work. It wasn't my best effort, but I hoped I'd get at least a C. I hit Send on the email and realized I'd need to hurry to catch the two fifteen bus back to our store.

When I walked in, Dad was waiting on a young man trying on dress loafers. Dad waved at me from the men's racks and looked relieved that I was there. I suppose he had shoe repairs to work on in his shop. Naturally Mom was nowhere around. Usually when she wasn't there and I was in class, she pressed Jon into service. He wasn't there either and frankly I was glad.

After not being able to concentrate on schoolwork, I discovered I wasn't too focused at the store, either. I kept replaying my wedding and probably had a silly grin on my face all afternoon. I messed up a couple of sales, too. The man buying the shoes when I first came in expected to use his discount coupon, but I forgot to apply it, meaning I had to redo the whole transaction. Then there was an elderly woman who chatted about how she'd been shopping here since Mr. Weinstein owned the store as she browsed through the small selection of handbags we had, and I absent-mindedly asked if she'd ever been here before. She gave me a funny look, and when I finally realized what I'd said, she was gone. I berated myself, because Caplan's needed all the sales it could get.

Try as I might, I just couldn't stay in the moment. On top of remembering the beautiful wedding ceremony, I was also fantasizing about tonight. Whatever Roman had planned, it was bound to be wonderful. The afternoon dragged on, so I was relieved when it was finally five o'clock and the store would be closing in an hour. I'd have to get ready pretty fast in order to make it back to the front of the public library in time for Phil to pick me up at seven in Roman's limo. I still didn't know what story I was going to tell Dad, but I figured I'd wing it.

I'd left my phone under the counter and hadn't checked it for several hours. When I pulled it out I saw I'd missed several texts. Some from Nora, some from Roman. I started with Nora's.

—*Call me! Urgent!*—

Then:

—*Roman is here with Mercer in the ER*—

I gasped. Did something happen to Roman? Nora's next text read:

182

—*Mercer has a head injury. Call Me!*—

I breathed a sigh of relief that my husband hadn't been injured, but then suffered a pang of guilt for my lack of compassion. Mercer had just stood up for Roman at our wedding mere hours ago, and now he was hurt. Nora's last message was more detailed.

—*Ty brought into ER, too. Where are you?*—

I was stunned. Ty was hurt, too? What the hell happened? I started to reply, but decided to read Roman's messages first.

—*Accident at Metro Community Center. We're at St. Stephens.*—

Then a few minutes later:

—*Julianne, please come to the hospital if you can.*—

There was a time gap before the next one came in.

—*Mercer's in a coma. I'm scared. Can you call me?*—

And the last one said:

—*The drs are taking him into surgery. I nee*—

Roman must have hit send before he could finish that one. He must be frantic. I hurriedly dialed Nora, who picked up on the first ring.

"Where have you been? I've been trying…"

"I know," I said. "I put my phone away while I was working. What's going on?"

"Apparently Mercer got into a shoving match with Ty at the gym," Nora said with a distinct edge to her voice. "Ty needed stitches, but Mercer has a hematoma. A blood clot. Usually Ty would be the one to do the surgery, but he's in no condition because he's got a concussion, so the on-call surgeon took Mercer to the O.R."

I was stunned. My new husband's best friend and Nora's colleague—our family friend—got in a fight? At the gym?

"Julianne, are you listening to me?" Nora said.

"Yes, I heard you." I swallowed hard. "But I still don't understand what happened."

"Just get here," she said, and disconnected.

Next I called Roman, but I stepped into the storeroom to make sure my end of the conversation wouldn't be overheard. Voice mail. "Roman, I'm so sorry. I just now got your messages. Nora tried to explain everything, but I'm really confused. I'm calling an Uber and I'll be at the hospital as soon as I can."

I disconnected, shoved my phone in my pocket, and walked back to Dad's repair shop. I didn't need to make up a story, but I did have to withhold some of the truth.

"Hi, Julianne," Dad said as he held a freshly-repaired shoe up to the light for inspection.

"Um, Dad, Nora called from the hospital. There's been an accident." My father's head snapped up. From the look on his face I could tell he thought something had happened to Nora. I shook my head. "Nora's fine. It's Ty Bolton. He was in some sort of altercation at the gym and has a concussion. I told Nora I'd be there as soon as I could."

"Thank God it wasn't Nora," Dad said, before tensing up. "But poor Ty. You go. I'll watch the shop till it's time to lock up."

I kissed my father on the cheek. "Thanks, Dad. I'll keep you posted.

****

Roman paced up and down the hospital corridor

outside the fourth floor waiting room. After an ambulance ride from Metro Community Center to St. Stephen's ER, medical personnel had taken his best friend first to an examining room, and then up an elevator to an operating room. Frantic, Roman had sought answers from Nora at the ER Nurses' Station. "What's going on?"

"Mercer needs surgery," Nora said, with what Roman thought was remarkable calm. Maybe it was her medical training, but her composure was eerie.

"I know that," he said. "Help me understand."

Nora looked up from her computer. "Mr. Montgomery," she said with professional aloofness, "this is information I can only share with family." She returned her attention to whatever was on her screen.

Roman was puzzled by her steely-eyed glare. It had been mere hours since she had stood next to his wife as maid of honor, yet now she acted as if they'd never met. "Nora, I *am* his family." When she didn't glance up, he said, "Okay, not technically, but he's an only child and his parents are out of the country. Right now I'm all he's got."

Nora seemed to wrestle with that information, and her shoulders relaxed a little. "The CAT scan showed that..." Nora broke off as another nurse walked by close enough to overhear. "Mr. Alvarez has a blood clot that needs to be removed immediately or it could be fatal."

Roman nearly collapsed. He gripped the nurse's station desk tightly with both fists to keep himself steady. "Fatal?" he whispered.

"Have you notified his family?"

Roman sucked in his breath. "I sent his dad a text,

but who knows when they'll get it?"

"After surgery, Mercer will be in recovery awhile, till he's stable." Nora pushed some keys on the laptop in front of her and glanced up. "He's been admitted. Do you know if he has insurance?"

Roman shrugged. "I guess. Maybe." He shook his head, realizing he hadn't paid much attention to his best friend lately. "No, I don't know, but if not, I'll cover his costs." He turned to Nora, pleading, "What should I do now?"

"Go upstairs to the fourth floor waiting area. I'll let you know about Mercer as soon as I hear anything."

"Thank you." He watched for signs of any emotion, but she was back to being all business.

Roman surveyed the upstairs waiting area. It consisted of semi-comfortable wooden chairs with vinyl upholstery in pastel shades, a few loveseats, lots of old magazines, and a television tuned to a home improvement network. Roman sighed, sat down in a chair, and thumbed through a six-month-old issue of *Sports Illustrated.* He tossed that aside and picked up a copy of *Parenting Magazine*, admiring the cute baby on the cover. But he couldn't focus on that either. He scouted around for other reading material, but except for the Gideon Bible and some children's magazines, there was nothing else. Finally he slumped in the chair and stared at the TV, not comprehending a word the host was saying. All he could think about was this morning, his wedding, and how happy he and Julianne had been.

Roman had managed to retrieve his gym bag and wedding ring from the locker before the ambulance arrived, but he now found himself wearing sweat-stained clothes. He would have liked to go to the chapel and light a candle for Mercer, but he was afraid to leave the waiting area in case Nora or the doctors came looking for him, so he said a silent prayer for Mercer and wished his wife was with him.

And then his phone pinged with a text. Relief washed over him as he read Mr. Alvarez's message, telling him he and Mercer's mother were on their way home from Mexico. Roman responded with an updated report on Mercer's condition.

And then another text pinged in. Roman's eyes grew wide as he read it.

—*Mr. Montgomery: The Metro Community Center strives to offer a safe family environment and in return, expects decorum from its members. After numerous warnings, this afternoon's altercation has forced me to rescind your membership. There will be no partial refund. Sincerely, Sylvester Prinze, Club Manager—*

Roman groaned. How could his wedding day have gone so wrong?

****

I was glad the Uber ride was short and relatively inexpensive. I texted Nora before I even got out of the car, asking where I could find her.

She responded:

—*4th floor—*

I was puzzled because Nora usually works in the ER.

I rang for the elevator in the lobby, but it seemed stuck on the twelfth floor, like someone had propped the door open. I banged on the Up button three times in succession and was about to hit it again when I noticed a woman next to me, also waiting for the elevator and scowling at my behavior. I took a deep breath to calm down as the elevator began to descend, one painstakingly slow floor at a time. I was anything but calm, though, because all I could think about was my friends' injuries and my husband's emotional pain. Finally the bell dinged, the doors swung open and I bounded out.

As many times as I'd been in this hospital, I'd never been above the main floor with its reception area, gift shop, and cafeteria. So it took me a minute to get my bearings. I looked up and down the corridors, but all I saw was patients' rooms. The whole floor seemed to go in one big circle, so I followed the hallway down to the right, and then another right, until I eventually found the Nurses' Station.

"Excuse me," I said to the nurse on duty, "I'm looking for Nora Coleman."

He glanced up from his computer. "Last I heard, she was in room four thirty-five." He pointed off to his left. "That way."

I found the room, but hesitated. After all, I certainly didn't want to intrude. The door was ajar, so I peered through the opening till I caught a glimpse of Nora, busily working around her patient's bed. But from the hallway, all I could see were his feet.

"Psst. Nora?" I whispered.

She glanced up from whatever machinery she was adjusting and hurried out into the hall. "Oh, thank God, Julianne." She gave me a hug, took my arm, and pulled me into the room.

The sight inside made me gasp. I had just seen Mercer a few hours ago at my wedding, happy, laughing, and eating cake, and now he was lying pale and unconscious in a hospital bed. His head had been shaved on one side and was covered in bandages, and he had tubes and IVs sticking out everywhere. Roman was pacing back and forth near Mercer's bedside as he alternately watched Nora work and glanced at the monitors. He looked like he'd been crying, and my heart went out to him as I tiptoed to his side.

We embraced. "Roman, what...?"

"It all happened so fast. Mercer and Ty were arguing about something stupid, and then shoving, and then..." His voice drifted off.

I turned to Nora. "Is Mercer going to be okay? And Ty...?"

"Ty's fine, more or less," Nora said. "Concussion, a couple of stitches. The resident sent him home, but he won't be back to work for a couple of weeks." She sighed, glared at Roman, and despite her insistence that she and Ty weren't romantically involved, at that moment I wasn't so sure. "As for Mercer, he's got a long road ahead."

"I called his parents," Roman told me. "They're on their way home from Cancun."

I nodded, but I could see how perturbed Nora was and how frightened Roman was. I turned to Roman. "Can we talk?" I tilted my head toward the hallway.

Roman followed me out, leaving Nora with Mercer and all the beeping monitors.

"Roman, I..."

He put his fingers to my lips as his eyes darted around the corridor. There were just a few nurses moving in and out of rooms and a couple of orderlies, and none of them even knew us, so I couldn't imagine why Roman was worried about being overheard. But as

I stood there, the creepiest feeling came over me. It was like those déjà vu moments people talk about, where you feel like you've been there before but rationally know you never have. I glanced around and swallowed hard as I took it all in. The hospital corridor outside a private room, personnel going about their duties, the sense of tragedy. It all reminded me of something I couldn't quite put my finger on. I wrapped my arms tightly around myself, chills running down my spine.

Roman seemed to feel it, too. He shivered, glanced around him looking for who-knows-what, sighed and finally waved his hand over his disheveled appearance. "I know I need to shower and change, but I can't leave Mercer until his parents get here."

"Of course not," I said. "I'd bring you some clothes, but..." I left the obvious end of that sentence unsaid.

"I'll call my driver." Roman leaned against the wall and stared up at the ceiling lights. "We have to tell our families," he finally said. "About us. My father will expect an explanation of what happened to Mercer, and to Bolton, and why." Tears welled up in his eyes. "And then there's Rosaline." Roman stared down at his feet.

"What about her?"

Roman shook his head. "She's got connections all over this city. She probably already knows what happened at the gym and is forming her own conclusions."

I took my husband's hand and noticed he was wearing his wedding ring. I pulled mine from inside my sweater on its chain. God, it was beautiful. Our wedding had been so romantic, but our future now hung in the balance. We made eye contact as I took my ring off the chain and held it out to him so he could slip it back on my left hand.

"Tomorrow, first thing," Roman said, "I'll go to Chicago, and when I get back we'll speak to your father."

I nodded as Roman pulled me in close and held on tight.

Chapter 13

I texted Dad that Ty would be fine, just a concussion, and let him know that Nora would drive me home at the end of her shift, sometime around midnight. His one-word reply, "*ok*," was typical, since he'd never been comfortable with modern technology.

I tossed and turned all night. I relived my fairy-tale elopement, but then my thoughts turned to the argument that ended up getting two of my friends injured. And then I agonized about my derailed wedding night, bringing me waves of guilt for being selfish. I went round and round with myself for defying my family and getting married in the first place. Then I'd loop back to where I started, with Ty hurt and Roman's best friend recovering from a brain injury.

I gave up trying to sleep and got up at six a.m. I took my phone and tiptoed into the kitchen to send my husband a text. I didn't expect him to see it at this hour, but I was desperate to connect with him on some level. I made coffee and thought about breakfast, but I was too keyed up to eat. Finally, I decided that getting some work done in the storeroom downstairs might keep my mind occupied.

I stood in the shower and let the warm water run over me while my brain continued on overdrive. I got married yesterday. My parents would freak out, but the Montgomerys would be furious, maybe even disown their son. Would Roman decide it was easier to annul the marriage and go back to Rosaline than fight them on it? *Would* it be easier to forget the whole thing?

There were no answers to any of those questions, at least none I could think of, and I still hadn't heard back from Roman. Maybe he'd spent the night at the hospital. I got dressed, took a travel mug of coffee downstairs, and set about logging in the newest shipment of shoes. Pretty soon I was totally absorbed in my work.

"Good morning, darling."

I nearly jumped out of my skin. I turned around to see Mom standing in the doorway. I hate when she calls me darling, like some throwback to a bygone era, and let's face it, Lydia has never been what you'd call a devoted mother. "Geez, Mom, don't sneak up on me like that." I went back to cataloging inventory. "What are you doing up at this hour anyway?"

"It's nearly ten a.m. and I told your father I'd open the store this morning."

Ten o'clock? I was surprised that the time had flown by so quickly, but Mom voluntarily working in the store was an even bigger surprise. She was a little overdressed for a workday, wearing a long-sleeved wrap dress with bone-colored pumps, but whatever. "Where's Dad?"

"Eye doctor appointment. Says he has eye strain from all the detail work he does on repairs." Mom tugged at the waistline of her dress and took one of her shoes off to rub her toes. The dress was too tight and she probably chose the wrong shoe size again, too, going for style over comfort.

"Well, thanks," I said. "I'm surprised you didn't

call Jon."

"Jon couldn't…has some…he's been…" Mom let that incoherent thought hang in the air. She put her shoe back on and turned to face me. "Your father said you have school. Aren't you going to be late for classes?"

Classes? Ohmigod, with everything that happened yesterday, I'd completely forgotten. I had just enough time to make it to my English class, but first I pulled my phone out of my pocket to see if Roman had responded. Yes, he'd texted back nearly an hour ago.

—*Can you come to my office this morning?*—

I fired off a quick:

—*Yes, on my way.*—

I glanced up at Mom. "You're right, I've got, um… Thanks for taking over here." I left the box I was unpacking on the storeroom floor and ran upstairs to grab my book bag and a jean jacket. The early April weather was mild, but there was still a chill in the air.

A short walk later, I pushed through the revolving entryway doors at Montgomery International Footwear Emporium and stopped to peruse the store map at the entryway.

Business offices, second floor.

Should I take the escalator or elevator? Elevator, probably, but where was it?

I walked around the entire lower level, which went in a giant circle, ogling the array of glamorous footwear as I passed by. Judging by the merchandise they offered and how many customers were already shopping this early on a weekday, it was no wonder Montgomery's was such a successful company.

I located the elevator at the back of the store near the public restrooms. Or lounges, as they were labeled.

When the elevator doors opened onto the second floor, I could see Men's Casual Footwear to my left and what looked like rather ordinary business offices to my right. I walked into a small reception area where a geeky-looking blond-haired man about Roman's age sat behind the desk, talking into a headset. He pushed a button on his ear, turned to me and said, "May I help you?"

"I'm here to see, that is, Roman called..."

The guy was all business, prepared to get rid of a nuisance in his boss's day. "And you are...?"

"Julianne," I told him.

The guy's face blanched. "Mrs. Montgomery?"

I gulped, unaware that Roman had told anyone about us. I had to hope this guy was trustworthy. And since that was the first time anyone had addressed me as Mrs., it felt a little weird. "Please, call me Julianne."

He reached out to shake my hand. "Ben Voss, Mr. Montgomery's Executive Assistant. It's a pleasure to meet you." Ben tapped his headset and spoke into it. "Sir, Mrs. Montgomery is here." He stood up, forced a smile, and opened a door to the office behind him.

I stood gaping through the doorway at Roman's office, which was nearly as big as our entire store. I glanced around at the leather and mahogany furnishings, the tightly-woven silk rug under the desk, and the large picture window overlooking Monument Circle. Before I could process all that, Roman stepped out from behind his desk, took my hand and led me into the room before embracing me. Looking over my head he said, "Thanks, Ben. Hold my calls." Ben closed the door and as soon as he did, Roman pulled me in close for a warm and increasingly passionate kiss.

Once I came up for air, I asked, "How's Mercer?" I had to take a step away from Roman because being this close to him made my heart beat faster and I was quickly getting overheated.

Roman helped me out of my jacket, hung it on an ornate, wooden coat rack near his desk, and then led me to the plush leather sofa under the window. We sat down facing each other. "Mercer's in ICU. His parents showed up in the wee hours, all stressed and upset about how he got hurt, so I left. I called the hospital this morning but they wouldn't give me any information about his condition because I'm not family." Roman let out an ironic snort. "Me. Not family." He frowned. "If Ty weren't already hurt, I'd be tempted to bash his head in."

I didn't like the sound of that. I hadn't heard the whole story of how the fight happened, but both Mercer and Ty got hurt. I pulled out my phone and fired off a text. "Nora," I said in response to Roman's quizzical expression. "She can find out about Mercer."

Roman wrapped his arms around me and I laid my head on his shoulder. Then he lifted up my chin and kissed me lightly. And then he kissed me again, and again, each kiss more urgent than the one before. I sucked in my breath as my husband pulled my sweater off over my head. Then he took my wedding ring off the chain around my neck, where I kept my beautiful ring hidden while at home, and slipped it back on my finger.

****

Roman hadn't intended for the first time being with his wife to happen in his office, on the sofa. His original plan for their wedding night, filled with romance, candles, and a gourmet dinner, was a no-go when his best friend got into a shoving match with Nora's wannabe-boyfriend. But the minute Julianne walked into his office, all he could think about was how much he wanted her. And it was as good as he'd fantasized it would be.

Roman pulled a throw blanket off the back of the couch and wrapped the two of them in it. He held her tightly, luxuriating in her womanly curves, kissing her flushed face, and brushing aside a stray lock of that thick, wild hair of hers. "I love you," he said.

She looked into his eyes. "I love you, too."

They lay there quietly for a time, listening to the phone ring in Ben's office and hearing his muffled voice talking into his headset. "Okay," Roman said, "now that we're officially husband and wife, we gotta make a plan."

Julianne nodded. "You got one?"

Roman thought for a moment. "This news is too big to break via Skype. I'm going to have Phil drive me to Chicago this afternoon so I can speak to my parents in person. I can be back by tonight. Tomorrow at the latest, depending on how long the yelling lasts." He winced. "Then we'll tell your parents together." He kissed the top of her head. "I'm sorry I couldn't ask your father for permission ahead of time, but hopefully he'll give us his blessing."

"Dad's gonna take some convincing." Julianne absent-mindedly ran a finger up and down Roman's arm. "But there's someone else you need to talk to."

Roman felt a pang of guilt. "Yeah, I gotta break off my engagement to Rosaline on account of having a wife." He grinned and kissed Julianne's nose, then got up to get dressed.

Julianne pulled on her underpants and jeans and reached for her sweater. "I had a bra," she said as she scouted out the office floor.

"It's..." Roman reached under the sofa and withdrew her pink bra. He watched as she turned her back to finish dressing, loving how modest she was. But at the last minute he turned away, afraid if he watched a moment longer they'd be back on the sofa again.

Instead he went over to his desk. "Where do you need to go?" Roman picked up his office phone and punched in a digit.

"Classes. They're gonna throw me out of school if I don't show up. And finals are in a few weeks."

"Ben," Roman said into the phone, "call Phil and tell him he needs to drive my wife to campus."

"Wow. What will my friends say when I arrive in a limo?"

Roman wrapped his arms around Julianne and kissed her again. "It doesn't matter what they say. Gossip can't hurt us."

Julianne's phone pinged and she pulled it out of her pocket for a quick glimpse. She grinned. "Mercer's awake."

Roman collapsed into his desk chair in relief. "Thank God. Can I see him?"

"Nora says you can visit him later today."

Roman nodded. "I'll drop by there on my way out of town." They both looked up when Ben knocked on the door before cautiously peeking inside. "Sir, Phil is downstairs in front, waiting on, uh, Mrs. Montgomery."

Roman helped his wife on with her jacket and gave

her a quick kiss goodbye. "And Ben, tell Phil I need him the rest of the day."

****

"Just let me out here," I told Phil as he pulled up in front of the student union. "And please, don't open any doors for me."

Phil grinned at me in his rearview mirror. "Yes, ma'am."

It was going to take some getting used to being called ma'am and Mrs. Montgomery. Just another reminder of how out of my league I was. And for all I knew, Roman was also wondering what he'd gotten himself into. Was he afraid he'd have to give up Sunday Mass for Friday night Shabbat? Easter or Passover? Hanukkah bush or Christmas tree? We had a lot to figure out.

And it was definitely weird arriving at Community College in a black stretch limo. A few students gave me the side eye when I got out of the backseat.

I knew I was late for English Comp class—way late—but I decided to risk possible embarrassment in order to put in an appearance. Dr. Knoll was well into his lecture when I tiptoed in the classroom's back door, but he paused and lifted an eyebrow at me, causing everyone to turn and stare. I quietly slid into an empty seat.

"Sorry," I said. "Traffic…"

Natalie looked over her shoulder from the front row and rolled her eyes before returning to her tablet and note-taking. I couldn't blame her for her disdain, since I'd pretty much blown off school lately. I took out some paper and a pen, scribbled on the paper when I realized the pen was running out of ink, and dug in my book bag for another one. All while trying not to make any noise and disturb the professor or the class any more than I already had.

After about a half hour, Dr. Knoll concluded his lesson about how to use correct documentation in our final research paper. *Wait. What?* Research paper? I metaphorically slapped my forehead. He'd told us the first day of class that we'd be expected to write one for our final exam grade, and that the grade we received could determine whether we passed or failed this class. I suddenly realized how far behind I was, because I hadn't even picked a topic, let alone started collecting sources or doing any writing. I sighed. I was going to have to beg for Natalie's help. Again.

The dismissal bell sounded. "I need your first drafts by next class," Dr. Knoll said. He gathered up his materials and left.

I groaned inwardly, because that meant I only had a few days to pick a topic and get something together. Never mind a new husband, a job, parents, and in-laws who were going to be shocked or angry, Nora's colleague Ty off work for a concussion, and Roman's best friend in the hospital. Now I had a paper to write, one that could determine whether I passed or failed.

I stuffed pen and paper back into my book bag, walked to the front of the classroom and sat down in the now-empty seat next to Natalie. "Did you...?"

"Get the notes?" She glared at me. "I got here on time, so yeah. Where have you been? And I don't just mean today. With that new rich boyfriend?"

I blew out a puff of air. How to explain? "He's not my boyfriend."

She slipped her arms into her jacket and hoisted her

bag onto one shoulder. "Friend with benefits. Whatever."

Natalie took off down the hallway, so I got up and hurried after her. "I'm sorry to be such a bother, but I really need your help. This will be the last time, I promise."

Eyes forward, she kept walking. "That's what you said last time. And the time before that." Natalie stopped to face me. "Julianne, you need to decide between love and school. I can't be bailing you out all the time."

I nodded, feeling guilty. I *had* imposed on her a lot, taking her help and friendship for granted. "I know and I'm sorry, but it's complicated."

She stamped a foot. "Then dump his complicated ass."

I looked down at my left hand and realized that I was still wearing my ring. I stuck it in Natalie's face. "I can't dump him."

Natalie gasped and her jaw dropped as she took my hand to scrutinize the two carat diamond. "Wow. Just…wow." She let go of my hand. "You're engaged?"

"Not exactly. More like married."

"What?"

"We eloped. A friend of his is a former priest, so…"

"A priest?" Natalie blinked. "Seriously? But you're Jewish." She gasped. "Wait. Are you…?"

"No!" I exclaimed, before lowering my voice and glancing around to see who might have heard. "And anyway, who gets married these days because they're pregnant?"

But then I stopped to think. My new husband and I

just made love for the first time a few hours ago, and we didn't use protection. In the heat of the moment, neither of us gave it a thought. At least I didn't, and Roman seemed pretty caught up as well. Huh. I shook it off. *Stop it, Julianne. Don't borrow trouble.*

Natalie's giggle brought me back to reality. "So then what was the rush?"

I took a cleansing breath, but I couldn't—or wouldn't—go into the reasons why we got married on the sly. "Like I said, complicated."

Natalie shook her head. "Your funeral, girl." She glanced up at the institutional wall clock. "I gotta go. I'll email you today's notes. But I swear, Julianne, this is the last time. Get your act together." And with that, she turned on her heel and sailed down the hallway toward the exit.

****

I went to the library, desperate to find a topic for my research paper. After kicking around a lot of ideas, most of which would take too long to research, I decided on Steps to Creating an Effective Advertising Campaign and planned to describe how I created the Valentine's Day Caplan's Shoe Lovers event. And hey, that topic could do double duty, since I also had a paper due in my marketing class.

Valentine's Day. The night I met Roman.

Thinking about that completely threw me off my game. Natalie was right—Dad was gonna freak. Big time. I scribbled a few notes, jotted down some sources I found on the library's in-house research database, and left. It was Friday and I promised myself I'd get caught up over the weekend.

I got to the store about an hour earlier than normal,

expecting to see Mom still on the floor. But instead I spotted Jon Parris, chatting it up with a well-dressed elderly gentleman wearing a yarmulke, who was paying for a pair of dress loafers. My first reaction was to wonder why he was here at Caplan's instead of down the street at Montgomery's, but as I got closer, I recognized him as the original owner of our store.

"Mr. Weinstein," I said as I dropped my book bag behind the counter and offered my hand to shake. "Thanks for patronizing our store."

Mr. Weinstein must have been close to ninety years old by now, but he winked at me as he accepted my extended hand, and then held on a bit too long. "I don't care what store moves into the neighborhood, Caplan's is the only place I'll ever buy shoes."

He pocketed his receipt, picked up the box of shoes off the counter, and shuffled his way to the door. I hurried ahead of him to open it. "Thanks for coming in, Mr. Weinstein. Enjoy your new shoes."

"I will, young lady," he said with a twinkle in his eye. He paused and whispered, "I'd ask you to join me for dinner, but I see some lucky man has already staked his claim."

Eek! I still had on my ring. As soon as he was gone, I hurriedly unclasped the chain around my neck, slipped the ring on it, and tucked the whole necklace underneath my sweater, patting it to make sure it was safe.

"Old guy has a crush," Jon said from behind the cash register. "Can't say I blame him."

I cringed. I turned to see him grinning, giving me two thumbs up, so I decided to change the subject. My gaze scouted out the empty store. "Did Mom leave?"

"She's still here, back in the repair shop with your dad. You're early."

"Oh, well, I…" I started to make up some excuse, but then realized the truth would actually work. "We have a research paper due in English Comp. I got finished in the library quicker than I'd expected."

By then Jon was staring at his phone and probably didn't even hear me. I shrugged and was about to get to work when both Mom and Dad appeared from the shop with what I thought were serious expressions.

"Hi…?" I braced myself. Could they possibly have found out? But how?

"Nora has told us something quite disturbing," Dad said.

My eyes widened, my pulse quickened, and I could feel sweat forming on my brow. Nora couldn't wait and let Roman and me tell them in our own way? "Dad, I was…we were going to tell you. See…"

Dad held up a hand. "She told us about the row at the gymnasium between Ty and that Montgomery boy and his friend. Disgraceful." Dad shook his head. "And Nora said you'd skipped some classes to check on Ty at the hospital. Is that true?"

My knees buckled and I almost fainted with relief. Apparently, Nora covered for me after all. "Yes. I was worried. But afterward I went to see the professor to ask if he'd give me time to get caught up," I lied.

"What did he say?" Dad asked.

I exhaled. "That I need a good grade on our final research paper or I'll flunk the class." At least that much was true.

Mom waved that away like it was a mere trifle. "I'm sure you'll catch up. I think you need a distraction."

Leave it to my mother to blow off something as serious as flunking out of school. "A distraction?"

Mom waved Jon over. "Jonathan has a wonderful idea, Julianne. Tell her, Jon."

Uh-oh.

Jon was practically giddy with excitement. "It's Electra-Con!" Like I'd know what that was. "You know, the big electronics convention they hold every year."

"Oh, right." No, I didn't know, and I was confused.

"Well, this year it's in Louisville, this weekend in fact, and I talked to your folks. They agreed to let you go with me. Take a couple of days off work and school. What do you say?"

My jaw dropped. I turned to Jon and said as politely as I could, "No, thanks." Embarrassed, I went to the cash register and pulled up a list of the day's receipts and began studying them. Except for Mr. Weinstein's purchase, there were only two other transactions, both for small amounts. So I could add possible bankruptcy to my list of worries.

"Julianne, darling, we really want you to go with Jonathan," Mom said.

Dad chimed in. "In fact, we insist."

I glanced up at the three of them. Never mind that I was married, Jon just wasn't my type. And being Jewish didn't count. "I just told you I'm behind in my schoolwork, and your suggestion is to take time off?"

"This is an excellent opportunity," Dad said. "A chance to get reacquainted with Jon. Plan your future."

Future? "My future consists of finishing my education." I narrowed my eyes at my parents. "Which

Dad's paying for."

"It concerns me, darling," Mom said, "that you're so absorbed in school and work and ignoring what's important. You and Jon need time to nurture your relationship."

"Relationship?" I couldn't take it anymore. I turned to Jon, hoping he didn't want to be manipulated any more than I did. "Jon, tell them," I pleaded. "We're just friends."

Jon grinned at me. "Well, it could be more if you'd go to Louisville with me."

My heart sank. I knew where this train was headed and I wanted off. Now. "Mom." I waited for her to look at me. "School's important to me, a career is important, and if anything were to happen to the store, God forbid, I'd need something to fall back on. Unlike you."

"Young lady, that's enough!" Dad roared. "First, you will apologize to your mother for that remark, and secondly, you'll accept Jon's invitation."

He was right about that snide comment to Mom, but I wouldn't be bullied. "I'm sorry, Mom." I turned to Dad, quivering. "The answer is no."

"After all I've done for you?" he thundered.

"What about what I've done for you?" I countered. "Running this store practically single-handedly…"

"Either go on this trip with Jonathan like you've been told or make arrangements to live somewhere else. I won't have my daughter disrespecting me in my own house."

I blinked in disbelief. Did I hear him right?

Dad scowled and stood his ground, and Mom stepped to his side in a rare show of solidarity. Jon's face turned a bright red as he scurried behind the cash register and poked at his phone. Dad was angry, but throwing me out was a pretty drastic reaction to my not wanting to go on a road trip with a guy I could barely tolerate.

"You can't be serious," I said.

Dad crossed his arms, a stern expression on his face. "I most certainly am."

It would only be a matter of time before I moved out anyway, so I held my head high. "Dad, I've always respected you, but if you want me out, I'm gone."

I picked up my book bag and stormed out. I prayed I could move in with my husband and not end up homeless.

Chapter 14

Roman's patience with the Chicago Friday afternoon traffic had run out. His stomach alternately rumbled with hunger and turned flip-flops with nerves, causing him to tap his foot and pound on the arm rest to relieve tension. By the time Phil finally inched his way through bumper-to-bumper gridlock, it was close to supper time.

At last Phil pulled the limo into a reserved parking space in front of Montgomery International Shoe Emporium, which housed not only their flagship store but the corporate business offices. Roman whipped out his phone and punched in the number for his father's personal assistant. "Ruby, is my father around?"

"No, Roman, it's Friday afternoon. He left hours ago."

"Do you know where he went?" Golf? Tennis? Drinks? The possibilities were endless.

"I believe you could reach him on his cell," Ruby offered.

"Thanks," he grumbled before disconnecting the call. Between traffic and his father's habit of leaving early for the weekend, Roman's original plan to speak to his father privately in his office had been derailed. Now he'd have to face both his parents at their penthouse.

He relayed the change of venue to his driver, and

then fired off texts to both of his parents, telling them he was in town and had something important to talk about.

Phil drove through more late-day traffic and eventually pulled the limo into the valet-attended circular drive in front of the high rise condo building. "Shall I wait for you?"

Roman shook his head. "Go get something to eat. I'll text you when I need you." He got out of the backseat of the limo, closed the door, and headed through the lobby toward the elevator bay.

The express elevator made its way up to the twentieth floor and opened onto his parents' private suite in the penthouse apartment. Roman stepped out but then froze, unable to make himself ring the bell. He paced back and forth, hoping to gather his courage. He'd had three hours in the limo to think through what he was going to say, then another hour stuck in rush-hour traffic. Yet he still wasn't sure how to explain the demise of his engagement and his spur-of-the-moment marriage. *It's now or never* he told himself and was about to knock when the penthouse door flew open.

"Roman, Smithson told me you were on your way up."

Roman should have realized the doorman would alert his father to his presence in the lobby. "Didn't you get my text?"

"I was on a conference call." Charles stepped aside to let Roman enter. "What the devil are you doing here, anyway? Has something happened at the Indianapolis store?"

Roman walked in and glanced around the penthouse. *Looks like Mother redecorated again.* Gone were the dark gray sofa and its matching lounge chair, as well as the heavy mahogany coffee table and coordinating end tables, replaced by tables in polished white and chrome. In fact, everything was now white— sectional sofa, loveseats, armless side chairs—and instead of the Tudor-style oak dining table, there was a new round glass table encircled by four black metal chairs, sitting on top of a white throw rug with a chevron pattern. The only colors in the room, if you could call them that, were the beige throw pillows stylishly karate-chopped and artfully arranged on the sofa.

"The store's fine, Dad," Roman said, not making eye contact. "Even showing a healthy profit." He started to lower himself onto the sofa, wondered if his mother would frown on him for mussing up the new furniture, and decided to remain standing. He crossed to the floor-to-ceiling glass windows that stretched the length of the room and overlooked downtown Chicago.

The only thing Roman had ever liked about this place was the spectacular view. The condo had never been his home. His parents had mostly left him in Indianapolis with staff or nannies during his growing up years, claiming they didn't want to disrupt his schooling. The older he'd gotten, the more he realized that was a convenient excuse to avoid parenting. This place was certainly a showpiece, but it wasn't a family home.

"Then why are you here?" Charles went to the wet bar near the window and pulled two bottles of beer from the fridge. He twisted the lid off his and offered the other one to Roman.

Roman shook his head. Alcohol on an empty

stomach was a bad idea any time, but he needed a clear head to get through what was sure to be an unpleasant conversation. "Did you hear about Mercer? He's…"

Charles nodded. "Rosaline sent your mother a text. Something about an altercation with a doctor, of all people, in a community center. What was Mercer thinking?"

Roman gazed out the window. "Oh, you know Mercer. Always a hothead." He turned to face his father. "But the doctor started it." At his father's quizzical look, Roman added, "I was there."

Charles raised an eyebrow. "And could have been injured as well. Rosaline says your membership in that club was revoked." He took a long pull from his bottle of beer. "Just as well. No son of mine should belong to a club where grown men get into public brawls."

So Roman had been right. Rosaline got the news from somewhere and spread the gossip. "The doctor's a friend of Jul…uh, the Caplan family."

"Who?"

"Julianne Caplan. Her father owns a shoe store not far from Montgomery's."

Charles frowned. "That Jewish girl you were seen dining with?"

Roman narrowed his eyes at his father. "Mercer's gonna be fine. Thanks for asking." He decided it was now or never. "Is Mother here?"

"Marla!" Charles called. "Roman's here!" He sat down on the sectional and set his bottle on the pristine coffee table, sans coaster.

Roman heard his mother's heels clacking down the hall as she chatted into her cell phone.

"Oh, yes, dear, I'm very excited." Marla paused to

listen to the person on the other end. "I agree, it's going to be a lovely garden party. The country club is the perfect setting for a bridal shower."

Roman cringed. Maybe he should have that beer after all. "Mother, good to see you." He crossed the room and gave her a quick peck on the cheek. To stall for time, he waved his arm around the room. "You outdid yourself."

Marla beamed. "I'm so glad you like it. I couldn't fathom hosting all the wedding parties here with that old, outdated furniture." She sat down on the new sectional sofa and glared at Charles until he pushed a coaster under his sweating beer bottle.

Roman groaned inwardly. His mother had gone to great expense to change the look of the room in anticipation of his big society wedding. She was planning bridal showers and who knew what else, and he had to put a stop to it. He clasped his hands behind his back in what he hoped was a strong stance, faced his parents, and took a deep breath. "The wedding's off."

Marla's face registered shock for a moment, but then she burst out laughing. "Don't be ridiculous, darling. I was just speaking to Rosaline…"

"Mother, I'm serious."

Marla stopped laughing and exchanged glances with her husband. "Roman, darling, what are you talking about?"

"I have news."

Charles scowled. "Is this about the store?"

"No. I already told you the store is fine. It's about Rosaline. I'm not marrying her."

Marla dismissed that with a wave of her hand. "Don't be absurd, darling. Of course you are. June twenty-seventh."

"No, Mother. Not that date or any other."

Marla's face contorted as she slowly rose to her feet. "And just why not, may I ask?" She put her hands on her slim hips and tapped her foot. "All the plans are made, Roman. Save-the-date cards just went out. St. Agnes Church in Indianapolis is reserved, the flowers are ordered, the caterers are hired…"

Roman could feel the heat rising on the back of his neck. "Mother, please stop. It's not happening."

Charles furrowed his brow. "Roman, I have to agree with your mother. If this is about that lovers' spat you and Rosaline had…"

"There was no spat. Rosaline and I just aren't compatible."

Charles jumped to his feet. "What the hell are you talking about, son?"

Roman stepped back for some much needed space. His eyes darted back and forth between his father with his reddening face and his mother who was turning pale. He inhaled and spit it out. "I can't marry Rosaline because I'm already married. To someone else."

His mother gasped as her hand flew to her throat, and the vein in his father's forehead throbbed.

"Someone else?" Marla whispered. She sank back onto the sofa, her head buried in her hands.

"This is outrageous," Charles exclaimed. "Whatever possessed you to do such a thing?"

How could he possibly explain his feelings for Julianne? Even he didn't quite understand how it had happened, just that it did and it felt more real than anything he'd ever had with anyone, especially Rosaline. "Please, let me explain." He hurriedly told them the whole story of how he met Julianne on Valentine's Day night, fell in love, and impulsively married her at Pop's Bakery last week.

"Married," his father thundered.

"Jewish?" his mother whimpered. She burst into tears, mascara running down her cheeks and smearing her rouge.

Roman had known his parents would be shocked, angry even, but he never expected his mother to cry. He started toward her but backed off when his father glared at him and put a protective arm around his wife.

"How will I ever hold my head up in society?" Marla moaned as she leaned her head on Charles's shoulder.

"This is untenable. How could you embarrass us like this, Roman? All the wedding plans, the Vandenbergs…" Charles released his wife, walked to the window, and stared out into the evening Chicago skyline.

Roman put an arm around his mother. "You'll like Julianne, really. She's warm, funny, smart, practically runs Caplan's Shoes all by herself…" Marla stepped away from him and went to stand beside Charles at the window.

"Shoes," Charles exclaimed. "*Our* family is in the shoe business. What could the daughter of a Jewish shop owner possibly know about the footwear industry?"

"It's a small, family-owned business, but it's been around for decades." Roman's mind scrambled for a way to convince them and then it hit him. He pulled off one of his loafers and offered it to his father.

Charles refused to take the shoe. "Why is my son

wearing low-end casual loafers in the middle of a workday?"

Roman turned the shoe over. "Mr. Caplan does excellent shoe repair work, and I wanted an excuse to see Julianne, so I deliberately damaged a new pair I bought off our showroom floor." He pointed to the sole. "See? You'd never know it. Good as new."

Charles glanced over at the shoe and harrumphed. "So the man knows how to fix shoes. Doesn't mean you should be involved with his daughter."

"I'm not 'involved,' Dad. I'm married."

Charles crossed his arms and growled, "This girl has obviously tricked you into a hasty marriage to get at your money. My God, what did she do? Get herself pregnant?"

Roman rolled his eyes at the misogynistic accusation. "She's not pregnant." His mind momentarily drifted back to his and Julianne's one and only time together. They hadn't been so careful. Could she...? No, no way. "And I wasn't tricked. In fact, I had to convince *her.*"

Charles went back to the wet bar and this time poured himself a glass of scotch, neat. "Well, since the girl isn't pregnant, you can get an annulment."

Roman gaped at his father. "We're not getting an annulment."

Charles studied Roman over the top of his glass as he swallowed several gulps. "Of course you are. You can't get a divorce and still expect to marry Rosaline in the Church."

Roman sighed. "You're not hearing me, Dad. Rosaline was your choice, not mine. I'm happy with Julianne and we're going to build a life together."

"The hell you are," Charles bellowed. "After that unwanted social media exposure a few weeks ago, the phone calls and arguments, all because of that Jewish girl…"

"Her name is Julianne."

"…we hoped it was a momentary lapse in judgment, sowing your wild oats, but that doesn't seem to be the case." Charles fixed Roman with a steely-eyed glare. "The Vandenbergs have honored our agreement, so you end this farce now, before it causes a rift between our families."

Roman glared right back. "I'm not a teenager you can order around. I'm an adult, and I made an adult decision."

"This isn't adult behavior, it's the actions of a petulant boy. One I entrusted with great responsibility. One who needs the right wife to help him further his career." Charles turned to Roman and said through gritted teeth, "Your mother and I need to talk. Please wait for us in my study."

Roman glanced at his mother, who wiped away tears and nodded her agreement, so he went down the hall to his father's office. He wanted to call Julianne, but he realized he'd also left Phil hanging, so he sent him a text.

—*Staying here tonight. Go ahead and check into the Athletic Club.*—

—*Kind of pricey*—Phil replied.

Since Roman's father kept a hotel room at the downtown club on retainer for overnight business guests, Roman assured his driver he'd be able to use the room for free.

—*Will do*—came the reply.

Phone in hand, Roman sank into his father's leather sofa and leaned his head back, hoping and praying that his parents would accept his marriage.

****

After I left the store, my home, my family, I thought I knew what I was going to do. But of course I hadn't thought it through. I wandered around aimlessly, afraid to spend what little money I had on bus fare, and eventually found myself outside Pop's Bakery. It was after six p.m. and the sign on his door said he closed at three. Dejected and fighting back tears, I sat down on the sidewalk in front of his store and sent a text to Nora.

She didn't reply. Maybe she was as mad at me as my parents were. Or maybe she was with a patient. That actually made more sense, but it didn't offer me any solutions to my immediate problem. I had nowhere to go. Moving in with Roman sounded great in my head, but he was in Chicago and I didn't even know where his house was. And even if I knew the address, I had no way to get inside.

So Nora was my only hope. I didn't really know what I thought she could do—talk sense to my parents about Jon, let me sleep in a bed at the hospital, or just be a shoulder to cry on. The only thing I knew for sure was that it was getting chilly outside, I had about twenty bucks in my wallet, and I was sitting like a homeless person on a sidewalk. Okay, not *like* a homeless person. Homeless.

I should swallow my pride and go home. That didn't sound too bad, but then it brought up all the ramifications. I'd either have to pretend to go along with my parents' matchmaking scheme and spend a long weekend with Jon Parris with all that entailed, or

I'd have to tell them I was already married and watch their heads explode.

I pulled out my phone again, hoping for a text from Roman, telling me he was on his way back to Indianapolis. But there was nothing. I drew my knees up under my chin, put my head down, and cried.

"Julianne, my goodness, what's wrong?"

I lifted my head and saw Pop, Father Al, standing over me. I hurriedly wiped away the tears and allowed him to help me to my feet.

Pop was wearing a lightweight athletic jacket, stocking cap, and had a satchel thrown over one arm. "Did something happen with Roman?"

I shook my head. "Something happened with my parents. They gave me an ultimatum and I walked out."

"And now you have no place to go," Pop said.

I guessed that as a priest he was used to listening to people's tales of woe. "Yeah, at the time I thought I was making a dramatic statement. Look where it got me." The tears started again.

"Now, now, dear, come inside and let me make you some coffee."

"Oh, no, I couldn't put you to the trouble. Looks like you're on your way home."

"Don't have much to go home to, except Felix." Pop smiled. "My cat." He unlocked the front door of his store and held it open for me. It was so warm and inviting, and the smell of freshly baked goods still lingered in the air. Pop flipped the lights on, disarmed the security system, and walked to the coffee machine, fiddling with buttons to get it up and running.

I felt guilty enough keeping him from going home, but letting him go to the trouble of restarting the coffeemaker seemed selfish. "I'd rather have a cup of tea, if you don't mind."

Pop lifted an eyebrow but nodded and went to the kitchen. He came right back with a box of flavored teas. I chose mint, and all he had to do was push the hot water button on the coffeemaker. Then he plopped a sweet roll onto a plate, motioned to a table, offered me a napkin, and placed the mug and the plate in front of me.

I sipped the hot tea and ate the pastry. "I guess I was hungrier than I thought."

"Now tell me what this is all about." Pop made his own cup of tea and sat down across from me.

I explained about the argument at home and why I couldn't go along with my parents' hare-brained scheme. "But if I'd told them why, that would have been a whole other fight. And anyway, Roman and I were going to tell them together."

Pop peered at me over his cup as he sipped his tea. "And where is your husband at the moment?"

"Chicago. Telling his parents. He wanted to do it alone."

Pop nodded. "Yes, I know the overbearing Mr. Montgomery and his society wife." He finished off his tea. "This is quite a conundrum, young lady. But you knew this wasn't going to be easy."

I did know. I was about to pour out my heart and ask for advice when my phone rang. I glanced at the caller ID and smiled at Pop. "Roman."

Pop winked at me, took our dirty dishes, and went to the kitchen.

"Hi. How'd it go?" I hoped Roman couldn't hear my voice quivering.

Roman dodged my question. "Where are you?"

"I'm…" I sighed. "Roman, my father threw me out of the house. He and Mom wanted me to go on a weekend trip with Jon…"

"Jon?"

"Yeah, a Jewish computer nerd they've been pushing on me. I refused, but since I couldn't tell them why…"

"You walked out?"

I knew I'd made a huge mistake, but I didn't know how to fix it. "At the moment I'm at Pop's. He took pity on me and made me a cup of tea, but now I have nowhere to go. I can't even get ahold of Nora." I stifled sobs as best I could. I didn't want to upset my husband, knowing the difficult conversation he must have just had and what he was facing with Rosaline.

Roman was silent a moment, "Okay, go to the Meridian Hotel and check in for the night. I'll call them and put the tab on my credit card. Order room service, whatever you like. Tomorrow we'll move you into my house."

I exhaled, and I didn't even realize I'd been holding my breath. "Thank you so much, Roman." I paused. "So how did it go on your end?"

"Not good. My dad exploded, my mother burst into tears, and now I'm in Dad's study waiting while they discuss what to do. Like they have any say in it."

"I'm sure they were shocked."

"We'll talk when I get back to town. I love you." Roman disconnected.

Pop poked his head out of the kitchen. "Everything settled?"

I nodded and allowed myself to smile for the first

time since I'd gotten there. "Roman's paying for a hotel room for me. We'll figure out the rest when he gets back."

Pop turned off the lights, let me out the door ahead of him, and then reset the alarm. "Ready?"

"Um..." I didn't know what I was supposed to be ready for.

"My car is out back. I'll drop you at your hotel."

"Oh, no, I can't ask you to do that."

Pop winked at me. "You didn't ask. Besides, Roman would never forgive me if I let you take off alone. And I live in that direction, so it's not out of the way."

I guess Roman and I were both lucky to have such a good friend in Father Al.

****

Nora finally called me back. She hadn't been ignoring me, she'd been assisting in surgery and hadn't seen my texts. I told her the whole sordid story, admitting to her and to myself that I was in a mess of my own making. Yes, I was in a luxury hotel room with access to a mini-bar, room service, and cable TV, but I was in it by myself. Plus, I had nothing but the clothes on my back.

After I talked to Nora, I took a shower, rinsed out my lingerie, and wrapped myself in one of the plush white bathrobes hanging in the closet. It was going on midnight, but despite the thousand-count bed sheets and extra firm pillows, I couldn't sleep. I had just turned on the television and started channel surfing when I heard a light rap on the door.

"Julianne? You in there?"

I got up and looked through the peephole, breathed

a sigh of relief and flung the door wide open, grabbing Nora's arm and pulling her into the room. I threw my arms around her and held on tight, fighting back tears.

Nora extricated herself and tossed an overnight bag onto the bed. "I packed a few things for you. Changes of clothes, toiletries, makeup." She glanced around the room. "It doesn't look like you're lacking for much."

I turned off the television and tossed the remote on the end table, then flopped onto the bed. "Looks can be deceiving."

Nora sat down on the bed next to me and put her arm around my shoulder. "Maybe you should give in to Samuel and Lydia, just for now. Tell them you've changed your mind about Jon. Then you can move back home."

I sat up straight and gaped at her. "Nora, you can't be serious. I can't go traipsing off to Louisville with a man who isn't my husband."

Nora stood up, hands on her hips. "Of course you can. If you have to. You and Jon are like brother and sister anyway, so even if you get stuck in a hotel room with him, it'd be totally platonic."

I sucked in my breath and studied Nora to see if she was serious. It looked like she was. "And what would I tell Roman?" I shook my head. "I can't do it."

"Well, then, I hope you have a plan, because I don't see Roman around here anywhere."

"He's…" I stopped. She was right. What if Roman couldn't extricate himself as easily as we'd hoped? I collapsed onto my back and stared up at the ceiling. "He's still up in Chicago. He told his parents about us, and I guess it didn't go well."

"Shocker." Nora reached for the door handle.

"Think about what I said. You can't stay here," she waved her arms around the room, "forever."

"I know, but I can't go home right now either."

"Never say never." Nora gave me a half-hearted smile and left me to my thoughts. And I didn't like what I was thinking, either, because it was possible I might have to go along with her idea to fake out Mom and Dad, at least until Roman showed back up.

Chapter 15

The early morning light streamed through the window in Charles's home office and woke Roman up. He'd fallen asleep on the leather sofa after waiting for hours for his parents to finish discussing his marriage. His father was probably still furious, and his mother would want to find a way to save face socially when the truth about him and Julianne came out. He rubbed his eyes, picked up his phone from where it had fallen, and checked for messages. There was one from Julianne, sent at seven a.m., which would have been six o'clock Chicago time.

—Going to classes. Might as well finish my semester and get the credits. Come home soon!—

Roman smiled. She missed him, and that renewed his determination. He was going to make this marriage work, and his parents' disapproval be damned. He typed in:

—Planning to leave in a few hours. Will text when I get to Indy.—

He hit Send, and then added:

—P.S. I'll be happy to pay for the rest of your schooling.—

The thought of being able to do that made him smile.

His stomach rumbled and he realized he hadn't eaten since breakfast the day before. He stood up, stretched to get the kinks out of his back after sleeping on a sofa, and went into the kitchen looking for food and coffee. His mother was sitting at the new marble countertop breakfast bar, drinking a protein shake and reading something on her phone.

"Good morning, darling," Marla said. She peered over her glasses at him and smiled.

Roman was a little unnerved. He'd expected anger or maybe the silent treatment. "Any coffee?" He glanced around the kitchen to locate the coffeemaker, which seemed to have moved during the renovation.

"Hannah made some cappuccino and baked some lovely strawberry muffins. They're still warm." Marla pointed to a plate under a warmer near the stove, piled high with pastries, and tilted her head toward a newly-installed coffee bar in the corner next to the double-wide stainless steel fridge.

Roman popped one of the housekeeper's delicacies in his mouth and moaned with pleasure. He opened a cabinet looking for a mug, closed it and tried a couple more till he found where the coffee mugs were now stored. He poured himself a cup of the freshly-brewed coffee, pulled a carton of creamer out of the fridge, and eyed his mother warily as she nonchalantly tapped at her phone. This behavior of hers, whether it was avoidance or denial, worried him. He felt like the other shoe was about to drop.

"The Vandenbergs will be joining us for supper this evening, darling. We'll be dining at the country club."

And there it was. Roman groaned inwardly and stalled for time by reaching for another muffin and slowly sipping his coffee, which he realized was nearly as good as Pop's. "I didn't know the Vandenbergs were in town."

"Oh, no, darling, they aren't. They're flying in this afternoon on their private jet, specifically to spend the evening with us. You need to speak to your fiancée."

On that they were agreed, but Roman wasn't a bit fooled. His parents probably hoped that seeing the Vandenbergs in person would change his mind and convince him to annul his marriage. No way was that happening. But even though he wanted to get home to his wife, he also needed closure with Rosaline. Perhaps it would be better to end their engagement in person, rather than with a cowardly email or text. And if the six of them were eating in a public place, it would limit the amount of histrionics. At least he hoped so.

"Okay, I'll agree to this, Mom. But then I'm going back to Indianapolis first thing tomorrow."

Marla removed her reading glasses and laid them on the counter next to her phone. "I'm afraid not, darling. Your father expects you to attend the Montgomery Board of Directors meeting tomorrow afternoon."

Roman blinked. "What?" He had just agreed to spend an uncomfortable evening with Justin, Elsie, and Rosaline Vandenberg, and now his dad wanted him at a Board of Directors meeting? "Since when? I'm never needed at those meetings."

"Well, this time you are."

Roman rolled his eyes. "Mom, you must have misunderstood Dad. Their meetings are mostly about Montgomery's corporate holdings. It has very little to do with the shoe fashion industry."

"I understood your father perfectly, and he expects

you to attend that meeting tomorrow." Marla stood, picked up her phone and glasses and said over her shoulder as she left the kitchen, "I have a Junior League luncheon. Dinner is at eight this evening."

Roman watched her walk away. This must be what his parents had been discussing so secretly last night: ways to trap him in Chicago. So far it was working. He thought about refusing to attend both the dinner and the board meeting, but he didn't want to appear childish. Maybe there was something on the Board's agenda he needed to know, and he certainly felt an obligation to break off his engagement to Rosaline in a gentlemanly way. He tossed his half-eaten muffin down the garbage disposal and sent another text to his wife.

—*Change of plans. Can't get back to Indy till tomorrow.*—

He waited for a response, but when none came, he figured Julianne was probably in class with her phone turned off.

****

Roman's eyes bugged out. "I thought you reserved the private dining room," he whispered to his mother as he glanced around the banquet room.

She patted his cheek like she used to do when he was ten. "Oh, no, darling, I'm sorry you misunderstood."

It wasn't just the six of them for a quiet dinner. In fact, the large room at the country club was filled with people. They were sipping cocktails, nibbling hors d'oeuvres, and chatting happily while a four-piece chamber orchestra played in the corner.

Roman realized he'd been had. Before he could make his excuses to his mother and hurry out, Rosaline appeared at his side. She gave him a wicked smile and linked her arm through his.

"Honestly, Roman, I thought you'd abandoned me." She tried for a kiss, but he pulled back.

Roman quietly withdrew his arm and turned his back on Rosaline. "Mom? What is all this?"

"Why, a cocktail party of course," Marla replied. She stood on her tiptoes and waved over his head. "Yoohoo, Elsie!" And off she went.

Roman turned back to Rosaline, the five-carat diamond engagement ring sparkling on her left hand. She was wearing a black lace sequined wrap dress that skimmed the top of her knees, and she'd paired it with glitter-encrusted pumps. He wasn't a fan of the shoes, but he thought the dress might have been pretty if it weren't accentuating every aspect of her bony frame. Roman briefly imagined Julianne in that dress and how nicely her curves would fill it out, but he put that fantasy right out of his mind. He didn't want his wife dressing like his former fiancée.

Rosaline grabbed his arm and dug her nails in. "Roman, can't you at least pretend to be happy to see me?"

Roman recognized that tone, the one she always used when he disappointed her in public, and it made him squirm. "Rosaline, we need to talk."

"About?" She released her grip on his arm and squeezed it affectionately, like she was trying to prove a point to anyone who might be watching. And make no mistake, people were watching. "Oh, you mean that fling with the little Jewish girl?" She nodded politely to some society matron. "I've given you plenty of time to get that out of your system, because our wedding is fast approaching."

Roman stopped mid-stride, his heart pounding. He could feel his face flush and sweat starting to form on his brow. Wedding? No, she couldn't possibly think... But wait, maybe she really didn't know. Come to think of it, how could she? He'd just last night told his parents about his marriage, so it was possible they hadn't yet mentioned it to Rosaline's parents, or they were going to let him tell her himself in private.

"Rosaline, I'm sorry, but our engagement is off."

Rosaline wouldn't look at him, preferring to smile and wave at party guests, but she said through gritted teeth, "Don't be ridiculous, Roman. Our engagement is *not* off."

Roman took ahold of Rosaline's shoulders and turned her to face him. "Yes, it is. I'd hoped you'd been told, but since you haven't, I eloped with Julianne Caplan a few days ago, so you and I..." His voice tapered off when he saw the steely glint in her eyes.

She took two glasses of champagne off a tray from a passing waiter and handed one to him. "I heard something of the sort, but your father assures me he's spoken to the attorneys and they're already working on the annulment. And I'm warning you, my love," she hissed, "that if that doesn't happen, that little Jewish whore and her family will be sorry."

Roman gaped at her. But instead of jumping to Julianne's defense, he tried to see things from Rosaline's viewpoint. After all, he'd hurt and embarrassed her. He got control of his anger and lowered his voice. "I'll take the ring back if you like, or you can sell it on Ebay, or throw it in the White River out of spite if it makes you feel better. But, Rosaline..."

He was interrupted when Charles Montgomery stepped to the microphone at the front of the room and tapped his champagne glass with a spoon. "Ladies and gentlemen, may I have your attention?" He tapped again until the hundred or so people quieted down. "I'd like to thank you for joining my wife Marla and me at this spur-of-the-moment engagement party for our son Roman and his lovely bride-to-be, Rosaline Vandenberg. So I'd like to offer a toast. To Roman and Rosaline. May their marriage be as long and happy as ours." Charles lifted his glass to a few shouts of "Hear hear!" and swallowed the entire contents in one gulp, slamming the empty flute on a nearby table.

Roman stood rooted to the floor, realizing this whole stunt was staged to make him acquiesce to their demands. He was tempted to rush out of the room, but before he could make his escape, he was surrounded by well-wishers. Rosaline had a death grip on his arm and was smiling and chatting happily with friends of her parents and his.

Roman panicked. Not only were his parents' friends and business associates being misled, everyone was behaving as if his real marriage didn't exist. And then chills went down his spine as he recalled how Rosaline had threatened Julianne's family. Knowing Rosaline, he didn't doubt for one minute she'd retaliate if she didn't get her way.

****

It wasn't supposed to be like this. I was supposed to support my husband as he faced his parents, and stand by his side as we announced our marriage to my parents and asked for their blessing. Instead, I'd spent over two weeks in a hotel, a luxurious one to be sure, but alone and anxious all the same. My parents hadn't reached out to me, and Roman kept putting off his return. He and I exchanged a number of texts, mostly about the various ways his parents found to detain him in Chicago.

To keep my mind off the predicament I was in, I tried to maintain something like a normal schedule, at least as far as school was concerned, since I no longer had a job to go to. I attended classes daily, much to Natalie's surprise, and then spent my afternoons at the library, alternately studying for exams, working on the English project, or texting my husband.

On the nineteenth day of our forced separation, I arrived at the hotel after classes to find an envelope with the hotel's logo slipped under my door, addressed to Mrs. Montgomery. It felt weird, but since Roman arranged everything and put it on his credit card, I guess he told them. I closed the door and opened it.

Dear Mrs. Montgomery:

We have been notified of a credit freeze on your husband's corporate account at the behest of the card owner. If you wish to continue your stay with us, you will need to make other payment arrangements.

I sank down on the bed in shock. Why had Roman's card been frozen? Identity theft? Unauthorized charges? Maybe I'd been using the mini-bar too much. Whatever the reason, this place cost a fortune, so I had to get out immediately. But that brought me back full circle to where I was when I first checked in. I had no place to go. I tried calling Roman, got his voice mail yet again, so I left him a message to please *please* return my call, and tried to explain my dilemma. In the meantime, I pulled the overnight bag

Nora had brought me from the closet and began packing what few things I had. I sniffled, wiped away a stray tear, and before I knew it the dam opened. Tears spilled down my cheeks as I threw myself onto the bed and sobbed into my pillow.

I cried and wailed, pounded the pillow, and cursed the gods until I was exhausted, my eyes red, and the pillow soaked. I sat up and spied the chocolate on the pillow. As I was nibbling on it, trying to figure out what to do next and wishing Roman would come home, my phone rang.

"Roman?" I glanced at the caller ID only after I'd picked up but sighed when I realized it wasn't him. "Oh, hi, Nora."

Nora didn't respond with her usual quip. "Julianne? You've got to come home. Now."

I didn't bother mentioning the change in my financial circumstances and that I'd have to do just that. But something about Nora's tone scared me. My mind jumped to all sorts of worst-case scenarios: my dad had had a heart attack; my mother had racked up near-bankruptcy-sized credit card charges; my folks had found out about my marriage; Nora had gotten fired... Despite my efforts, panic creeped into my voice. "What's going on?"

"I'll explain when you get here," she said, and hung up.

Wait. *Here?* She said "come" home rather than "go home." Why was she there this time of day? By now Nora should be at the hospital, starting her evening shift. I stared at the dead phone, wondering what I'd find when I got there after weeks of stubbornly refusing to communicate with my parents. I sighed and finished packing, and then left the room key where the maid would find it. The door clicked to a close as I sneaked down the back stairs, because if I'd racked up any extra charges, I certainly couldn't pay them.

What was next? Divorce? A forced engagement to Jon? I shuddered as I walked to the bus stop.

The buses were running behind schedule, so what should have taken me a half hour to get to the store ended up being over an hour. Despite the urgent summons from Nora, I wondered what sort of reception I'd get from Dad and Mom. I gathered my courage and went inside.

"Julianne. Thank God!" Nora pulled me into a hug, giving me a chance to look over her shoulder at the disarray in the store. It didn't look like anything had been done since I left. Shoe boxes were piled up near the counter when by now they should have been arranged on the shelves with display samples. The floor hadn't been swept, let alone mopped, and I could see dust collecting on the checkout counter. Next to the computer I spotted a large stack of unopened mail. That meant the utility bills and merchandise invoices had been ignored.

"This place is…" *in bad shape* is how I'd probably finish that sentence, but I clamped my mouth shut before pulling out of Nora's grasp. My gaze drifted back to the stack of bills. "Is the electricity being cut off?"

"I wish it was that simple," Dad said. He sat off in a corner on the footstool I always kept near the counter so I could reach the higher shelves. He was pale, sweating, and had his head in his hands.

"Dad! You look awful!" I rushed over to him. "Are

you sick?" I glanced over at Nora who shook her head. "Where's Mom?" I asked her.

"Lydia and Jon went to see if anything can be done."

My stomach churned, my pulse raced, and sweat trickled down the back of my neck. "Done about what?"

Apparently Dad did open at least one piece of mail, because he handed me an envelope with its flap ripped. The outside return address read Vandenberg Commercial Realty Company, with an address on Monument Circle in downtown Indianapolis. Just seeing that name made me feel queasy. With a shaking hand I pulled the letter out and read it.

Dear Mr. Caplan:

It is with regret that we send you this notice. Caplan's Shoes and Repair is the only viable business currently occupying our property, the Kramer Building on Alabama Street, and rent payments from you have been sporadic in recent months. In addition to your delinquency, the building's vacancy rate has remained unchanged for several years, costing us additional profits. The building itself is in disrepair and estimates to fix it run into the hundreds of thousands of dollars. Therefore, we have made the difficult decision to sell the property to a development company, which plans to convert it into overflow parking for Lucas Oil Stadium and the downtown shopping corridor.

Demolition begins July 1, 2020. We trust this gives you enough time to either relocate your shop or sell off your inventory.

Sincerely,
Justin Vandenberg, CEO

My knees went weak, my vision blurred, and my stomach roiled. I clapped a hand over my mouth and took off running to our apartment upstairs, barely reaching the bathroom before I puked my guts out. After I'd emptied the contents of my stomach, I collapsed onto the worn bath mat on the familiar penny tile floor and waited till the room quit spinning. When the nausea had passed and my pulse had calmed down, I wetted a cloth and wiped my face and mouth.

I stared at my reflection in the mirror, and the girl looking back at me was a total stranger. Due to the spring humidity, my hair was even frizzier than usual, but it was my dull, bloodshot eyes and pale face that rendered me unrecognizable. If anyone else had looked as bad as I did after retching, I'd say they were hung over. But I knew I wasn't. It had to be the shock of our impending eviction.

"Rosaline Vandenberg," I muttered as I slowly walked back down the stairs to the store. Being jilted obviously didn't sit well with her. And now we were being thrown out of our home and our business, and it was all my fault. I gathered my courage and walked into the store. Dad and Nora were waiting anxiously for me, and Mom and Jon were there, too, looking grim.

"Are you okay?" Nora rushed to my side. She felt my forehead and looked into my eyes.

I pushed her hand away. "I'm fine. Don't go all nursey on me."

"Julianne," Dad said, "you don't look fine. Are you sure...?"

"It's a shock." I turned to Jon since Mom was never much help in a crisis anyway. "What did you find out?"

"We went to the Vandenberg offices and tried to see Justin Vandenberg, but since we didn't have an appointment, the receptionist said he was"—Jon used air quotes—" 'in a meeting.' " Wearing his trademark torn jeans and faded rock band t-shirt, he couldn't have made a very good impression at a corporate office.

"His assistant told us the sale had already gone through and the building is being demolished in a matter of weeks." Jon shook his head, put an arm around my mother and squeezed her shoulder as she started to sob.

Nora turned to face me and narrowed her eyes. "You've got to tell them, Julianne. If you don't, I will."

I shuddered at the very idea of coming clean with my family, but Nora was right. They had to know my part in all this.

"Tell us what?" Dad asked.

I exchanged glances with Nora, who nodded encouragement. I reached into my blouse, fished out the chain with my wedding ring on it, and placed it on my left hand, both admiring its beauty and hating the pain it would cause them.

Despite the seriousness of the moment, Mom rushed over, picked up my hand, and gaped at the two carat diamond. "Oh, my goodness. That's gorgeous! Where did you get this?"

I steadied myself as I looked her in the eye. "From my husband. Roman Montgomery."

Mom gasped, dropped my hand like it was on fire and backed away. Jon blanched, and Dad got so red in the face I thought he was going to have a stroke. Nora helped him back to the footstool, took his pulse and looked into his pupils. "Breathe in through your nose,

Samuel. Someone get some water."

Jon took off for the storeroom and returned with a plastic water bottle. He twisted the lid off too fast and water splashed onto the dusty floor, creating a muddy stain. My first instinct was to grab a mop, but then I realized it didn't matter how dirty our store got. It had an appointment with a wrecking ball.

Dad sipped the water and took a few deep breaths. Finally his color returned to something like normal and his breathing slowed. "Julianne, did I hear you correctly? You married that boy?"

"We were going to tell you..."

Dad gaped at me. Mom burst into tears. But I felt the worst for Jon, who looked like a wounded puppy.

"My baby," Mom exclaimed. "Married to a millionaire, and I didn't even get to be there." She sniffled. "Whatever would I have worn?"

Dad slowly stood, walked over, and searched my face for signs I was making all this up. He glanced from Nora to me, before turning back to her. "Nora, why aren't you as surprised as the rest of us?"

"I was there," Nora said.

Without a word or a backward glance, Jon stormed out of the store. Mom ran after him, leaving me, Dad and Nora alone.

"How could you betray me like this?" Dad demanded before turning to Nora. "Both of you."

"I'm so sorry, Dad. Roman and I were going to tell you together, but he went up to Chicago to tell his parents, and they've kept him up there for weeks, practically under lock and key."

"He's a grown man," Dad harrumphed. "He should have been ready to face the consequences of his

reckless behavior instead of cowering up in Chicago."
He took my shoulders and looked me in the eye. "How
did you think this marriage would ever work out,
Julianne? You're Jewish, he's Catholic."

I sighed and stepped back. "I know all that, Dad.
We're still trying to figure it out." I reached for my
father's hand, but he pulled it out of reach. "This may
have been hasty, but Dad, I love him. We want to start a
life together."

"Tell him the rest," Nora said.

I groaned. This was even harder than admitting I'd
gotten married without my family's blessing. I turned to
face my father, whose scowl was deepening. "In order
to marry me, Roman had to break off his engagement.
To Rosaline Vandenberg."

Dad's eyes widened and he began pacing back and
forth in front of the counter. "Vandenberg? As in…"

"Yes," I said.

"My, God, Julianne! What were you thinking?
Look what you've brought down on us."

I hung my head and fought back tears and more
nausea. "I'm so sorry. I just never thought…"

"No, you didn't think at all." With one last frown,
Dad stomped off and I heard the door slam as he went
upstairs to our apartment.

I turned to Nora for sympathy. "Now what?"

She crossed her arms and glared at me. "Talk to
that husband of yours. See if he can get the
Vandenbergs to back off. Otherwise we're all screwed."

I nodded, but it might already be too late.

Chapter 16

After the disastrous cocktail party Roman's mother sprang on him, an engagement party for a married man no less, his father insisted Roman was needed in the corporate offices. So he'd taken meeting after meeting for days, been forced to put on a fake smile, and even dine with his "fiancée" in public, pretending all was well as they posed for the paparazzi.

On the nineteenth day of Roman's frustrating stay in Chicago, he awoke early to a text from his father, telling him he was expected in his office promptly at ten a.m. Roman sighed, wondering what other stalling tactic his dad had thought up, but he put on a suit and went. He nodded to his dad's assistant Ruby who waved him through, but instead of Charles, Roman found one of his father's attorneys waiting for him.

"We need your initials here and your signature right there, Roman." The attorney handed him a pen and pointed to the spots with yellow Xs.

"What am I signing?"

"Annulment papers," came the reply.

Roman tossed the pen on the desk, turned, and walked out.

In his father's limo on the ride back to his parents' penthouse, Charles called. "Roman, why didn't you sign those annulment papers?"

"I already told you I'm not getting a divorce."

"Annulment."

Roman's jaw tightened. "Whatever. The sooner you and Mom accept my marriage, the better."

Charles was silent for a moment, but Roman detected irritation in his voice when he finally spoke. "Son, the company is planning to expand overseas in this tight global market. We can't afford a scandal, and your ill-advised elopement with a Jewish girl could cause our stocks to plummet."

Roman couldn't believe his ears. After all, this was the year 2020, not the 1950s. "Look, Dad, the limo just pulled up in front of your penthouse. I'm done. I'm going inside, pack my stuff and go back to Indianapolis."

"And just how are you planning to get there?"

Was Charles kidding? Roman rolled his eyes as the driver opened the back door for him. "I'll call Phil." Roman felt like adding *Duh* but decided that was immature.

"Yeah, let me know how that works out." Charles abruptly hung up.

Puzzled, Roman stared at the disconnected phone an extra moment before returning it to the holder at his belt. He was angry at his father, yes, but mostly disgusted with himself for allowing all the manipulation. He was an adult and he knew what he wanted, which was Julianne and the life they planned to build in Indianapolis. Roman went inside, shoved clothes he'd had to buy into the travel bag he'd been forced to purchase, and sent Phil a text, asking him to pick him up within the hour.

Roman hadn't been in touch with his driver for weeks, but he'd just assumed Phil was still cooling his heels at the downtown athletic club. Phil's reply left him dumbfounded.

—Mr. Montgomery terminated my employment with a very generous severance. I'm in the Bahamas.—

Roman felt lightheaded and nearly collapsed onto the guest room bed, now covered with his clothes and toiletries. His parents were determined to run his life. Ruin his life. Maybe they thought if they stalled him in Chicago long enough, threw him in Rosaline's path often enough, paraded him through society and corporate meetings, that he'd forget about Julianne. Just annul the marriage and be done with her.

Not a chance.

So without a driver, Roman decided to rent a car and drive back to Indianapolis on his own. He scrolled around on his phone till he found a nearby car rental company and dialed. He placed an order for a late model mid-sized sedan but was stunned when his credit card was declined. He tried another card. Declined. A third one was no good either.

Roman called his credit card companies and their answers were all shockingly alike. His corporate accounts had been frozen by Mr. Charles Montgomery, the co-signer. Roman berated himself for having always relied on his father's money, never bothering to open any credit cards in his own name. Now he couldn't rent a car, buy a plane ticket, or even purchase bus fare. Charles was playing his trump card: holding Roman's finances hostage until he agreed to divorce Julianne. He groaned, changed his clothes, and went for a run along Lake Michigan, staying gone for hours until he was certain his parents would have gone out for dinner and he wouldn't have to face them.

The next morning Roman rolled over and popped open an eye to peer at the digital bedside clock. It was after ten o'clock. He never slept this late at home, but what did he have to get up for? *Day twenty of my exile,* he thought. He sat up and stretched his aching back. Night after night of sleeping on the too-soft mattress in his mother's frou-frou guest room had caused kinks in every muscle. He longed to go back to Indianapolis, get back to work, find a new gym since he'd been kicked out of the Metro, and make love to his wife.

He pulled on his jeans and a t-shirt and ambled barefoot into the kitchen in search of coffee and one of Hannah's fresh-baked pastries. Just like every other day, the muffins were sitting under the warmer on a plate, and the coffee smelled freshly brewed. He took one of the mugs off the neatly-arranged display on the coffee bar and was about to pour a cup when his cell phone pinged. It was from Julianne.

—Call me ASAP!—

He sighed. Lately he'd been dodging his wife's calls and texts, having run out of excuses as to why he was still in Chicago.

Roman dumped sugar into his coffee and blew on it, thinking about the predicament he was in. Thanks to his dad's financial manipulations, Roman was truly stranded in his parents' luxurious penthouse. Dejected, he took another sip of his coffee and punched in Julianne's number. He needed some comfort and hoped the sound of her voice would boost his spirits. It rang so many times he thought it was going to voice mail, but at the last minute she picked up, out of breath.

"I just got your text," Roman said. "Is everything okay? Where are you?"

"School. I'm late to class."

He waited till her breathing slowed. He thought about all the time that had passed since he'd last seen her and realized her semester would be ending soon. Finals could be stressful, especially freshman year. Maybe that's why she was so upset. That and his seeming abandonment of her. "What's up?"

Julianne told him in agonizing detail about how her father had gotten the letter from Vandenberg Realty, their impending eviction, and her suspicions about Rosaline's involvement. "Is there anything you can do?"

Roman whistled softly. "I knew Rosaline could be underhanded when crossed, but this is low even for her. But there's probably no way to fix it if the building's already sold."

"Can you at least come home? We need to figure this out together."

"But your parents don't know…"

"Yes, they do," Julianne said. "I had to tell them. Roman, this is no way to start a marriage. We've been apart for weeks, and worse yet, I've seen pictures of you and Rosaline on social media…" Her voice trailed off.

"Part of Charles and Marla's whole plan to force me to…" Roman broke off. No sense telling her what they'd really been planning. "It means nothing. Rosaline means nothing." He sipped some of his now-cooling coffee and bit into one of the muffins, both of which left a bitter taste in his mouth. "But Dad cancelled all my credit cards," he said with a sigh.

"I know," Julianne said. "I had to leave the Meridian Hotel yesterday."

Roman thought through this whole fiasco and a spark of an idea came to him. He decided to fix things once and for all. "I'll be there tonight, I promise. Where can I find you?"

"At the store," Julianne said. "Packing."

Roman disconnected the phone and then punched in another phone number. He hoped this call wouldn't go to voice mail. It didn't. "Mercer, how are you feeling?"

"Better," Mercer said. "Almost back to normal."

"Good. I need your help. Can you drive up to Chicago and pick me up? I'll explain when you get here."

****

Roman had called just as I was entering the building at school for class, so the conversation made me late. And I'd been doing so well with my attendance. I sighed as I hurried in and took my seat, enduring a scowl from the professor and a lifted eyebrow from Natalie.

"Sorry," I mumbled.

Dr. Knoll continued his lecture, and then put up a link on the overhead monitor. "This is your online review for the final exam." He held up his hand to quiet the clamor of students complaining that the final project *was* the final exam. "This is only for those of you who don't turn in your project or earn a grade less than C." Amid groans and eye rolls from the students, Dr. Knoll turned off the monitor, picked up his briefcase and left.

I gathered my belongings, stood up and found myself face to face with Natalie. So close, in fact, that I nearly bumped into her. "Hi?"

"Project's due in a couple of days. You gonna be

done?"

I nodded. "Don't look so shocked. I've had plenty of time to finish." After my forced exile in a luxury hotel, followed by several more days of living with but avoiding my angry parents, I'd at least gotten caught up on schoolwork.

"Okay, good," Natalie said.

We walked out of the classroom together. "Hey, you want to…" I started, but she didn't give me a word or glance as she hurried past me in the hallway. I knew I'd probably lost her friendship, one more casualty of my rushed marriage.

It was a beautiful spring day, but I was feeling really tired. Probably the stress of school, telling my family I was married, and the prospect of Roman facing my parents when he showed up tonight. *If* he showed up, which he might not if past history proved anything. So to clear my head, I went outside and sat down on a cement bench under one of the trees in the commons area. It was peaceful there, surrounded by greenery coming to life after the long winter, and white flowers blooming on the Bradford Pear trees. It hardly seemed possible that it was already May. So much time had gone by since I met Roman, got married in early April, and now faced my first college final exams. Not to mention an uncertain future with my husband.

I was contemplating all of that, with no real solution in sight, when the smell of the flowers unexpectedly sent a wave of nausea over me. Even though the Bradford Pear blossoms were lovely and a sign that spring was truly here, some people thought they smell like rotten fish. It never bothered me before, but today I couldn't take it. I got up and ran for the nearest restroom.

As I was washing my hands and splashing water in my puffy face, it occurred to me that I'd been throwing up a lot lately. Was I coming down with something? I didn't feel sick, other than the occasional bout of nausea and lack of interest in breakfast…

Oh. My. God. I forced back the lump in my throat as I hurried out of the restroom. I had to get to a drug store immediately.

****

"There's no place to park," Mercer told Roman. There were several parking meters outside Caplan's, but they were all full, as were the public parking garages they had driven by. Mercer turned right at the corner stoplight to circle the block again.

Roman glanced around him. "What's going on?"

"Man, you haven't been gone that long. It's May and tomorrow's the Marathon. Tourists are everywhere."

Roman shifted in his seat and stared out the passenger-side window. Mercer was right, people were everywhere, many of them wearing clothing featuring checkered black and white in honor of The Indianapolis 500 later in the month. But the partying always started with the annual twenty-six mile marathon race the first weekend of May.

"Maybe you could slide into a handicap slot, just to let me out," Roman said.

Mercer looked sideways at Roman and shook his head. "No way. You owe me big as it is. I left work early to drive up and rescue you in Chicago. I'm not risking a parking ticket."

"How was I supposed to know you'd gotten a job?"

"You haven't exactly been in touch," Mercer said.

"I was sort of busy, trying to convince my parents that they'd like Julianne if they took the time to get to know her." Roman sighed. "And fending off everyone's efforts to shove me back to Rosaline." He rolled his eyes. "Tell me about your job."

Mercer grinned. "Part time customer service at The Humane Society."

"So the guy with the master's degree in finance is cleaning up dog poop?"

"I'm easing into the job market," Mercer sniffed. "Still recovering from brain surgery, you know, and anyway accounting jobs are… Hey! Look! A parking space." Mercer zipped his small economy car into the empty spot and slid the gear shift into park. "And right here in front of Caplan's." He turned off the engine and grinned. "You're welcome."

Roman's shoulders slumped. He scrutinized Mercer for residual signs of the head injury he'd received only a month ago. Except for the scar on his forehead, Mercer seemed to have made a quick recovery. "Sorry. I know I haven't been much of a friend lately. But I appreciate this, I really do. And I'll pay you back for the gas as soon as…"

"…Daddy lets loose of the purse strings," Mercer finished for him.

Roman got out of the car and stared at the storefront. "I'm half excited and half scared to go in there." It was after business hours and the inside lights had been turned off. "Come with me, okay? Store's closed so I've got to go around back."

Mercer's eyes widened. "You want me to walk down a dark alley with you?"

Roman fought off the urge to groan. "It's only seven o'clock and still light out. Come on." He needed the moral support and wasn't ready to admit to himself or Mercer that he was nervous about seeing Julianne after all this time. Never mind facing her father. That terrified him.

They made their way around the side of the building to the back door. The dumpster reeked of stale garbage, and there were a few broken liquor bottles and cigarette butts littering the ground near it, adding distinct odors of their own. Funny, he didn't remember any of this from his one other time back here, Valentine's Day. Well, okay, it had been past midnight and frigid outside, and at the time he'd been so focused on Julianne that whatever trash was behind their store didn't register.

Roman knocked on the back door of the store. No response. He knocked again louder, exchanged glances with Mercer, and was about to give up when he heard footsteps on the stairs. The chain lock on the door opened a crack, an eye peeked out, and then Julianne slid the lock and opened the door wide. She was beaming.

"Hello, husband," she said, blushing, her green eyes twinkling.

Roman felt a little shy himself. He smiled at her. "Hello, wife." Hesitantly he pulled her into his arms. She was wearing black jeans and a soft gray, lightweight cropped sweater. When she stood on tiptoes to throw her arms around him, her bare waist was exposed, giving Roman distinctly romantic thoughts. Her hair smelled of herbal shampoo and she felt so natural in his arms that he almost forgot they'd been apart. He leaned down for a long, passionate kiss.

Mercer elbowed Roman. "Get a room, you two."

Roman reluctantly released her.

Julianne crooked her finger. "Come in." Roman and Mercer followed her through the storeroom and up the stairs to her apartment. "Be it ever so humble…" she said.

As Roman crossed the threshold into his wife's home, he was ashamed of himself for thinking she lived in poverty. It might be small but it was surprisingly attractive. Someone in the family had a flair for decorating, because the living area was decked out in modern furnishings, the kitchen was updated with granite countertops and stainless steel appliances, and the hardwood floors were polished and gleaming. Too bad it was about to be torn down, along with the rest of this historic building.

"Mom," Julianne said as she followed Roman's gaze around the room. "She did all the decorating. As far as I know, Dad's still paying for it."

A hallway door opened and Nora stepped out. "Hey, Jul…" She stopped short. "Oh. I didn't know we had company."

"It's good to see you again, Nora," Roman said.

"It really is," Mercer said, looking her over with a gleam in his eye.

Nora was dressed in tight-fitting jeans, a white sheer blouse, and ballet slippers, her short hair framing her face in a bob. "Nice to see you, too." She tore her gaze away from Mercer and glanced at Roman. "Both of you."

Roman cleared his throat, mostly to get Mercer's eyes off Julianne's aunt. "Julianne, can I talk to you?

Privately?"

She nodded and led him down a short hallway.

****

"My bedroom," I told him as I opened the door. "Since we're married, I guess it's okay to have a boy in here." I winked at him.

Roman followed me in and I shut the door behind us. Almost immediately we were locked in an embrace, kissing passionately and falling onto the twin bed. Before I knew it, he'd pulled my shirt off over my head and was fumbling with my bra.

"Wait!" I said. I sat up to catch my breath. I couldn't think straight when we were in the throes of passion.

"Don't worry," he whispered. "I've got a condom."

"No, that's not..." I pulled away and stood up. "We need to talk." I picked up my sweater from the floor and put it back on.

Roman sighed and sat up. "Yeah, okay." He ran his fingers through his hair.

"I..." he said, at the same time I said, "We..."

"You first," I told him.

Roman swung his feet around to the edge of the bed and leaned back on his elbows. "My parents are furious." He glanced at me and then looked away, his face flushing with embarrassment.

"Mine aren't too happy either." My stomach roiled, but I forced down the fear and nausea. "And because both your family *and* your ex are angry, my family is being forced out of our home and business." I clenched my fists at my side. "You know, I was even feeling a little sorry for Rosaline when I saw the two of you on social media, knowing how she must have felt when she

250

heard about us." I shook my head. "But not anymore. She's a mean-spirited, jealous…"

Roman stood and put his fingers to my lips. "Yes, I know." He wrapped his arms around me. "Let's not talk about her. I want to talk about us."

I buried my face in his chest. "What are we going to do?"

"I'm not sure." He thought for a moment. "What about your parents? And Nora? Do they have a plan? A place to go when…" Roman's voice trailed off.

"Nora's moving into Ty's Canal Street condo." I shrugged. "He offered his spare room and she accepted. Mom and Dad are…" How did I explain the emotional roller coaster we'd all been on? Their anger and shock defied description, and there had been no way to ease my guilty conscience. "They can't seem to make any decisions." I turned to face Roman. "Is there any way you could help them out? At least give them the down payment for an apartment until they can relocate the business? My parents don't have any savings."

Roman groaned and slumped back down on the bed, burying his head in his hands.

That wasn't the reaction I'd expected. After all, it was his rejection of Rosaline that got us into this mess. Well, that and our hasty marriage.

"There's another problem," he said. "And it's bad."

How much worse could it get? "Okay…?"

"Since I wouldn't agree to an annulment…"

"Wait, what? Annulment?"

"Yeah, my parents tried to force me to sign annulment papers so Rosaline and I could be married in the Catholic Church as planned. When I refused, my father cut me off."

I had been deliberately keeping my distance because our hormones could override this desperately-needed discussion, but now I allowed myself to step in close and put my arms around him. "What do you mean, cut you off?"

He glanced up at me from the edge of my bed. "Financially. All the corporate accounts are frozen. Dad fired my driver. That's why I couldn't get out of Chicago and Mercer had to pick me up today."

This can't be happening I thought as I sank down onto the bed next to Roman. "I already knew about the corporate credit cards, but surely you've got your own money?"

Roman let out a sardonic chuckle. "I have a personal savings account with not much in it, but I never seemed to get around to opening that Amex card in my own name. Twenty-twenty hindsight, huh?"

My heart sank. The one thing I was counting on was Roman's money. Not that I'd married him because he was rich, because I didn't, but I'd been clinging to the hope that his wealth could be a temporary solution to my family's current nightmare. "I've got less than a hundred dollars in my debit account," I whispered. The nausea came back. I picked up an open can of soda off my nightstand and took a sip. It was warm and flat, but sipping it slowly helped calm my queasiness.

Roman sighed as he pulled his shoes back on. "I need to go to the store and see if I've still got a job there. For all I know, Dad's hired a new general manager."

"Seriously?" Roman shrugged in response to my question. "So what are you saying?"

"I know I said we'd move you into my house, but

maybe we need to hold off." His eyes pleaded with me for understanding. "Just for a little while, till I can sort all this out. I want to be sure I can support you."

I thought about that for a moment. Maybe now wasn't the right time to abandon my family, but still... I shook my head. "We knew what we were up against. We're adults, we're married, we're starting..." I couldn't finish that sentence.

"Starting...?" he prompted.

I stood up and put my hands on my hips as I let out a puff of air. "Starting our lives together. Unless you want a divorce so you can marry the woman of your parents' dreams."

Just then I heard loud voices in the living room, and I knew my father had come home. I glanced at the door. Sooner or later we'd have to face my father, so in a show of solidarity we walked out of my bedroom hand-in-hand. Mercer and Nora had retreated to the corner of the sofa, looking like they wished they were invisible.

"Well, well," Dad said with a snarl. "If it isn't my new son-in-law."

Roman extended his hand to shake, but Dad just glared at him, so Roman pulled his hand back and wiped his palm on his jeans. "Good to see you again, sir."

Dad turned to me, holding up the paper carryout bag. "Shrimp fried rice, since that's all you seem to want to eat lately." He set the bag on the kitchen table and turned to Roman. "I'd welcome you to the family, but I'm all out of goodwill at the moment."

Roman swallowed hard. "We'd still like your blessing, Mr. Caplan."

"Get out of my house. While I've still got one." Dad turned his back on both of us and went to his bedroom, slamming the door.

"I think we need to do as he says." Mercer stood up and started for the door.

Roman nodded and kissed me lightly on the forehead. "I'll call you tomorrow," he whispered.

Once they were gone, Nora lifted an eyebrow at me. "So…?"

I sighed. "His father cut off his money and he's got to figure some stuff out." My stomach growled and the Chinese food smelled divine, so I went to the kitchen and started eating right out of the cartons.

"You didn't tell him, did you?" Nora said, following me into the kitchen.

I shook my head. "He might decide his parents were right and sign those annulment papers."

Nora's jaw dropped. "Annulment?"

I shrugged and kept eating.

"Well, married or not, that doesn't change the facts." Nora rummaged through the white paper bag, pulled an egg roll from the paper wrapper and bit into it.

"I know, but I just couldn't bring myself to tell him. He said he'd call me tomorrow, once he figures out his work situation." I put down my fork. "And I've got finals in the morning, so I'd better get studying."

I knew Nora was all set to argue with me, but right now I didn't have any answers, so I went to my bedroom and closed the door. I could still smell my husband's cologne in the room, and the thought of losing him brought tears to my eyes.

Chapter 17

Roman checked the BMW's gas gauge. Relieved that the tank was nearly full, he turned on the motor, adjusted his rearview mirror, and backed his car out of the garage. It had been weeks since he'd driven his own vehicle, and it felt good to be in the driver's seat again.

He pulled into the street and then flipped on the windshield wipers. The gray day and drizzly rain suited his mood perfectly. His abrupt departure from his parents' penthouse yesterday, his wife's disappointment, the cold shoulder from her father—it was all a dark cloud hanging over his head.

The music blasting from the car radio was some unrecognizable heavy metal song, so he adjusted the volume down and surfed through the channels till he hit on an easy-listening jazz station. As he drove from the Meridian Kessler corridor downtown to Montgomery's, he tried not to think about what might be awaiting him at the store, especially after all this time away.

The rain slowed down traffic, already crawling along Meridian Street, giving him even more time to think about the predicament he was in. Finally, he got to the store's underground parking garage and was about to whip his car into his reserved space when he discovered another car already parked there. *What the hell*, he thought. He was forced to drive in circles searching for another parking spot, finally locating one next to a new Jeep with its dealer tags still attached, taking up more than its fair share of the space. Luckily a Smart car was on the other side, so he squeezed his Beemer in between the two. He beeped the car locked and headed for the express elevator that would take him directly to the business offices. But his key didn't work in the lock. *Why have the elevator locks been changed?* Roman shook his head and took the back service stairs.

The stairwell opened onto a service hallway, littered with unopened boxes of shoes to be inventoried and put out on floor display. He eased around the mess, making a mental note to have housekeeping clear the hallway. That could be a trip hazard, which he discovered firsthand as he collided with a rolling cart left askew in the middle of the hall.

Roman opened the door to the business office and blinked. Instead of Ben Voss, his trusted administrative assistant, there at the reception desk sat a middle-aged woman he'd never seen before. He steeled himself and walked up to her.

"Hi, I'm Roman Montgomery."

She looked up from her computer and removed her reading glasses. "Roman Montgomery?" She smirked. "Mr. Voss told me that if you showed up, he was to be notified."

Mr. Voss?

She picked up her desk phone, spoke into it, and hung up. "Follow me, please." The woman stood up and walked ahead of him, as if he didn't know the way down the corridor. She reached for his office's door handle, but Roman beat her to it. What he saw confounded him.

"Ben, what the hell?" he bellowed as he burst in.

"Thank you, Mrs. Greenley," Ben said. "I'll take it from here." She quietly closed the door behind her.

Ben was ensconced in the large leather chair behind the antique desk, and he didn't even stand up as Roman entered the room. Roman thought the guy looked awfully comfortable.

"What do you think you're doing?" Roman had a good look around the office. The furnishings were the same, but all his personal items were missing. Gone were his college fraternity photos taken with Mercer and their sorority dates, the pictures of the Hawaiian sunset he'd taken just last summer on vacation, and his framed college degree. Also missing, which he didn't really care about, was the oversized framed selfie of Rosaline flaunting that five carat diamond engagement ring.

"What happened to..." Roman waved his arms around his office, bewildered.

Ben shrugged. "We tried to soldier on here without you, but the ship was rudderless."

"Oh, cut the metaphorical crap," Roman said.

"I was running the store during your extended absence. Your father called me yesterday and offered me the position of General Manager. Said you'd decided to take your life in a different direction." Ben stood up and reached for something under the desk.

Roman glared at him. "I don't understand how you could stab me in the back like this. I thought you were my friend."

Ben retrieved a cardboard box and slammed it down on top of the desk. "Friend? I worked really hard here, Roman, getting the store ready to open, seeing to the day-to-day operations. Covering your ass every time you ducked out without explanation. Making you look good to your father, to the company's Board of Directors, the New York buyers. Not to mention the city of Indianapolis. All for a pittance of a salary, I might add. I deserved the promotion. And the raise." He shoved the box toward Roman. "Leave your keys with Mrs. Greenley. Have a nice day."

Roman picked up the box, filled with his personal effects and what was left of his short management career, and walked out the door without another word.

He tossed the cardboard box in the trunk of his car, fired off a text to Julianne, backed out of the parking space, and squealed the tires as he pulled out of the parking garage. It was raining pretty hard now, so he had to slow down and turn his wipers on high speed. He navigated the circle around The Soldiers and Sailors Monument and headed north on Illinois Street. It wasn't even nine o'clock in the morning.

On the way home he stopped at a branch of his bank, parked the car and went inside. A friendly teller greeted him.

"I'd like to check my balance," he told her as he handed her his photo ID.

She glanced at it, nodded, and tapped keys on her computer, then frowned. "Oh, I'm sorry, Mr. Montgomery. It seems your business accounts have been…"

"Yeah, I know. Frozen. But I'd like to see the balance in my personal savings account. It's listed under my name, not the company's."

"Oh, of course." She punched in more information, smiled politely at him as she waited for the information to come up, and then turned the screen around so he could see it. "Here it is. Twelve hundred and fifty-seven dollars, plus change." She printed it out for him.

Roman got back into his car, but before starting the motor, he checked his phone. No messages from Julianne, adding to his frustration. He turned off the radio and drove home in silence. Once inside his garage, Roman turned off the engine, and leaned his head against the headrest.

Twelve hundred dollars, a car he owned outright, and his personal possessions. That was all he had in the world. Hell, he could come home one day and find the locks changed on the house and his belongings piled up on the curb. Part of him wondered if Julianne would stick with him "for richer or poorer," but somehow he didn't see her as a gold digger.

He slammed his fist against the steering wheel. "No, dammit, I'm not giving up." He went into the house and set the coffee pot to brew. Then he sent a text to Nora.

—*Can't reach Julianne. ???*—

The coffee pot had time to finish brewing and Roman was already on his second cup when Nora finally replied.

—*Probably in her Business final.*—

Oh, of course. Final exams. It crossed his mind that his plan to pay for the rest of her education had evaporated. He went into his living room, flopped down on the sofa and turned on the TV. He flipped through the channels, finally landing on an episode of House Hunters. A young couple was looking for a house they could afford in Honolulu, and for some reason he sat up and gave the program his undivided attention. Maybe it was the photography, but he felt like paradise was calling to him. Roman muted the TV and called his wife's voice mail.

"Hey, Julianne, Nora told me you're taking exams. I've got some bad news. More bad news, I guess. Call me when you get this."

****

I came out of my final exam, Business Management 101, confident I'd done well. Short on time and ideas, I'd turned in a copy of my English research paper to the Business teacher, hoping I'd get at least a B on the project in both classes. I just hoped the teachers didn't compare notes.

My phone was displaying the Voice Mail icon, so I clicked on it and listened to Roman's message. More bad news? How much worse could it get?

It was pouring rain outside, so I went into the ladies' room and closed the stall door. I always hated it when other women had phone conversations in the toilet, but I didn't have a choice if I wanted any privacy.

"Roman?" I said when he picked up. I listened as he explained about losing his job and what little he thought he had left. I groaned inwardly at this bad turn, but I also felt sorry for him. Roman Montgomery didn't know how to be poor.

"I know this isn't what you expected when you married me," he said, "but…"

"Roman, stop. I married you because I love you, not because you're rich." I could almost hear him breathe a sigh of relief. "Look, you still have a house to live in, a car to drive, and a college degree. You can get another job. We'll be fine."

"We? Oh, God, Julianne, you don't know how

happy it makes me to hear you say that," he whispered, his voice catching with emotion. "Can we meet somewhere? Figure this out?"

I thought for a minute. Yes, we did need to figure out what our next step was, but we needed help. "I've got something important to tell you, too, but it has to be in person. And I've still got final exams. How 'bout in a few days at…"

"Pop's" he finished for me.

We were already thinking alike, a sign we truly were soul mates.

"I'll see you then. And Julianne. I love you."

The toilet next to me flushed, so I knew my conversation had been overhead, at least partially, but for once I didn't care. "Me, too."

****

It had been raining on and off for days. The TV weather guys said we'd had close to four inches, and flood warnings were posted all around the state. I could hear rain pattering against our apartment building's tin roof, and if I was right, leaking into the bathroom window like it always did. It was only six a.m., but I had to pee. Sure enough, the window was fogged up and water was dripping down the wall. I got a large towel out of the linen closet and stuffed it around the ledge, hoping to stem the tide. I'd been after Dad for months to call a handyman, or at least get some caulk, but he'd never gotten around to it. Now that the building was marked for demolition, it didn't matter anymore.

I used the restroom and went back to bed, but I couldn't fall back to sleep. After a while I got up, showered, dressed, and went into the kitchen for a bowl of cereal. Nora came out of her room, yawning and eyeing me suspiciously.

"You okay?" She glanced at the clock on the stove. Seven thirty.

"Fine," I said around a mouthful of granola. "By the way, have you seen Mom? She hasn't been here in a couple of days."

Nora shrugged. "Maybe she and Samuel had an argument. You should call her. Tell her your big news."

I glanced up and pointed my spoon at her. "Tell my forty-year-old mother who thinks she's twentysomething that she's about to become a grandmother? Right." I finished off my bowl of cereal and poured another one, liberally sprinkling on the sugar.

Nora lifted an eyebrow and pointed at my breakfast. "You're gonna get gestational diabetes if you keep that up. And Roman's insurance may not cover it, either."

I kept my eyes down. "Roman got fired." I pushed the bowl aside, my appetite suddenly gone.

She gasped. "From his own company?"

"More of his father's strong-arm tactics until he divorces me and marries Rosaline Vandenberg."

"That bitch?" Nora snorted. "The Montgomery family can't get rid of you that easily." She studied me closely. "You have told Roman, right?"

I avoided her gaze. "Not yet. Today, I promise."

She gave me a look and I knew what she meant. I'd been stalling for days, but I couldn't put this off any longer.

****

Roman rummaged through his house and car to

scrounge up whatever cash he could. After searching for change in the car's glove box, under the living room sofa cushions, emptying out the ashtray-turned-change holder on top of his dresser, and digging through pants pockets in the closet, he came up with just under twenty dollars. That would at least buy a few groceries until he could get a job and a paycheck.

This was a whole new world for Roman, and he didn't like living in it. Having to scramble for enough cash to stay afloat was terrifying. He hadn't realized how easy it was to just swipe the credit card. He was starting to sympathize with Ben, and the fact that he'd been underpaying his former employee suddenly caused him a fair amount of guilt. Lesson learned: if he was ever again in a position to hire employees, he'd be generous with their salaries. But for now, he had to get to Pop's to meet Julianne.

He glanced out the bedroom window. It was still raining, had been most of the night and for days before that. The flower beds were looking bedraggled, and running water overflowed the storm drains in the street. He'd heard on the news that other parts of the state were already under water from rising rivers and lakes, and he hoped the weather would break before flooding set in locally.

Roman showered, dressed in jeans and a golf shirt, but he put on heavy waterproof boots instead of loafers. He put the newly-discovered change in his pocket and the dollar bills into his wallet, grabbed his umbrella and keys, and backed the BMW out of the driveway. The rain was coming down pretty hard, forcing him to drive slowly, which made the expected fifteen minute trip twice as long. Halfway downtown his stomach started growling. After the amount of money he'd paid to rent out Pop's for his wedding, he acknowledged the irony of hoping Pop would offer him some free coffee and a pastry.

Roman lucked into a parking space within a half block of Pop's Bakery, and even better, it still had time on the meter. He opened up his umbrella and made a mad dash for the coffee shop. He arrived at the entry and ducked under the awning, not surprised that he didn't see any customers inside. Business must be slow in this weather. Roman was almost relieved, knowing he and Julianne needed Pop's undivided attention.

"Pop?" Roman called out. He shook out his umbrella and left it by the front door, and then kicked the rain off his boots before walking all the way inside the store.

Dishtowel in hand, Pop appeared from the kitchen and smiled at Roman. He opened his arms and pulled Roman into a warm hug, patting him affectionately on the back. "What brings you out on a day like this?"

"I'm meeting Julianne," Roman said. The enticing smell of coffee and freshly-baked pastries made his mouth water and his stomach gurgle with hunger.

"Meeting her?" Pop released Roman and took a step back to peer quizzically at him. "Aren't you living with your wife?"

"I wanted to. I went to tell my folks, but..."

"They didn't take it well, I presume."

Roman snorted and sat down at the nearest table. "My parents tried to force me to annul the marriage. When I wouldn't agree, my father cut off my income, fired me, and basically turned his back on me."

Almost as if he could read Roman's mind, Pop

went to the espresso machine and prepared Roman's favorite beverage. He set it down in front of Roman, along with a slice of banana bread that was still warm. Roman nodded his thanks, picked up a fork and tucked in.

"Son, you knew this marriage would be difficult, but 'what God hath joined together...' "

"I know, Father." Roman swallowed a mouthful of pastry. " '...let no man put asunder.' Dad apparently forgot that part."

"The Catholic Church views marriage vows as sacred," Pop told him. "Even if they're exchanged with someone outside the faith."

Pop was refilling Roman's cup when the door opened and Julianne stepped in. She shook the water off her athletic shoes, a pair that were at least five years old, Roman noticed. She set her soaked umbrella alongside Roman's by the door and dropped her backpack next to it.

Roman crossed the room and hugged her. "Ugh, you're wet."

"It's raining," Julianne said. She pulled her hooded sweatshirt off over her head and hung it on a coat hook near the entrance.

Roman tried not to think about how far Julianne had had to walk from the bus stop in those old shoes and wet clothes. "I should have come to pick you up." But then his mind flashed to his half-empty gas tank.

She shrugged. "Well, maybe you could drive me home."

"Once you decide where home is," Pop said from across the room. He dipped a tea bag into a cup of hot water and placed it on the table where Roman had been sitting, along with another slice of the banana bread.

Julianne looked at the bag of herbal tea and glanced up at Pop. "How did you know I'd want tea instead of coffee?"

Pop winked at her. "Years of waiting on customers has given me a sort of sixth sense about these things. I'll just leave the two of you to talk. I've got something in the oven."

She accepted the dry dish towel Pop handed her on his way to the kitchen and tried to towel off her wet, tousled hair, but the humid weather made it even more unruly. "So. I need to tell you..." she said as Roman said, "I have to tell you..."

Julianne smiled and leaned over to kiss Roman, a long, slow romantic kiss that he eagerly returned.

"We keep doing this," she said. "Talking at the same time." She blew on her steaming cup of tea and took a tentative sip.

"Well, I went to my bank," Roman said, gazing into her eyes. Even wet, she was beautiful. In fact, her green eyes sparkled with a glow he hadn't seen before. What was different? He didn't know.

Julianne peered at him over the rim of her cup. "Okay, the bank?"

Roman leaned his elbows on the table. "Since my father froze me out of my accounts and my job, all I've got left is my personal savings account. Twelve hundred dollars." He watched for her reaction.

She forced a half smile. "That's more than I've got."

Could she really be so blasé about it? Since his whole life had been defined by his wealth, Roman was flummoxed to find himself without it now and for the foreseeable future. Or forever, if his father didn't relent.

Julianne took another sip of her tea, set the cup down, and sighed. "Welcome to the real world." She reached for his hand. "Roman, I don't care about your money. I never did. I love you, and I hope that's enough for you. But you have to admit we're kind of in a situation here."

Roman nodded, withdrew his hand and took another bite of banana bread. To his mind, it was the best thing he'd ever eaten. "I need to get a job."

"Have you been looking for one?"

Roman shrugged and polished off the bread. "I've put in some online applications, but no response yet."

"Well, you kinda need to hurry it up, because I'm pregnant."

Roman's eyes widened. He set his coffee down as he gasped and coughed. "What?" he squeaked out.

"Pregnant."

Roman felt the color drain from his face. This was a complication he hadn't counted on. He'd been about to suggest they continue living separately until he found another job, or until her family was evicted, whichever came first. He'd convinced himself they could move in together once he was gainfully employed. Now baby was about to make three, drastically changing everything.

Roman slumped down in his chair and stared up at the ceiling. "Oh. My. God."

Julianne stood up and walked to the window which overlooked the street. "I know, I was surprised, too, but..." She shrugged.

Roman went to the window and looked out at the rapidly flooding streets and the wet pedestrians scurrying by, soiling their shoes, and slopping water onto passersby. If it didn't stop raining soon, the city was going to be in trouble. "Are you sure? Because this is terrible timing, Julianne. No money, no job, families feuding, did I mention no money?" He tried to put his arm around her, but to his surprise, she pushed him off.

Her jaw set, she said, "I didn't make this baby alone, Roman. Yes, it's bad timing, but money or not, job or not, in about eight months we're gonna be parents."

He tried to catch his breath, but he felt like he was having a panic attack. "I have no idea how long it will take me to find a new job. Or get back on my feet financially. Right now, three is about two more than I can afford to support."

Julianne's jaw dropped. "Seriously? You're bailing on me?"

Roman couldn't look her in the eye. He was too embarrassed about the financial predicament he was in and how poorly he was dealing with what should have been terrific news. "Not forever, just…" The fear rising in his throat choked off the rest of that statement.

Julianne folded her arms in front of her chest and glared at him. "Fine. I can take care of myself. And the baby. We don't need your help. Sign the annulment papers, go back to your cushy life, and forget I ever existed." Despite the pouring rain, she bolted out the door and into the street, leaving her backpack and umbrella behind.

Roman stood there, dumbfounded.

Pop poked his head out of the kitchen. "Did Julianne leave?"

Roman tried to grasp what just happened. "My

wife just ran out into the rain, telling me it's over."

"Go after her," Pop exclaimed. "You can't leave your pregnant wife alone out there in this kind of weather."

"How did you know...?"

"Like I said, sixth sense. Now go!"

Roman picked up his umbrella, Julianne's backpack, and darted out into the rain, ducking for cover till he got into his car. He didn't see Julianne anywhere, but the rain was coming down so hard he could barely see anything at all. He started the car and pulled out of the space, windshield wipers flapping wildly.

Where would she go? The answer was, he had no idea. And despite the fact that it was mid-May, it was chilly outside and it worried him that she'd left her rain-drenched sweatshirt at Pop's. She'd be soaked to the skin and could possibly catch cold, definitely not good for the baby.

Baby. He sucked in his breath.

Roman turned north on Illinois Street, thinking she might have tried to seek shelter at a covered bus stop. Driving slowly, his eyes darted in all directions. After a half mile or so, he thought he spotted her. He pulled up to the curb, rolled down the window and called out to the woman. She stepped a little closer to his car and he realized it wasn't Julianne. "Sorry, I thought you were someone else." He rolled the window back up and kept driving, for blocks and blocks, around and around Fall Creek, driving in circles for nearly an hour, all while the rain continued pelting down.

He'd heard about people who had panic attacks, shortness of breath, sweating and chest pains mimicking a heart attack, and always thought they were either faking or exaggerating. At that moment he became a believer, because his heart pounded loudly as he scouted out the nearly empty streets. Julianne seemed to have vanished. Did she really leave him for good? That kicked the panic attack into high gear. Yes, he'd said some stupid things out of pride, but all this was so new. Never before had he been without money, and he was embarrassed. But his wife, his baby, their life together...

And then Roman spotted her, huddled up to the side of a building under a dripping awning. She was wet, shivering, her lips turning blue, but he'd never been so relieved in his life. "Julianne!" Roman called out. "Get in!"

Julianne stepped out of the shadows and relaxed a little when she saw Roman. She opened the passenger side door and slid in, but kept her eyes facing forward. "I'm going to ruin your leather seats."

Roman grabbed her and held on tight. "I don't care. I found you and that's all that matters. Please don't ever scare me like that again." He turned on the car's heater full blast as tears came to his eyes. He pointed to her back pack on the floor at her feet. "Do you have a change of clothes in there?"

She nodded, extricated herself from his firm grip and pulled out a dry Old Navy t-shirt, quickly changing out of her soaked sweater. Then she rubbed her hands against the heat vent but still didn't make eye contact with him. "You can drop me at home now."

"No. Not till we talk."

"What's to talk about?" Julianne cast him a sideways glance. "I'm an inconvenience."

He reached for her hand, the one with the ring on it, and kissed it. "No. Never. I can't live without you. Either of you."

"Not what you said a little while ago." She withdrew her hand and turned her face to the window.

"I was an idiot. Please don't leave me."

"Right now I can't see any other way." Julianne glanced over at him and then quickly turned away again, wiping tears off her face. "Sorry, hormones."

He sighed as he put the car in gear. "It's okay. I love you and all your mood swings." Roman refocused on his driving as he proceeded slowly north on Illinois Street, hindered by the pouring rain and the rapidly flooding streets. He turned on the radio.

"Folks," the announcer said, "it's dangerous out there. The Weather Service now reports four more inches of rain in the last twenty-four hours, on top of the six we've gotten over the last several days. Many streets are flooded. If you don't need to go out, you're advised to stay indoors. The White River is nearing flood stage, and there have been reports of slide-offs near Fall Creek Parkway. Current visibility is limited, too, due to heavy rain and fog."

Roman and Julianne exchanged glances. "We need to get out of this," Julianne whispered.

Roman nodded. They were right in the area the announcer had just said was dangerous. He made the turn onto Fall Creek Parkway, but the street running alongside the historic bridge was flooded and up ahead was more high water. He stopped in the middle of the deserted street as he remembered the old adage, "Turn around, don't drown." After everything he and Julianne had faced, Roman wasn't about to let that happen. What was the best way out of here? And where could they go where the streets weren't also flooded? Maybe...

"Roman, look out!" Julianne shouted.

Roman snapped out of his head. He glanced over at Julianne with her still-unfastened seatbelt, but he didn't have time to warn her. Because out of nowhere a white Everlasting Batteries Company truck appeared, crossed the center line and was barreling straight at them, careening out of control. Something felt familiar about that company logo, but he didn't have time to puzzle it out.

He veered sharply right to avoid a head-on collision. Tires squealed, the truck's horn blared, and then the Beemer went into a spin. Roman fought desperately to regain control on the wet street by turning into the spin like he'd been taught. But he couldn't make the correction in time, and the car crashed into the hundred- year old concrete bridge.

****

"Lettie, Lettie. Wake up!"

I could faintly hear a woman's voice calling to me, like through a fog, but I couldn't force my eyes open. What happened? I couldn't remember.

"Lettie! You and Romeo have to get out of the car. It's going over the edge."

Why was that woman calling me such a strange name?

I was able to pop one eye open and take in my surroundings. I was still in the passenger seat of Roman's car, now with a broken windshield and mangled dashboard. Outside the car stood a beautiful woman I felt I should know, surrounded by a sort of golden glowing light, and she was pounding on the dented window. I forced open my other eye, and despite the rain, she wasn't at all wet, but she did look frightened. I glanced over at Roman who was slumped over the steering wheel. *Please don't let him be dead* I prayed.

"Lettie," she called out. "Can you hear me?"

I nodded, trying to recall what just happened. There was street flooding, no other cars around except us, and then that Everlasting Battery Company truck appeared out of nowhere and ran us off the road. Just before I lost consciousness, that logo triggered something in my memory. Not even my memory, really, but deep within my soul. I grasped at flashes of a scene I knew I'd been a part of but couldn't quite bring into view. I instinctively knew Roman had been there, too, as was this woman shouting at me outside the car window. Why couldn't I remember?

And then it came to me like a lightning flash. *Everlasting.* That was the code word Roman and I were supposed to remember if we veered off course in this life. And of course we had, literally and figuratively. In spite of my throbbing head, I concentrated and everything came rushing back to me. Things that had happened long before the car crash, long before this life, things that had happened in our past lives.

I slowly turned to the window. "Celeste?" I croaked. "Are we dead again?"

"No," she said. "But you will be if you don't get out of that car."

I felt around my body to assess my physical condition. I reached up to my throbbing forehead and discovered a gash above my eye that was oozing blood, and swiped at it with the back of my hand. Other than that I thought I was okay, because I could move my arms and legs. If Roman hadn't been driving so slowly due to the weather conditions, the airbags would have deployed, causing us serious injuries.

"Roman." I tried shaking him. "Are you okay?" I held my breath, fear gripping my insides.

He moaned and moved a little. "What happened?"

I exhaled with relief. "We have to get out of the car. Like now!"

He slowly lifted his head and tried to glance around him, but he was still too dazed. It was up to me. I tried to open the passenger door, but it was pinned against the concrete railing. I tossed my backpack into the backseat and crawled over the seat after it. I managed to open the door behind the driver's side, sling my backpack over my shoulder and scoot out.

Roman's car was totaled, the front end dangling precariously over the side of the bridge. I could smell gas leaking, too. I tugged on Roman's door and it wouldn't budge, but I wasn't giving up. Celeste was still there, and now there was a young man next to her who seemed vaguely familiar. "Celeste, one last favor. Please?"

"Henry," Celeste instructed, "help her."

Henry appeared at my side and laid his hand on mine, giving me strength. I tugged on the door one more time and it cranked open enough for me to reach inside.

I shook Roman's shoulder as the smell of leaking gas nearly made me puke. "Roman, get out. The car's going to explode." Time seemed to slow down as I gave his left arm a good yank but couldn't free him because his seatbelt was still fastened. *No no no* I screamed internally. *After all this, all our past efforts, I can't let this be the end!* I said a quick prayer, stretched as far as I could across Roman, and after a couple of unsuccessful tries, finally yanked the seatbelt open. Then I frantically tugged and tugged until I got him through the narrow opening and out onto the pavement, where he landed on his backside.

Roman looked as disoriented as I felt. He slowly pulled himself to a standing position. "My car," he moaned.

I threw my arms around him. I was still wet from before, but now both of us were drenched and starting to shiver. "We're both alive and that's what counts," I whispered.

He pulled me in close. "Julianne, did you see that truck?"

"The Everlasting Battery truck? Yes, but..." I craned my neck around him but didn't see the truck anywhere, or Celeste and Henry for that matter. Did I imagine them? And where did the truck go? It should be wrecked in the middle of the street, but it was almost like it vanished into the ether.

Roman did a visual search of the area. "Something about that truck was familiar."

"It was our wakeup call," I told him in hushed tones. Roman and I turned to each other as a distant memory flashed through my mind. From the look on his face, he was remembering, too. We were supposed to be together in this final life, unite our families, and bring love and acceptance to all of them. Instead, Roman and I had each let our pride get in the way and had almost blown this last opportunity.

By now police, first responders, or at least

bystanders should have arrived, but we were the only people there and it was eerily quiet. The stillness was broken by Roman's car as it groaned and teetered on the edge of the bridge. We exchanged frantic glances, clasped hands, and rushed across the street to safety. Engulfed in a ball of fire and smoke, Roman's Beemer exploded and toppled over the bridge and crashed into the White River below. It quickly sank beneath the flood waters.

We stood staring after it. "We have to call the police," I said. "Do you have your cell phone?"

Roman shook his head. "No. You?"

I sighed. My cell phone battery was dead this morning and I'd left it at home on the charger. "No."

"Car's not salvageable anyway," Roman said. We were both soaked to the skin and stranded in the middle of a deserted street. "We need to regroup. Maybe get a cab, or…"

"I have a better idea." I took Roman's hand and led him down the block to a covered bus stop. I perused the schedule and asked, "Where to?"

"My house?"

****

My mouth was agape as I walked through Roman's five-bedroom, five-bath house in an elite neighborhood near downtown Indianapolis. Each room seemed bigger and more elaborately decorated than the one before. But even as I took in the luxurious furnishings in what Roman said was actually his parents' house, I knew this would never be my home. Our home.

The only clothes I had were on my back. I borrowed a pair of his sweat pants and a dry t-shirt, cleaned the blood off my forehead and applied a bandage, and put my wet clothes in the washer. Then Roman made us both a cup of hot tea. We sat down in his open-concept living room on the very expensive leather sectional sofa to discuss our future.

I took a sip of tea. "We need to contact our families. They're going to hear about the car accident and think we're dead. That our bodies are floating in the White River somewhere."

Roman was quiet for a long time, intermittently sipping tea and staring off into space. Finally, he set the cup down on the antique mahogany coffee table and turned sideways on the sofa to face me. "Let them."

I nearly choked on my tea. "Let them what? Think we died?" Carefully I set my tea cup down next to his, wondering if maybe there was a coaster I should use.

"It would buy us some time." Roman rubbed his forehead. A lump was forming where he'd hit his head on the dashboard.

"Oh, Roman, I don't know. That seems, well, heartless."

Roman thought for a moment. "Okay, how about this? We let Pop know we're okay." He reached over and pushed a lock of hair out of my face. "It won't be forever, just till we get our lives on track."

I considered it, but it seemed impossible. "How could we even get in touch with Pop? No cell phones." I glanced around the room. "You don't have a landline, and if we get online…"

A smile came over Roman's face as he took my hand. "We'll do it the old-fashioned way—send him a letter." A faraway look flickered across his face. "We nearly allowed our families to pull us apart, all because of money and pride." Roman leaned his forehead against mine and whispered, "We weren't supposed to let that happen this time, Lettie."

His statement confirmed what I already suspected. Roman—Romeo—and I had both recalled the pact we made when we came into this life.

"All I want is to be with you," Roman said. "And our baby, when she arrives."

"He," I shot back.

Roman winked at me. "Whatever."

I sighed and rubbed my belly, noticing a slight bump that wasn't there a few days ago. "But we can't just hide out here. Sooner or later…"

He put a finger to my lips. "Let's get out of here. Out of Indianapolis."

My eyes widened. "And go where?"

"Do you remember the night we first met, on Valentine's Day? Your Sole Mates activity?" Roman seemed energized, even animated. "Both of our nametags said our ideal place was Hawaii."

"Of course I remember." Hawaii? Life in paradise would be a dream come true, but still… I gulped. "How could we afford it?"

Roman stood up and started pacing. "I've got that money in my savings account. It's not much, but it could buy airfare. And you've got some savings, right?"

An idea came to me and I threw myself into Roman's arms. "We have this!" I stuck my left hand in his face and wiggled the two-carat diamond on my finger.

Roman frowned. "No. That's yours, and it's a symbol of our love and commitment."

I shook my head. "Our love and commitment is stronger than ever, and I'd be very happy with a plain band. This thing's worth…" I held my hand up to the light and watched it sparkle… "well, a lot. Enough for a new start in Hawaii."

He kissed me passionately. "Are you sure?" I nodded. "Okay, but I promise to buy you a wedding band as soon as we get there."

"Oh, but wait." I stepped back when yet another dose of reality hit me. "If we fly to Hawaii, we'll have to show our photo IDs to board the plane."

Roman lifted my chin for another kiss. "Julianne, we're not criminals on some do-not-fly list."

I looked up at this man I love, have loved for centuries, and I'd never felt such joy.

Chapter 18

Honolulu, Hawaii, January 2022

"You ready, babe?"

Even though my heart was pounding, I nodded and sat down on the loveseat in our tiny Hawaiian beach house. "As ready as I'll ever be, I guess."

Roman sat down next to me, hit the video record button, and aimed the phone at us selfie-style. "Hi, Mom, hi Dad!"

I leaned in and waved. "Hi, Dad, Mom, Nora! Greetings from Oahu."

"We know this is a shock," Roman said, looking to me for confirmation, "but if you check the date and time stamp, you'll see this is for real. We wanted to let you know we're okay and we've made a good life for ourselves. I got a job working in a shoe store at the mall, and they just promoted me to manager. It's not Montgomery's, but I'm happy."

I leaned in a little closer. "And I'm working in a daycare because..." I stood up. "I want you to meet someone." Roman followed me with the camera as I went to the second, very small bedroom that served as a nursery. The baby had recently learned to stand, so he was leaning on the railing and grinning at me when I picked him up out of the crib. "This is Christopher Montgomery-Caplan. He just turned a year old, and

280

already he's trying to walk." I picked up his little hand and helped him wave. "And don't worry, Dad. I called a rabbi before he was circumcised at the hospital." I nuzzled my nose into his pink little face. "Smile for all the nice people watching this, Chris." He giggled adorably.

I took the baby with me back to the sofa and let him dance on my lap. I had to peek around the wiggly baby to continue speaking into the phone Roman was holding over us. "I'm allowed to take Christopher to the daycare with me when I work. And Nora, I've been taking online classes, too, trying to finish my marketing degree."

Roman aimed the camera at himself. "We love you all and hope you'll give us a call after you get this." We waved at the camera one last time before he switched it off.

We exchanged glances. "Now what?" I asked.

"Now we wait," he replied.

It didn't take long, either. I'd no more put Chris back in his crib than Roman's cell phone rang. *Nora Alvarez* the caller ID said. *Alvarez?* He handed the phone to me and I put it on speaker.

"Nora?"

"You don't call. You don't write," she harrumphed before bursting into tears. "We've been through hell for a year and a half. I could throttle you."

Tears flooded my eyes. "I know, but we had to make a fresh start." I swiped at my wet cheeks. "Alvarez?"

"A lot has happened since you've been gone. At first Mercer and I were just helping each other through our grief, but then we fell in love and got married about six months ago. Samuel walked me down the aisle, and Pop officiated."

"Congratulations," I said. "And Mom and Dad? Are they okay?"

"I guess they will be now. But Lydia and Samuel got a divorce."

I was stunned. "Was I the cause?"

"Sort of," she said. "But the real cause was their unhappiness with each other. Shortly after your, uh, death, Lydia ran off with Jon Parris. Seems his tech company's worth a few million dollars."

I let that news sit for a minute. Well, Mom got what she'd always wanted: a second chance at youth via a much-younger, very rich man. "And Dad?"

"He's doing okay. Great actually. At Father Al's insistence, Roman's dad showed up at Caplan's right before it was torn down. They talked, cried, shook hands, and then Charles set Samuel up with a shoe repair shop in a newly-created area of Montgomery's Footwear. Your dad's business is better than ever." She paused for a moment. "Wait. Did Pop know…?"

I ignored that question. "Nora, you and Mercer come visit us as soon as you can. I want you to meet your new great-nephew." She and I expressed our love before I disconnected the call.

Roman and I grinned at each other. "Mission accomplished," we both said with a fist bump, right before the phone rang again. The caller ID said Charles Montgomery, so I handed the phone to Roman.

He grimaced as he answered. "Dad?"

"Oh, God, Roman. I thought…we thought you'd… I'm in shock. Just shocked. Your mother and I watched the video and couldn't believe our eyes. She was so overcome that she had to go lie down. Felt a migraine coming on. We...we..." Charles sobbed openly, but then got control of himself and growled, "I could strangle you for letting us believe..."

Roman smiled and pushed mute for a second. "There's the Dad I know and love." He returned to his father. "The car accident was just that—an accident, but it was the excuse Julianne and I needed to get out on our own. I'm sorry it took this long, but we had a lot to figure out."

"Your mother's been ill, Son. She never quite recovered from losing her only child, so she's spent most of her days either in bed or at the spa getting massages. And then almost immediately after your, uh, well, we had a memorial service for you."

Roman frowned. "How is Mom now?"

"Better, but your mother's nerves couldn't take any more shocks. She was in the hospital for a while after we got news of Rosaline Vandenberg's elopement with the oldest Caldwell boy."

"Who?" I whispered.

Roman pushed mute. "Harvey Caldwell. Billionaire hedge fund trader."

I rolled my eyes. So Rosaline landed on her feet. Figured.

"Please tell Mom I'm fine," Roman said. "And Dad, I can't tell you how much it means to me that you reached out to Samuel Caplan."

Charles sighed. "He was as distraught as I was. And now it seems we have a grandson in common. We'll all be on the next flight to Honolulu. I'll text you and the three of you had better meet us at the airport."

Roman disconnected the phone and tossed it aside

as he pulled me into his arms. "That went a lot better than I'd thought." He kissed me.

I smiled up at him. "They'll have to get a hotel room. We don't have any extra space in our seven-hundred square foot house."

"Dad can afford to put all of them up at a five-star resort hotel on Waikiki Beach."

I held my left hand up to the light and admired my white gold wedding band. Roman had reluctantly sold my diamond ring to a jeweler in Indianapolis before we left town, but as promised, once we got settled in Hawaii he let me pick out my own ring. It's dainty, with a tiny diamond chip, and it suits me perfectly. "Roman, I love our life here. It's simple, and I've never been happier." As soon as we got off the plane in Oahu, I felt like I'd come home. I glanced up at my husband. "Do you think your father will try to force us to go back?"

Roman wrapped his arms protectively around me. "No one can force us to do anything, Julianne. We have good jobs, a house of our own, be it ever so humble, and a growing savings account. Our lives are here."

I nodded agreement. We finally accomplished what we've tried for centuries to do: live our lives together and help our families move past their centuries-old grudges. As we kissed, I noticed a bright light and lifted my eyes. Counselor Everman, Celeste, and Henry were floating near the ceiling, all of them smiling, and Celeste was giving us the thumbs-up sign.

I sighed contentedly and rested my head on Roman's chest. "I guess this means we're no longer star-crossed lovers."

A word from the author...

I am a former high school English teacher and author of *Confessions of a Teenage Psychic* (The Wild Rose Press, 2010), which was a 2011 Epic Ebook Contest finalist. My YA novel *Genius Summer* was released in November 2014. It was a finalist in the 2013 San Francisco Writers Contest. *Certainly Sensible* (The Wild Rose Press, 2015) won the Literary Classic's 2016 Gold Award in the Female Audience category. *Teenage Psychic on Campus* (The Wild Rose Press, 2017) has garnered rave reviews on Amazon.

I live in Noblesville, Indiana (just north of Indianapolis) with my two rescue cats, and work part-time at a living history museum.

https://www.facebook.com/pages/Pamela-Woods-Jackson/1523690337865060?ref=ay